I0657959

CHINCHUBA

By: K. Michael Casey

Published by: Emporium Press
*The Publishing Division of Professor Theophilus' Emporium
of Imagination, Inc.*
Magnolia, Arkansas

Chinchuba. Copyright © 2005
by Kevin Michael Casey
Published by:
EMPORIUM PRESS
The Publishing Division of Professor Theophilus' Emporium
of Imagination, Inc.
Magnolia, Arkansas

Cover Design by: Timothy D. Wise

Library of Congress Control Number: 2005932530

First Edition
ISBN: 0-9725549-6-3

The story contained in the following pages is fiction. Any names, characters, or scenes are creations from the author's imagination and, therefore, any resemblance to any person, company, or event is coincidental. Many of the places, such as the Stennis Space Center, are real, but all employees and incidents related to these locations are purely figments of the author's imagination.

DEDICATION:

To my wife, Diane, for all her support.

ACKNOWLEDGEMENTS

I want to thank all the individuals who have read at least one of the countless versions of this novel and offered encouragement and/or feedback. My wife, Diane, probably has the book memorized by now. My son, Mike Jr., also gave me some critical feedback and spurred me forward. I will also thank my daughter, Lindsey, for being a good kid, even though she hasn't read my novel!

Tony Prothro, a close personal friend with similar tastes in fiction, provided some invaluable suggestions (including changing the title). Maria Ross, a friend and fellow avid reader, encouraged me greatly on another novel. Without that impetus I might have stopped writing. A special thanks to all the dreamers out there who also pushed me to continue, some of them unknowingly. Andy McCullin, Don Johnson, David Ashby, Hal Jacobs, Gary Klein, Dan Flaherty, Bob Ellis, Selwyn Ellis, Ron and Karen Barnard, Victor Puleo, Gary Linn, Mike Watters, Pat Cantrell, and Mary Barnard, (and even Cindy Lotz!!!) all provided encouragement at one time or another. My brother Bill Harness let me bounce crazy ideas off him and made me laugh. Thanks to Myrtle Covington and John Thomas Casey, my mom and dad, for buying all those *National Geographic* magazines and encyclopedia sets that stimulated my desire to learn.

I want to acknowledge three individuals who have impacted my life and thus contributed to this work. Becky Evans, Esther Bittle, and Pam Fulmer all taught me English at one time or another at Rose Bud, Arkansas. It's not their fault I didn't learn it. I apologize to them for all the grammatical violations I've committed (some of them knowingly). Mentioning their names in no way indicates they endorse this novel, the writing style, or any content. In fact, they might disagree vehemently with all of the above. I still want to thank them for a first class education and a love for reading that was inspired somewhere about that time. Please know that you do impact lives, and many of us remember.

A special thanks to Dr. Tim Wise; my publisher and cover designer, fellow author, and fellow dreamer. You came along at the right time. I believe it was a "God thing." My hope and prayer is that anyone that reads this novel will enjoy it, recommend it to their friends, and it might even cause someone to get curious. Above all, I want to thank God for this blessing and opportunity. I apologize in advance for anyone I've neglected to thank. I did not intentionally omit anyone, although I know I have.

PROLOGUE

Mississippi Gulf Coast. Singing River, 1542 A.D.;

The small child wriggled in Katanwa's arms as the morning sun's orange glow peeked over the horizon. Sweat beaded across the Biloxi's large forehead and smooth upper lip in spite of the cool breeze.

What if he did not make it in time?

Katanwa walked faster. He held the fate of the tribe in his hands and too many warriors had already perished. The River God's anger at Katanwa's people demanded tribute, and only he could provide that tribute.

Making his way down the narrow rarely trodden path, he picked up speed as the light grew. Katanwa felt the spirits watching him as he traversed the way of death. The swamp, normally alive with sound, did not speak today. No birds singing. No insects buzzing. Nothing except silence. The *Chinchuba* would be hungry soon.

Katanwa suppressed a shudder and steeled himself against what was to come. Maybe the pure one, his newborn son, would appease the River God.

All had been quiet in his lifetime. Until sixty sunrises ago. Then, without warning, the disappearances started again. Nine members of the tribe, seven of them warriors, had vanished. The tribe's strength drained with each loss. Soon they would not be able to protect themselves against other tribes. The River God must be very angry.

The Grandfathers remembered the last time the *Chinchuba*

visited their tribe. The old men told stories and sang songs of the terror and the mighty warriors who could not conquer the *Chinchuba*. And now the evil had returned.

For many days the tribe had been in prayer and worship to the great god. Yet the deaths continued. The River God demanded sacrifice. Only sacrifice would appease the River God and convince him to call the *Chinchuba* back into the pit from which it came.

The Grandfathers made their decision through purification by fire and communion with the dream world. Katanwa was the chosen one. His seed would provide the sacrifice and with pride he would stand before the River God and plead the tribe's case. Whatever transgression the Biloxi tribe had committed, they would remedy. If only the River God would show them their grievous mistake.

Katanwa wore a suit of the finest doeskin, softened by long hours of chewing by the old women, their hardened gums removing all the stiffness. Dyed shell beadwork that bore the image of the *Chinchuba* adorned the front and back of his garment. One Grandfather saw the shirt in a vision and ordered its creation. The women of the Grandfathers labored over twenty sunrises on the intricate beadwork, purifying themselves daily with burning cedar so that they might be found worthy to complete the task.

The last time the River God grew angry with the tribe, a warrior wearing a similar shirt had conquered the *Chinchuba*. This time the honor belonged to Katanwa. He glanced at the pure one squirming in his arms. His woman handed Katanwa their newborn male child that morning. A single tear ran down her cheek, but she knew there was no other way. Holding her head high, she had retreated into their dwelling to grieve and pray. The Gods had honored her with their choice.

Katanwa approached the river's bank, drawing near to the underwater realm of the River God and the home of the *Chinchuba*. He strode forward, his back proud and straight. The River God would be pleased with the Biloxi people.

Katanwa laid his newborn son on the bank, careful to avoid eye contact with the sedated child. He removed the small pack from his back and spread its contents before him. Using the finest animal skins he covered the bare earth, and then placed four intricately carved sacred stones facing in each of the four directions. He performed the sacred ritual revealed by the Grandfather's dream and placed his newborn son in the center of the skins.

Moving back about an arm's length, he seated himself cross-legged on a well-tanned deerskin. Katanwa began to chant. Softly at first, but louder as his courage grew. Katanwa gained strength with the chant.

His child was silent. Earlier that morning, his woman fed the unnamed male child tea made from mushrooms to keep him quiet and content. The River God would be displeased with a crying sacrifice. Katanwa sang the sacred chant. The tribe's fate depended on him.

Katanwa's gaze did not rest upon his first born when the murky waters parted and the *Chinchuba* appeared. The Grandfathers had so instructed. Katanwa chanted louder. The *Chinchuba* seemed pleased with the child and, with little sound, took Katanwa's son and returned to the water.

He prayed the sacrifice would appease the River God.

Katanwa waited for the *Chinchuba* to present the child to the River God. He continued to chant and pray as instructed.

He would wait until the sun rose high overhead and, if the *Chinchuba* had not returned by that time, the tribe would be safe. However, Katanwa did not wait long. The waters moved and the *Chinchuba* emerged for a second time.

Katanwa's chant grew louder.

The sacrifice had not pleased the River God. The *Chinchuba* had returned for him.

The *Chinchuba* approached slowly. Katanwa felt its hot putrid breath on his face. He chanted louder and tried to block the pain when the *Chinchuba* seized him and started back to the river. Katanwa chanted to keep from screaming. He felt unbearable pain but he would not disgrace his tribe. The River God would not be pleased.

The murky waters welcomed Katanwa and the *Chinchuba*. His chanting ceased when the water flowed into his lungs.

Maybe now his people would be safe.

He hoped that his life would appease the River God. Katanwa would carry great honor in the afterlife and his people would sing about his deed for years. His mind was at peace as the Chinchuba carried him deeper to meet the River God.

CHAPTER 1

New Orleans, Louisiana, French Quarter, present day:

He would kill tonight, and the thought pleased him.

Doctor John stood on the stoop and drew deep, intoxicating breaths of the city. A hint of fear carried on the wind, and it beckoned to him enticingly. Yes, tonight would be a good night.

The composite smell of New Orleans, a city with a myriad of odors winging through the air as colorfully as the many-hued birds in the Audubon aviary, never grew old to him. Midnight approached and his heightened olfactory nerves detected bacon frying, sweat from a thousand overindulged bodies, a trace of pineapple from someone's pina colada, and the acrid aroma of New Orleans coffee. Expensive perfumes mingled with the ever-present smell of stale beer, sex, urine and vomit. He savored the moment, testing each breeze in the same manner a house cat tested the air before going outside, his nostrils slightly flared. Aromatic assailants bombarded him from all directions, all of them stimulating.

No matter how thoroughly the clean-up crew hosed the streets in the morning, the smell never changed. It permeated the asphalt pavement and the flagstone sidewalks. It rose from the sewers and gutters. It soaked into every fiber of the French Quarter. Hundreds of years of odor all culminated in creating a unique scent signature that pleased Doctor John. New Orleans, the greatest city in America, had welcomed him and his exceptional abilities from the moment he stepped off the boat. And Doctor John loved New Orleans. Everything about it.

He stepped off of the stoop and into the revelry of Bourbon Street. Even the most drunken of the throng parted to allow his passage. Doctor John was an imposing figure anywhere and he cultivated an image that, even in New Orleans, caused people to step out of the way. During the daytime, when the families toured Jackson Square en masse, mothers and fathers would catch their children's hands when he strolled by and pretend they didn't notice him. Their fear praised him.

And tonight he could smell the fear. Rarely was the presence of fear this strong. Tonight would be a special night. The time approached to honor Vodu. Vodu, in due time, would reveal just how special the night would become. Maybe, if Doctor John's sacrifice pleased him, Vodu would speak to him.

For now he must prepare. He had much to do in the next thirty minutes. Doctor John reached his home and, deceptively quiet for a man of his size, ascended the two flights of stairs to a portion of the house off-limits to everyone but him. He entered a small room and slowly stripped the clothing from his upper body, revealing the taut muscles of one with great strength. The tepid water in the basin beside the room's only other door provided him with a quick sponge bath. He was ready to begin.

With the reverence of any priest in the presence of his god, he entered an adjacent room and seated himself on the floor. Doctor John removed a small vial from his pocket, tapped the contents onto the back of his hand, and inhaled the fine white powder while he waited for the magic to begin. Soon his senses would heighten and enable him to read the sacred bones with great clarity.

He sat cross-legged on the floor and rested his huge hands on his knees, palms upward. The journey was as important as the destination, the anticipation almost as intoxicating as the drug. Something magical would happen tonight. A smile, revealing a hint of gold, played across his scarified face. It was now midnight and a full moon, an ideal time for prayer and offering. Vodu would speak soon.

The small room glowed with the feeble light from a dozen flickering candles. An eerie shadow ballet played out on the walls, physical evidence of the raging battle between the darkness and the light. A porcelain bowl, indistinguishable from the ones thousands would soon eat their morning cereal from, occupied the center of a large circle drawn on the floor. Red and black concentric lines formed the perimeter, broken only by four large candles marking the north, south, east and west. A white rooster, tethered with a short length of twine tied to an eyebolt secured to the floor, pecked at a few crumbs of bread sprinkled near the bowl. The only other furnishings in the room were two antique armoires placed against the north and south walls.

The time had come. Doctor John knelt and entered the circle on his knees. He caught the now-vocal rooster and raised the struggling bird to his mouth. With his tongue he felt the life pulsing through the bird's veins just beneath the feathers. Using an efficiency and skill one only develops from repetition, he bit through the bird's neck. The salty flavor of the rooster's blood met his tongue.

He pulled the bird away from his mouth and held it by its legs and head, allowing the beating heart to pump the crimson elixir into the porcelain bowl. The rooster's struggles weakened until the bird ceased to move altogether. A trickle of bright red blood, newly exposed to the oxygen, dripped from Doctor John's chin.

He placed the rooster's carcass to one side and focused on the contents of the bowl. With one hand he cupped the bowl while the other hand shook the contents of a small leather pouch into the warm liquid. Several small vertebrae, taken years ago from a sacrificed black cat, disappeared beneath the red surface.

Doctor John closed his eyes and cupped the bowl in both hands, raising it over his head as a toast to all four directions. A phrase unintelligible to any living being escaped his lips before he consumed the warm blood. Satisfied, he placed the bowl reverently in the center of the floor before opening his eyes. The bones would reveal their secrets now. Secrets known only to the other side and on special occasions revealed to Doctor John.

He studied the pattern, intent on every subtle nuance the position of the bones would tell him. Today they told him much.

Was it possible? Such a thing came along so infrequently that, at first, he rejected it. But it had to be true. Vodu had spoken.

He stood and crossed to the ornate armoire on the south side of the room. It's twin rested behind him against the north wall. The only difference between the two armoires, other than contents, lay in the intricate carvings decorating the two large doors. Doctor John placed his large hands on the carving and traced the outline of the small baby carved into the door. A father would do a similar act on the photograph of his newborn child.

Another smile visiting his face, Doctor John opened the door to reveal a portion of the contents. Two small bodies, their smoke-blackened corpses resembling the mummified remains of some ancient culture, dangled from their respective chains. Remembering the pleasure at the moment of sacrifice, Doctor John removed one of the small dried bodies and cradled it to his chest. The child, a newborn, had been only three days old when he killed it with the ornate dagger resting in the cabinet drawer. It had been his first and would always remain special. His power had multiplied exponentially with the act, and also his reputation and fortune.

Doctor John swelled with anticipation. The time approached when he would once again be allowed to sacrifce the goat without horns. One did not take such an honor lightly. He had much preparation to do. And this time not just any child would do. Only a special child would gain him tremendous power. Already the most powerful voodoo chieftain in New Orleans, there were others more powerful elsewhere. Soon, that would change.

Doctor John could be patient. Vodu had honored him and he would reveal the chosen child to Doctor John at the proper time. The bones would not lie, but could be difficult to interpret, often revealing the hidden things bit by bit. He replaced the small mummy in its cabinet and his smile broadened, turning into a laugh.

A deep, booming laugh.

A maniacal, feral laugh that caused hair follicles to contract and sent icy chills through the hallways of the mind of anyone within hearing distance.

The other occupants of the house heard, but made no outward response. After all, he was their master.

* * *

Elsewhere in the French Quarter, Kevin Croix stared at the ceiling of his bedroom. However, the total darkness prevented him from seeing it. In the light, one could see it wasn't an ordinary ceiling. It was the lid of a coffin closed over the man. The red-velvet-linedoak crypt reminded him of his own mortality.

Tonight the reminder was especially vivid.

He could sense a major battle in the spirit realm. Soon it would manifest and he must be ready. Over the next few days he had much to do. He knew better than anyone that most of the battle's outcome would be determined by that preparation.

For now he would sleep. He must be at his peak for what lay ahead. Kevin closed his eyes. A tom cat screamed outside. A drunken reveler yelled at a prostitute. The man in the coffin did not move. He heard neither sound. He was asleep.

* * *

Kat Abnaki sighed and turned over yet again. Her mind wandered as sleep eluded her. The muggy coastal Mississippi night was awash with night sounds; sounds that usually comforted her, but not tonight. It was silly she knew, but an irrational fear overwhelmed her. One of those times when she couldn't put her finger on what was bothering her, but she was bothered nonetheless.

Earlier, she had managed to catch a few winks, but now she was wide awake, staring at the ceiling fan, and wondering what had awakened her. Careful to make no sound, she'd slid deeper under the covers. The security of the heavy quilt pulled up to her chin comforted her.

Kat watched the dark corners of her bedroom and contemplated turning on a light. However, rationality won out. She refused to give in completely to the panic attack. She shifted her thoughts to Nathan and his boxes of junk in the living room. What was next for both of them?

Hours later, the night nearly spent, mental and physical exhaustion overcame anxiety. Kat closed her eyes and drifted into a fitful sleep populated with the shadowy images of ancient warriors.

The warriors were in a fight. A battle with something not quite human, something her subconscious mind could not quite make out.

CHAPTER 2

Mississippi Gulf Coast. Singing River;

"Did you hear that?"
"Hear what?"
"That chirping sound."
"I ain't heard a thing." Billy wiped the back of a bait-stained hand across his plentiful forehead. The stifling heat caused it to glisten in the dark, making nice runway landing lights for the 737 sized mosquitoes he was constantly flagging away on their approach. "Toss me another beer."

Lou's hand dipped into the murky cooler water and emerged with a half cold Bud that immediately sailed through the air in Billy's general direction. Two or three fist-sized pieces of ice fought a losing battle with the heat but managed to cool the exterior of the beer cans somewhat. Billy snatched the can out of the air like a star outfielder and rubbed it over his ample forehead before popping it open.

"You got that one baited yet?" Billy slapped another mosquito, the sound loud and ominous in the middle of the dark night. "If I'd wanted to give blood I'd have gone down to the Red Cross." He chuckled at his own wit. A few more beers and he'd really think he was funny.

"I told you to bring the bug dope." Lou's gyrations, alternating between baiting the trotline and frantically waving and slapping at the persistent insects, resembled some form of redneck aerobics.

"I know, I know, mother." Billy shined the spotlight on Lou to check his progress and chuckled at his brother's antics.

"Would you quit that? All you're doing is drawing them to me." Lou mumbled some profanities under his breath as Billy switched the light off. "Why don't you just coat me with sugar water and stake me out to an anthill? It would probably be a quicker death."

"Shut up! I'm getting tired of your lip." Billy took a long swig on his beer. He felt something firm, decidedly un-beer-like, pass through his teeth. He swallowed quickly to keep from gagging.

Nothing like some bug protein in your brew!

The slogan, 'tastes great, less filling,' popped into his head but he couldn't think of a twist on it to share with Lou. Besides, Lou was as cranky as his old lady was tonight.

Lou swished his hands in the water to wash off some of the blood from the bait. They were using beef liver that had soaked in chicken blood all day. The stuff smelled to high heaven so the catfish ought to go crazy over it. Both anticipated several large flathead catfish to greet them in the morning.

"There it is again."

"There's what?" Billy belched loudly after downing the remaining half can of beer in one gulp.

"The noise, you moron!"

"I'll knock your scrawny butt outta this boat you call me a moron again." Lou had *little man's syndrome*. Always trying to prove how tough he was to compensate for being a runt. He could be a real pain, even if he was his brother.

The threat had no effect on Lou. Billy was drunk enough that he could take him tonight, size advantage or not. He shined his high beam spotlight around, searching for the source of the noise.

Nothing. No ripples or disturbance. Just the flat water's surface on a windless night in the swamp.

Lou turned the light off before too many of the vampire insects used it for a homing beacon. He couldn't remember the mosquitoes ever being this bad.

"Move the boat over to that stump." Lou gestured to a shadow rising from the water about 30 feet to Billy's right. "Let me tie off one more line and we'll run it out between those two big cypress trees."

Billy nodded. Lou knew how to catch catfish. Their daddy had managed to impart that sacred knowledge to Lou, but like most knowledge, it had somehow failed to stick with Billy. Maybe it was just a sixth sense and couldn't be learned. You were either born with the ability to catch big catfish, or you weren't.

The trolling motor hummed as Billy expertly positioned Lou close to the stump. He crumpled the empty beer can in his hand and tossed it overboard, "Hey, pitch me another beer."

"Are you gonna drink all of them before I get a couple?"

"Shut up and throw me a beer." It was Lou's problem if he didn't get any. "We got another case back at camp. Besides," Billy smiled to himself, "I'm on vacation and my blood alcohol level is getting dangerously low."

Lou obliged and repeated the ritual. Another can sailed Billy's direction. Digging around in the flat-bottom boat, Lou soon found what he was looking for. It was a short trotline, maybe twenty hooks in all, but perfect for this location. He knew, as sure as he knew Billy was as dumb as a rock, that this one would have at least one good fish on it in the morning.

Expertly he reached both arms into the murky water and tied the end of the line to the stump. It needed to be well below water line to keep others from finding it and to keep boat props from cutting it. Not much danger of either in this place, but he didn't want to take any chances.

Billy worked the motor, keeping the line tight, while Lou quickly unwound the trotline from the piece of Styrofoam he'd used to take it up the last time he'd gone fishing. Styrofoam worked best because, as he retrieved the line, he had somewhere to put the hooks to keep it from getting tangled. And there was nothing worse than a tangled trotline.

Lou motioned for Billy to stop when he reached the end. He grabbed an old window weight kept for just such occasions, tied it to the end of the trotline, and let it sink to the bottom. Catfish fed on the bottom.

"Let's bait her up, Billy." Lou opened the box of liver and looked inside, "This one will be a good one. I've got a good feeling about it."

Billy cocked his head, "I think I heard it now."

"What's that?"

"That noise you were talking about."

Lou raised his head and listened. Hearing nothing, he shrugged. "Oh well. Put me back up to the stump and I'll get this line baited."

Again Billy positioned the boat perfectly. He switched his light on and panned the surroundings while Lou dipped his arm into the water to grab the end of the line.

"I wish I knew what that noise was." Billy could find nothing in the light.

"How many times I gotta tell you to turn that thing off?" Lou groused.

Billy obediently turned the light off and pitched it in the bottom of the boat.

"It's probably noth . . . . Hey! What was that?"

"What?" Billy really didn't care that much. He was feeling a good buzz and Lou was getting on his nerves.

"Turn the light back on a minute. Something brushed against my hand."

Billy groped for the light. "Turn the light off. Turn the light on. Maybe I don't want to."

Lou, frustrated with his brother, stuck his hand underwater and grabbed the trotline. He could bait it by feel if he had to. Just as he grabbed it, the line jerked and set one of the large barbed hooks deep into the fleshy part of his hand.

"Aaaahhhh! You hooked me, you stupid moron."

"I didn't hook you, and I told you not to call me a moron again." Billy was yelling now, completely fed up with Lou.

"Turn the light on and hand me the knife. I'm gonna have to

cut the line."

"No. I think I'll drink another beer." Billy could hear Lou rustling in the front of the boat. He propped his feet up on the cooler and leaned back in his seat.

"Billy, if you don't quit jerking on that line, I swear to God I'll kill you when I get this hook out."

"I ain't jerking on anything."

Lou's imagination was beginning to kick into overdrive. What if Billy really wasn't pulling on the trotline? Who, or what, was? He felt a lump of cold fear rise in his throat as something brushed against his hand again.

Frantic, Lou yelled. "I ain't fooling around, Billy. You better...."

Billy interrupted Lou's sentence sarcastically. "Yeah, yeah, yeah. I'm really scared."

"Hey! Who's there? What are you do...." Lou stopped in mid sentence and screamed. "Billy! Qu...."

A loud splash silenced the cries.

Lou must have fallen overboard. Served him right.

Billy finished his beer in the dark, waiting to hear Lou sputter to the surface and fly into a cussing fit. A few minutes passed and Lou still hadn't appeared. Lou, always a prankster, was probably up to something. Billy fumbled for the light and turned it on, shining the beam toward the front of the boat where Lou had been baiting the line. He panned the immediate surroundings, suspecting he'd find Lou sneaking up on him to jerk him overboard. Only he didn't find him there.

Two hours later, even alcohol impaired Billy knew it was hopeless. Lou was gone. He had vanished without a trace. Lou was probably playing a trick on him. But what if he wasn't?

Billy tried to remember the few seconds before Lou disappeared. Was Lou talking to someone right before he fell overboard?

* * *

"Is that him?" Neil 'Hawk' Hawkins, the Hancock county sheriff, nodded in Billy's direction. His piercing namesake eyes methodically dissected the larger Blanchert brother, cataloging every detail and filing them away in his mental file cabinet.

"I'm afraid so, Hawk." The speaker was a slightly built man, five foot four inches tall and weighing in at a solid 110 pounds. There was no outward indication of the inner strength Hawk knew resided within that small frame.

Ed Hebert and Hawk had known each other since childhood. The two men graduated from Bay St. Louis High School over fifteen years ago with NFL dreams. A knee injury for Hawk and Pop Warner size for Ed pushed both men other directions, coincidentally into law enforcement. Ed was the newly appointed chief of the Bay St. Louis police force.

"Billy Blanchert, huh?" Hawk knew the man's reputation but had never seen him. He was no stranger to Ed. "Can't suppress your true nature, I guess."

Before Hawk had been elected sheriff, Billy had been a chief suspect in Tara Hocum's disappearance. After the election, he'd spent some time reviewing all the unsolved cases over the last ten years. There weren't that many, so it hadn't taken too much time. The coast had been a low crime area until the last couple of years.

Even though he'd always maintained his innocence, Billy had always been the odds-on favorite. They had never found enough evidence to arrest anyone and Tara's body had never surfaced. The district attorney's office refused to charge Billy Blanchert, knowing they would lose, and double jeopardy would prevent his conviction if any evidence surfaced later.

Meanwhile, everyone kept their ear to the ground for that one witness they needed to convict. Someone would stumble over the girl's remains eventually. And, hopefully, with all that DNA magic the forensics lab could conjure up, they would be able to convict. The courts seemed receptive to that type of evidence, so Billy wasn't off the hook yet.

"Who was it this time?" The dispatcher had only notified him that someone had disappeared and provided him with the location. Turtle Creek Landing.

Turtle Creek was a small meandering tributary that ultimately wound its way to the Pearl River. Incidentally, it was only a few miles from where an eyewitness, albeit a questionable one, had sworn they had seen Billy Blanchert and Tara Hocum get in a small boat together. That fact, coupled with the pair's known stormy relationship, pointed to Billy. But someone had dropped the ball and Billy Blanchert left the coast for greener pastures in Texas. The case remained unsolved.

"Lou Blanchert." Ed's face revealed nothing.

"His brother? Kept it in the family this time, huh?" Hawk had little sympathy. Lou Blanchert he did know and he had been a constant thorn in the flesh of the local authorities, always in trouble over one thing or another. Bootlegging beer for minors, growing pot, petty larceny, you name it. The only problem was that Lou was brighter than Billy and covered himself well enough to prevent arrest. Hawk suspected him of a number of crimes, but none terrible enough to warrant wasting too many scarce resources on him.

"He's the one who reported it, Hawk."

"Think that means anything?" Hawk searched Ed's face. He respected Ed's opinions. They were childhood buddies and had an unusually good working relationship. They still fished and hunted together several times a year.

"He seems shook up pretty bad. I just never figured him for that good of an actor." Ed nodded in Billy's direction. "I remember how he was when we questioned him about Tara. He was all nervous and defensive. Now he's just terrified. Like he's really afraid of something and I don't think it's us."

Ed was right. Billy was a wreck. His hand trembled as he assaulted a cigarette he'd bummed off one of the deputies. One deep drag followed another as if he needed to convert the tobacco to ashes for some mysterious purpose. The normally soothing nicotine was having little impact.

"What's his story?"

"Billy claims they were setting trotlines and he heard a splash and Lou just disappeared. Says he heard Lou talking to somebody right before he fell overboard."

Hawk shrugged. "So, they were drunk and Lou hit his head on a stump and drowned. Seems open and shut to me." He gave Ed a whimsical look. "And that bit about talking to someone? What were they doing? Wading around in the swamp?"

"Where's the body, Hawk? There's no current here. Lou's body should be floating on the surface or the divers should find it within a few feet of where they were fishing." Ed glanced at his watch. "They've been searching for almost two hours now and haven't found a thing."

"It'll turn up soon. Billy probably doesn't even remember where they were fishing anyway. What makes you certain that you're even looking in the right area?"

"We found the trotline they were setting out. Billy took us to the exact spot."

"Well, it's possible he's a better actor than you give him credit for, Ed. Maybe we should find out how well him and Lou were getting along."

Ed nodded. "Could be you're right. Something's not ringing true here. That's for sure."

"Ed! Hawk! You guys better see this." A uniformed officer waved them over to a small flat-bottom boat. Another ashen-faced deputy held a garbage bag at arm's length, like a new father on diaper disposal duty. Ed and Hawk headed toward the bag to view the man's find.

Both men peered into the bag. A severed hand, wrinkled from long exposure to the water, lay like a dead fish in the bottom. The white shard of wrist bone protruded a couple of inches out of the flesh and stood in sharp contrast with the black plastic garbage bag. A number two galvanized fishhook was imbedded in the heel of the hand.

Ed and Hawk exchanged telling glances. Billy Blanchert would

have a hard time explaining this one.
They had him this time!
Even a blind hog finds an acorn once in a while.

CHAPTER 3

John C. Stennis Space Center, Remote Sensing Research Laboratory, Coastal Mississippi

Harlin studied the imagery. New photos, still warm from the recent processing, covered the large table in front of him. Banks of shallow drawers lined all four sides of the room containing thousands more similar photos and topographic maps for almost every area on the globe. Huge maps covered every square inch of available wall space while four computer workstations shared the center of the room with a large map table in the center.

Oblivious to everything else, Harlin scanned the photos to see if anything jumped out at him. He moved a bottle of spring water out of the way and soaked up the condensation ring with a paper towel. The "NO FOOD OR DRINK ALLOWED" sign posted yesterday still rankled him, but he knew better than to get caught disregarding Humsinger's orders with something as blatant as a bottled drink.

Humsinger was a crotchety old coot but controlled the keys to the Holy Grail, the post-doctoral fellowship, and Harlin needed the training. A Ph.D. in archeology had seemed like a good choice when he entered the doctoral program but now, with student loans staring him in the face and no job prospects, he wasn't so sure. That's why this post-doctoral fellowship was so important. All previous fellows had landed jobs, and good ones at that.

Footsteps in the hall caused Harlin to scramble. The water bottle made it to the trash seconds before the door opened. A furtive glance at the map table made him wince. A candy wrapper, wadded into a ball, remained in plain view. Nathan Young strode through the door, noticed the candy wrapper, and smiled.

"You better be glad it wasn't Humsinger. He'd skin you alive and nail your hide to the outside door." Nathan paused, contemplating Humsinger's reaction. "He might even use the skin for a nice map."

"Or worse, kick me off the post-doc team."

Nathan had been here almost two full years now. Harlin only eleven months. Both men had faced stiff competition for the coveted two-year fellowships and had been selected based on merit.

"Anything's possible with Humsinger. He's a loose canon."

Harlin's face twisted into a grimace. "Don't I know it. I think I've already made his black list."

"You've just got to learn to play the game, Harlin."

"Politics was never my strong suit."

Nathan smiled derisively, "You hide it so well, Harlin." He pointed to the photos, "What's up?"

"I'm not sure." Humsinger forgotten, Harlin pointed to an area he'd been studying, "It looks like someone's been digging right here. I was just going to pull last month's shot and compare the two."

"For the life of me I can't see how you can remember what the last flyover looked like." Nathan shook his head in amazement. Harlin had an uncanny ability to look at the newest remote photos and immediately detect even the slightest difference from the previous month's photos. Not an easy chore when they saw hundreds of these photos a week.

"I only remember the ones around here." Harlin tapped the photo site with his index finger. "I've been dying to dig that mound and just haven't had time. Now, it looks like some pot hunter beat me to it."

Harlin went to the map drawers and pulled out a thick sheaf of photos. His already practiced hand ruffled through the stack and found the right one. He returned to the table and spread it out beside the new one. Both were taken from a remote satellite flying overhead at an altitude of more than one hundred thousand feet. The detail the camera could get from such great distance was amazing.

Nathan studied the photographs. The color patterns were obvious to the trained eye. To anyone else they looked like what they had to him almost two years ago. A kaleidoscope of reds, browns and greens that meant absolutely nothing.

Harlin, as usual, was right on target. Someone had been digging. Freshly turned dirt reflected light in a vastly different manner than undisturbed ground. It also held heat longer and would show up on infrared as a disturbance.

"Somebody's been digging alright. We might as well notify the authorities, Harlin." Nathan knew the illegal digging frustrated Harlin. His training dictated a controlled dig, cataloging every find, meticulously uncovering and documenting all traces of ancient civilization. However, with artifact prices high enough to put your children through college, pot hunters and grave robbers were destroying archeological sites faster than they could even be recorded, much less excavated. Important historical evidence was being destroyed that could never be recovered.

Disgusted, Harlin shook his head, the cowlick in front bobbing up and down emphatically. "Yeah, and they'll get around to going over there in a month or two."

Nathan understood his friend's reaction. They had reported several such violations of Federal law in the last few months and so far little had been done. Bureaucracies moved maddeningly slow.

"Now you know why I've been so worked up about the dead zone." The remote sensing fellowships were open to anyone with a doctorate in the sciences and Nathan's specialty was marine biology. Chemical runoff into the Gulf of Mexico had created a vast dead zone where nothing lived. No fish, no plankton, no algae, no life of any kind. He had been trying for months, with a consortium of other scientists, to get something done about it. So far to no avail.

"Well, I'm tired of doing nothing while the government allows these sites to be ransacked." Harlin's zeal, fresh from the doctoral program, was admirable. Nathan had been out for so long that he'd lost that passion.

What a difference a year can make.

Constantly butting his head against a bureaucratic stone wall had only gotten him one thing besides a month of wasted hours. A sore head, literally and figuratively. Often his temples would throb from dealing with the rampant apathy and stupidity. Apparently, apathy was contagious, because lately it had been easier and easier to let the consortium work slide.

"Harlin, you'll have to save the world later. Right now we've got a meeting with the big boys." Certain that Harlin had probably forgotten the meeting, Nathan had come to remind him.

Harlin's facial expression told Nathan he'd been right. "Couldn't you have forgotten about me just once?"

"No way. You think Humsinger's a freak over the trash? You should miss a meeting." Nathan raised his eyebrows and nodded in the affirmative. "You'll only do it once."

Nathan knew that Harlin would test the boundaries once he left. In five days his fellowship was over. Then he had a full month before his academic appointment started. A month to relax and do nothing.

"Well, maybe this should be my one time."

"Not on my watch." Nathan adopted his old tenured professor scowl and did his best "retired-on-the-job-but-I-remember-when-I-was-young impression."

"Why, you young pups don't have any discipline anymore. Back when I was a doctoral student, tenured faculty members were gods. You're all spoiled now."

Even though Harlin was in another specialty and had gone to a different school, he could relate to Nathan's routine. It was the same everywhere. Humsinger epitomized everyone's dissertation supervisor. The one who crawled on his hands and knees uphill through the snow in 100-degree weather while writing his dissertation with a sharp stick pressing each letter into wet clay. Things were always so much easier for the ones that came later. Forget about the fact that the amount of knowledge a student had to learn expanded exponentially from year to year. Forget about the fact that every professor always felt like his protégé should jump at least one more hurdle than he had. Forget about the fact that advances in computing resources expanded everyone's expectations since you could crunch more data in five minutes than your professor could in five months with the old punch cards.

Harlin smiled over Nathan's mock lecture. Finishing his degree had eliminated some of the pressure, but the fellowship was similar in many ways. He had merely replaced his dissertation supervisor with Humsinger. His upcoming position would probably be the same. Humsinger would be replaced by a department chair or dean. The cycle of life continues. Harlin couldn't help but wonder when he would pass over the imaginary boundary and make the switch from the perpetual student to the wizened scholar.

"All right, all right. Let's go." Harlin carefully put the photographs back in their drawer, "But I'm going to check it out tomorrow."

"Another martyr," Nathan said in feigned admiration. "You can't do anything about it, Harlin. Why don't you just forget it."

"I only want to see what they're up to." Nathan could tell that Harlin was still irritated. At him or the circumstances, he couldn't tell.

"Why don't you run out there with me?" Harlin suggested.

Apparently Harlin wasn't irritated at him. "I can't tomorrow. I've got an appointment. Let's do it Saturday."

"Done." Harlin said, "I'll bring a camera and we can document everything."

Nathan looked at his watch, "We better get to the meeting

before Humsinger gets wild-eyed." They stopped at the door while Harlin ran back and snatched the candy wrapper off the table and stuffed it in his pocket. A derisive smile played across his face. "I wouldn't want the trash police to ticket me."

* * *

"Look, Nathan. I'm fed up." Kat's black eyes flashed fire. Their ten-minute argument had grown louder and more embarrassing by the second. "I'm sick of trying to patch things up."

"Kat, please give us another chance. I still love you," Nathan pleaded. Shouting had failed to produce the desired result.

"Shut up, Nathan. All you ever do is whine. You act like a three-year old." Kat turned to enter the auditorium and couldn't resist throwing another verbal jab over her shoulder. "I wanted a man, not a child."

Kat, mad at the world, stomped into the crowded room. She realized that last blow had been below the belt, but Nathan pushed her to it. Their separation grew uglier the closer they got to the end of the mandatory waiting period. Now all she wanted to do was find a seat before the tears came. Never one to cry, she'd been exceptionally teary lately.

The meeting hall buzzed with activity as everyone speculated about the cause of the impromptu gathering. The various research centers at Stennis operated under a fairly structured system and it was a rare occurrence for there not to be at least a week's notice before any meeting. This one had been called only yesterday via e-mail. No hint had been given as to the reason and, as a result, speculation ran amok.

Kat, forced to mingle, chatted with some of her acquaintances from other divisions. However, she managed to steer clear of anyone from the Remote Sensing Project. She wasn't in the mood to discuss her personal life, particularly after the recent public argument.

Not that it mattered.

The topic of her impending divorce would surface anyway. Particularly among several male colleagues who were secretly hoping for the breakup between her and Nathan. She was flattered by their attention, but also not ready for it, and didn't particularly understand it.

In the past, the male population had barely acknowledged she existed. Somewhat bookish while growing up, she had been more interested in science than in boys. Only recently, since meeting Nathan, had she started noticing the furtive glances of fellow graduate students and co-workers.

Even so, Kat didn't consider herself attractive. Her hair, the color of cloud-covered midnight, had always been too straight to suit her. Lately she had taken to wearing it short to save time. She was a little too thin and not quite filled out in the places the boys in high school were concerned about. Self-consciously she folded her arms across her chest as she strolled through the crowd. Nathan had been her first true love.

And only true love, for that matter.

And Nathan had been enamored with her looks, constantly telling her she was beautiful. Before Nathan, she had accepted the fact that she was intelligent and plain. Now, because he'd pointed it out to her, she noticed that she did seem to draw a lot of attention.

Kat eavesdropped on several conversations where numerous theories were being offered about the reason for the meeting as everyone milled around. Her academic mind sorted the various offerings and quickly categorized the results. As far as she could tell, there were two broad categories; the doomsday group and the euphoric group.

The first group, the doomsdayers, assured everyone that funding cuts were inevitable and this meeting was to announce the extent of the damage. Rumors hinted at loss of funding; either across the board cuts of varying percentages or total loss of a particular research division. Government funding had been increasingly difficult to obtain for a number of research proposals.

Starting about a decade ago, money had been drying up for research projects that didn't have a clear link to potential commercial applications. Lately, the battles had become even more difficult. The economy was doing well and no one saw a real need for technologies that might create entirely new industries in the future.

Why worry about tomorrow when everything is fine today?

In part to battle that line of reasoning, Stennis had developed the Technology Transfer Center geared toward finding commercial applications for any of the research generated under the umbrella of the John C. Stennis Space Center.

The main mission of Stennis remained the same. To test and certify the engines used to power the space shuttle. Back in its heyday, when NASA's space program received a lot of attention, there were as many as 5,000 total employees. Over the years, budget cuts had trimmed that number to about 3,500. For the most part, the doomsday camp was led by what Kat called the old guard. The old guard consisted of scientists and technicians who had been at Stennis for 20 years or more and remembered the glory days. They had all survived the congressional chopping block many times but were scarred from near misses and recollections of colleagues who had not been as fortunate.

The other group, the one she'd dubbed the euphoric group, insisted that the reason for the meeting was to announce new funding, either for another research division or increased funding for one of the several continuing operations. Oceanic groups, meteorology groups, and the remote sensing group seemed to be the odds-on favorites for this type of blessing. These were the current areas that could most easily extend their applications to the commercial realm. The biometrics group, doing work in iris identification and voice recognition, should also have a decent shot at additional funding but they weren't good at public relations. The computer jocks in biometrics were too introverted, overly concerned with solving the problem at hand and not concerned enough about potential applications of their discoveries.

The huge auditorium was filled to capacity. Of course it always was for a general meeting. A general meeting usually meant a visiting dignitary or eminent scholar was delivering a presentation and the Stennis community came out *en masse* to either. Dignitaries were potential allies in government funding battles and therefore deemed worthy to waste valuable time on while listening to some boring presentation. Eminent scholars usually had something worthwhile to say and often generated a spirited debate after their presentation. The Stennis community lived for such moments.

Someone clearing his throat at the podium created a scramble for seats. Everyone had waited long enough. Kat settled in to the comfortable theater seat beside someone she didn't know. She noted the Remote Sensing Group seated in their usual section. She averted her eyes and scooted down in the seat when she saw Nathan scanning the auditorium, no doubt looking for her. The older man beside her, probably one of the old guard, gave her a curious sidewise glance and then returned his attention to center stage. Ray Tennison, the center director, was standing at the podium waiting for the room to quiet. He didn't wait long because everyone was curious.

"Good morning, everyone." Ray smiled at his audience, a polished smile perfected from years of political battles and behind-the-scenes lobbying for funds. She wondered if it were pure chance that Tennison was here, or if he had scheduled this meeting. He spent most of his time in Washington or *en route* to some corporate headquarters or private foundation. Kat noticed he did appear to be at ease, however. Maybe that was a good sign. Even though her postdoctoral appointment was almost over, she remained an ardent supporter of the many separate research endeavors currently underway at Stennis and hoped for continued funding.

"I won't keep you in suspense for long." He paused for effect. "I have good news."

Tennison's speech was halted by a collective sigh from the

audience and a smattering of applause. He held up his hands for silence. "We have just received the largest private donation in the history of Stennis." Instantly the room grew quiet. "And, I'll answer the obvious question about which of you will benefit from the donation before I give the amount. All of you will receive a portion of the monies with the lion's share going to the remote sensing group."

"The donation will total twenty million dollars over a five-year period." Tennison stepped back a moment to enjoy the reaction. The news stunned everyone, including Kat. She knew the total operating budget for the remote sensing group was less than two million dollars a year. Their satellite had been dedicated to them and therefore didn't cost anything. And the facilities had been constructed and paid for in the Apollo era. They were allocated access to the Cray supercomputer at various times to do their major computing chores. The only real expenses of the remote sensing group were labor and some clerical supplies. The employee list included four full-time Ph.D's, a dozen low-paid postdoctoral slaves, and four secretaries. Supplies were minimal.

Kat didn't hear the remainder of Tennison's report. Her mind wandered elsewhere. There was a slight possibility that this meeting might benefit her after all!

CHAPTER 4

Nathan heard the phone ringing and tried to focus enough to determine the source of the annoying sound. Slowly, as if seeing a semi truck approaching through the fog, the sound registered. He scrambled for the phone and tripped over his suitcase on the floor. At the last second he caught himself by grabbing the nearby stack of book boxes filled to capacity with academic biology tomes. He'd be moving again soon and unpacking seemed like fruitless labor.

He found the elusive phone and snatched the receiver, "Hello."

"Nathan? Can you come over today and get the rest of your stuff?"

No pleasantries.

Just demands.

In spite of that, Kat's voice on the other end filled him with regret. The only relationship he had ever wanted to succeed and it had fallen apart.

"I'm supposed to go with Harlin today." Nathan stifled a yawn as he looked for a clock. It was only six o'clock in the morning. "We're going to check out a dig site."

"Can't you do that some other time?" Kat's voice was insistent. Not the least bit friendly.

"I'll come by tomorrow and pick it up." Nathan wondered why she'd called so early. What was the big deal about his junk?

"Look, Nathan. You told me you'd pick it up last week and the week before that." Her voice was growing colder if that was possible, "Nothing like a man of his word." The sarcasm dripped from the receiver like cold pancake syrup.

Nathan held his tongue. He didn't want to fight any more. That's why he'd moved out.

"Let me put it this way." Kat paused for just a second, "I'm throwing your junk in the dumpster if it's not gone by this afternoon."

Nathan heard the crash of the slamming receiver and then the blissful dial tone rescued him from her tirade. Luckily she'd hung up before he lost his cool and responded in kind. The hallmark of their rocky relationship.

He looked at the clock, knowing he'd better call Harlin and cancel. It was too early though. Harlin probably wouldn't be up. He could wait and catch him later. Right now he wanted to catch a few more winks if he could get Kat off his mind. She was the best thing and the worst thing that had ever happened to him.

Maybe the relationship had been doomed from the start.

Their post-doc appointments under Humsinger were almost as demanding as their respective doctoral programs. Like Harlin, Kat was an archeologist. She and Nathan had both landed fellowships at the same time.

Each year, six of the coveted slots were opened up for competition. The fellowships began in May and lasted a little over two years. The jobs ended in August, allowing the recipients some summer support before they took their respective jobs. Most of the time the jobs were in the academic community so new positions always started in the fall of any given year.

Occasionally one of the fellows would opt to move into industry research. Nathan knew of two people who had taken "real-world" jobs as they were called, for substantially more money than academe with substantially less control over their work. They traded autonomy for financial security. He'd considered it himself, but ultimately opted for the freedom of the university. At least his research agenda was his own, no matter how esoteric the 'powers-that-be' deemed it. Until the tenure decision.

One of his and Kat's most bitter arguments was about Nathan even considering a corporate research job. Kat had gone ballistic when she discovered several pharmaceutical companies with employment opportunities had approached him. One would think she would have been happy because both of them had combined school debts to repay that surpassed several small countries' gross domestic product.

Now Nathan wondered if she was just jealous.

With a doctorate in archeology, Kat didn't face the same employment prospects. In fact, she was yet to find a university post. There simply wasn't a huge demand for her specialty. If she would abandon her "holier-than-thou" attitude about industry, she could get a job. She just needed to focus on the skills she had obtained during this fellowship.

But Kat didn't want an industry job. She wanted an academic post. She and 500 other unemployed Ph.D. archeologists scattered around the globe. Kat might change her tune after repeating the question, "Paper or plastic?," about ten thousand times.

Nathan clasped his hands behind his head and stared at the ceiling. Kat was stubborn, high-spirited and aggravating. Yet beautiful, tantalizing and intelligent. On the other hand, so maddening, arrogant and frustrating. And so much still his wife.

At least for a little while longer.

She would have to be the one to file for divorce. Nathan certainly did not intend to make it easy for her. If he closed his eyes, he could generate the sensual aroma he had grown to associate with Kat.

* * *

Harlin stopped the pickup under the shade of a huge live oak. With a diameter of over seven feet at the base, Harlin estimated the tree to be at least 600 years old. Spanish moss draped from the limbs and several gray squirrels chattered at him, noisily wondering what type of creature had invaded their territory. Several of the limbs had grown so heavy that the forces of Sir

Newton had pulled them back to the earth twenty or thirty feet from the trunk before they swept majestically upward again.

Harlin marveled at the tree, thankful that the coast community had enough foresight to protect these ancient residents. It was illegal to cut an oak, pecan or magnolia in any of the coastal counties.

He turned his attention back to the road. The rest of the way would be on foot. Four-wheel drive enthusiasts had rutted the road to the point of impasse for ordinary vehicles. A quad runner would be nice about now. Just drop the tailgate of his old pickup and take off in one of those new Hondas with automatic transmissions and reverse. Someday he would buy one if he ever managed to whittle his school debt down, he thought wistfully. The list of wants grew longer as he approached real employment. The fellowship paid the bills, but left no room for extras. His pay barely exceeded the stipend he'd received as a graduate assistant at Berkeley.

With practiced ease, Harlin filled his small daypack with the necessities. A packet of sandwiches and granola bars for lunch, three one-liter bottles of water, a change of socks, matches and extra film for his camera. The camera he slung around his neck. The electronic global positioning unit he had borrowed from Stennis was already safely secured on his belt, preprogrammed with the site coordinates. A topographic map, encased in a waterproof Ziplock® bag, fit into his back pocket. To complete the ensemble he added his new Gerber knife to his belt. A birthday present from everyone at work. Harlin found it hard to believe that he had just turned thirty-one years old. The older he got, the faster the years rolled by.

Harlin checked his watch and wondered why Nathan hadn't shown. Probably something to do with Kat again. It was a wonder Nathan or Kat got any work done lately. All they did was fight when they were together. Or, if he happened to be alone with one of them, they talked incessantly about how incompatible they were and how much their individual lives would be better without the other.

Harlin had grown sick of the whole mess, and he'd regretted inviting Nathan along. At the time he had been so engrossed in the new remote sensing photographs it had slipped his mind that Nathan and Kat were people he wanted to avoid lately. He certainly hadn't called Nathan when he didn't show up at the appointed time. He considered Nathan and Kat to be good friends, but preferred solitude over their companionship at this stage of their relationship. Early on, he had tried to help them work through their differences, but counseling had never been his *forte'*.

Harlin slid the pack over his shoulder and started off. It promised to be another wonderfully hot humid day and he had about a three-mile hike ahead of him. Better to get it over with before the heat became unbearable.

* * *

Quin Laroche's dark skin glistened in the morning sun. Not even nine o'clock and already too hot to work. He stole a look at Specky, doing nothing as usual, poking around with a stick at something on the ground. Specky worked at looking busy. Always had since Quin had known him. Specky Vore was the laziest man Quin had ever seen. And a white man at that. Three days on this job and they still hadn't found a thing. At least today he'd thought to bring a fishing pole and put it out with some stink bait before they started digging again. The edge of the slough was only a few paces from the ancient burial mound they were busy desecrating. Or, more accurately, the mound Quin was busy desecrating. Specky had done little of the actual work.

"Specky! You gonna help me?"

"I'm just lookin' around a little."

"If you ain't going to help, at least get me something to drink."

Specky sneered. "What do you want me to do? Spit in a cup for you?"

"What? You ain't brought no water?" Quin snorted his disgust. "You're about as worthless as teats on a boar hog."

"You want some cheese with that whine?" Specky figured his humor would fly right over Quin's head.

"Oh. You're so funny." Quin slapped his knee in false amusement, and then added. "I wish the boss man would fire you. I'm gettin' tired of doin' all the work."

"Yeah, yeah. You're just a regular workaholic." Specky snickered, "You ain't seen a shovel in ten years before I got you this job."

Quin held out his palm. A newly opened blister looked red and ugly with the clear fluid creating a dirt stained halo around the offended area, "How many of these you got?"

Specky rubbed his hands together, "You don't get em if you got calluses already."

Quin threw his shovel in Specky's general direction. It skidded to a stop a few feet away from Specky's boots. "Pick it up. I ain't doing another thing until you start helping. I ain't hired on to be your yard boy, Specky."

Specky's lip curled up in a sneer. "You ain't being paid to stand around either."

Specky thumped his chest with an unwashed hand. The fingernails had enough topsoil under them to grow a good garden.

"Who's the super on this job, Quin?"

Without waiting for Quin to answer, Specky continued. "I am. That's who. And what I say goes."

Specky spat on the fresh mound of dirt heaped up by the two men in the last few days, "And you'll get a cool two grand for your time."

Specky cocked his head and squinted at Quin. He resembled one of those fighting roosters with his chest all puffed out just about ready to spur somebody. "Maybe more if you get off your butt and we find something."

"I'm about fed up with you, Specky." Quin outweighed Specky by an easy eighty or ninety pounds and he was through putting up with Specky's superior attitude. "If you don't help me dig this stinking hole I'm gonna kick your sorry butt from here to the road."

"All right, all right. Quit your crying." Specky acted hurt, but he knew Quin would do what he said. "I was trying to do you a favor and you get all bent out of shape on me. I thought you needed money."

Quin sighed. " I do, Specky. But I don't like digging up no graves. Why didn't you tell me that before we got here?"

Specky snorted. "What did you think we was doing with a shovel that would pay you a couple of thousand dollars for a week's work? Digging taters?"

Quin stammered. "I don't know. I didn't think about it."

"Say cheese, guys." Harlin's voice took them by surprise. Specky and Quin had been so engrossed in their argument that they hadn't even noticed when he walked within ten yards of them. In unison they turned toward the voice just as the camera flashed. The man quickly snapped several more photographs while they remained immobile.

Specky reacted first. "Gimme that camera."

Specky brandished the shovel and moved menacingly toward the man. Quin noted the man was bigger than Specky, but not much bigger.

Harlin snapped more pictures of Specky waving the shovel around and then stopped, realizing he might be in danger. His hand drifted to his belt and the new knife.

"He's going for the knife, Specky." Quin had yet to move, uncertain about what he should do.

Specky reacted fast. In two steps he was on the man and swinging the shovel hard. He connected, but dealt only a glancing blow to Harlin's shoulder. Harlin managed to get the knife out but another shovel blow knocked it from his hands. Quin watched both men scramble for the knife, Specky still holding the shovel awkwardly. The knife landed next to the water of the slough. Harlin reached it first with Specky just a split-second behind him. Harlin dove on the knife and Specky landed on him, astride Harlin's back like a bull-rider at a rodeo. The tangle of arms and legs that ensued was almost comical to Quin but he knew Specky was in real danger of being overpowered and carved up by the larger knife-wielding man.

Quin had taken about two steps towards the struggling pair when the apparition appeared and engulfed the fighters. Blood spurted from Specky's punctured jugular vein and splayed across Quin's cheek. Brief screams erupted from two terror-stricken throats before the murky waters silenced the cries. The water roiled for a moment and then calmed. A spreading red stain on the water's surface remained the only indication of the quick nightmare event.

Quin would relive the horror-filled moment several more times before his life was over.

For now he ran.

Ran like he had never run before. Twenty minutes later he found Harlin's abandoned truck and, hands trembling, hot-wired the ignition. Saying a silent prayer he fingered the pouch suspended from a chain around his neck and headed for New Orleans. There was a man he had to see that terrified him almost as much as the sight he had just witnessed.

Almost.

CHAPTER 5

"Kat, I swear to you something's happened. I'm worried about Harlin. He didn't show up for work today and Humsinger said he didn't call in sick either."

"He's a big boy, Nathan. Harlin is quite capable of taking care of himself. He'll show up in a day or two." She furrowed her brow and her gorgeous dark eyes glinted with anger. "And besides, I'm not speaking to you any more."

Kat stomped off, slamming the map room door behind her, still furious from the weekend's events. He'd made it to her place on Saturday to pick up his few belongings and they had gotten into another one of their infamous fights. Only this one had been so bad the neighbors had called the police on them for domestic disturbance. The whole sordid scene embarrassed Kat beyond belief. Two scientists with freshly minted doctorates acting like drunken white trash on the newest episode of *Cops*.

He had to admit it was more than a little embarrassing himself. They had gotten into such a heated argument that neither had realized how loud they were getting. Explaining that to Hancock county's finest had been humbling to say the least. Fortunately the officer had merely given them a warning after they satisfied him they weren't drinking and dangerous. Calling Humsinger to bail them out of jail would have been a nightmare.

Nathan hunched over the newest photos and tried to remember the exact location Harlin had identified last week. He'd drifted off to sleep Saturday and, by the time he called, Harlin had already left. And now Harlin hadn't shown up for work. Nathan could imagine Harlin breaking a leg and lying there all weekend unable to crawl out. Or worse yet, getting bitten by a poisonous snake. Water moccasins and copperheads thrived in the swampy coastal region.

Nathan narrowed the likely area down to three sites. He wished he had paid more attention to the particular map Harlin had been studying that day. He had verified Harlin's assessment of someone digging but had failed to note which particular photo that had caught Harlin's attention. Nathan knew it was in northern Hancock county, so he had started with those photos and narrowed it down to the three that showed the color signature of recent ground disturbance that he couldn't link to agriculture or recent building permits.

He studied all three photos and closed his eyes, trying to dredge up the memory of the photo from last Thursday.

Which one was it?

Something odd tugged at the corner of his mind, but he couldn't quite pin it down. Nathan was so deep in thought that he failed to hear the door open.

"Meditating, Nathan?" The deep voice resonated throughout the room.

Nathan jumped, startled by the intrusion on his thoughts. "You surprised me, Dr. Humsinger."

Brian Humsinger looked the part of elder scholar. He was approaching sixty years old but surprisingly trim and fit for a man that age. His silver hair merely made him appear more distinguished. A geologist by training, he had landed the highly sought-after position as head of the remote sensing group when the project first began over twenty years ago. Humsinger was truly one of the remote sensing pioneers with over fifty papers published in respected journals on the subject. His mind was still as brilliant and alert as it had been thirty years ago.

Humsinger ran the remote sensing group almost like a military unit; he gave orders and expected them to be obeyed. In spite of his sometimes-harsh management style, his protégés respected him. He was the true undisputed expert in his field and a post-doctoral appointment under him meant a jump-start to most academic careers.

"Still no word from our wayward scholar?" Humsinger

queried.

"Nothing, sir. I'm concerned something might have happened to him." Nathan paused, weighing the consequences of his next statement. He decided he had to risk it, "I think he went out to a site he found on one of the photos. He was concerned about relic hunters."

Humsinger frowned. "He knew that was strictly forbidden. You have all been instructed to report suspected violations directly to me and allow me to contact the appropriate authorities."

Humsinger looked askance at Nathan. "Why didn't you report it to me if you knew about it?"

"I'm sorry about that. It slipped my mind with the announcement about the donation." Nathan knew his excuse sounded lame, but he really had no good explanation. Harlin would report it when he came back from investigating the site so there had been no need for him to concern himself with it. That excuse wouldn't carry much weight with Humsinger at the moment. It was a breach of protocol either way.

Humsinger nodded at the photos, "Hunting for the proverbial needle in the haystack, eh?"

Nathan felt relieved. Humsinger appeared to be dropping the rule violation in light of the current circumstances. "Yes, but at least I've narrowed it down to these three possibilities."

Nathan indicated the three locations, each marked with a small brightly-colored sticky note. "I wasn't paying enough attention to which particular photo Harlin was studying the other day."

Nathan swallowed expecting another mild reprimand. Humsinger prided himself on paying attention to detail. He harped on that fact being what separated the good scientists from the great ones. He demanded that his students develop that same ability. At the moment, Nathan realized he wasn't exhibiting the coveted trait. Humsinger, however, apparently decided to ignore the lapse of Nathan's powers of observation and bent over the map table.

"Well, it shouldn't be this site. It's too far away from water." Humsinger was right as usual. Ancient villages, including burial sites, normally were located within a few hundred feet of water. Nathan felt foolish but his normal quarry was located in the water. Marine biology and archeology were two separate fields.

"Pull last month's photo on these other two, Nathan." Humsinger was a master at solving puzzles and Nathan still admired watching the man work, in spite of his boss's normally gruff demeanor.

Nathan pulled the requested photos and spread them out on the table. Humsinger bent over the photos and compared them with the ones still on the table. A moment later, he tapped his finger on the table, indicating one of the sites, "It could be either, but this one is the most recent."

Humsinger, always the teacher, studied the photos some more and then traced a color pattern on one of them with his index finger. "Note how the red is slightly more intense here? That small area is retaining heat in a manner more consistent with freshly turned earth. I'd guess in the last day or two given the soil moisture now. The other site appears to be a little older, and it's also not too far from this house." Humsinger tapped a small square that indicated a structure. "Most of the recent relic hunting has been in more isolated areas."

He looked up at Nathan. "Let's take a ride over there in the morning and see if we can find out if Harlin visited the site."

Humsinger exhibited a genuine interest over Harlin's welfare that Nathan would never have expected. It was a side of the man rarely seen by any of the post-doc fellows.

"I appreciate that, sir." Nathan hesitated, "But, would it be possible to go now?"

"I have an appointment in ten minutes and then a luncheon with Dr. Tennison regarding our recent benefactor. It would be impossible for me to go this afternoon."

Humsinger smiled in a fatherly manner, "Have a vehicle checked out of the car pool and ready to go. I'll stop by your office, or the map room, shortly after nine."

Nathan sighed and carefully replaced the photos in the proper drawer. A few more hours wouldn't matter. He considered calling the police, but he doubted they would do anything about someone missing no longer than Harlin had been missing.

* * *

Kat tentatively knocked on the door.

"Come in, Miss Young." Humsinger's voice resonated through the door. Kat had waited almost thirty minutes and the courage she had summoned this morning to request Humsinger's earliest available meeting time had long since ebbed. Twice she had stopped herself from chewing her fingernails. She had developed the nasty habit as a nervous child and, in times of stress, caught herself unconsciously moving her hand toward her mouth. The habit had been as difficult to break as someone quitting smoking.

Humsinger's one-hour luncheon had turned into an hour and a half. Kat now regretted making the appointment. She should have attempted to run into Humsinger in the hall, or casually asked him while going over some work. But the problem with that plan was that she had wanted to ask him alone. Rejection would be less painful without a crowd of onlookers.

Kat breathed deeply and entered the office. She had been there many times over the last two years but was always amazed. His office was as large as any four of the other offices combined and crammed with a lifetime of academic memorabilia. It wasn't messy or unorganized, just full. Floor to ceiling bookshelves, harboring souvenirs of every conceivable type, lined the walls. Some people might call Humsinger's collection clutter, but to Kat it was wonderful.

Humsinger was a geologist by training, so a collection of rock and mineral specimens dominated the space. In addition, there were numerous fossils and artifacts that he had collected from around the globe. A mastodon tooth served as a desk ornament while a framed case of beautiful Midwestern flint arrow points occupied a prominent position on the wall behind him.

On the opposite wall hung a limited edition artist rendering of the Space Shuttle that had been autographed by one of the shuttle crews. After all, the engines had been tested here at Stennis. Kat marveled at the treasures every time and almost always discovered something she hadn't seen before. She actually relished the few times she had been in his office and he'd taken a phone call. Those times presented opportunities for her to visually explore every conceivable cranny.

"Good afternoon, Dr. Humsinger. Thank you for agreeing to see me." Kat hoped that her voice didn't reveal her nervousness.

"I always try to be accessible. I know you and Nathan will be leaving us soon and things will get exceptionally busy around here. I'm excited about receiving the grant money but it will also increase my workload in the short run." Humsinger leaned back comfortably in his leather chair. "What can I help you with today?"

Kat, uncertain how to proceed, jumped in full force. "Actually, you breached the topic already. I have yet to find an academic appointment and..." Kat stammered but continued rapidly before she lost her nerve. "I was wondering if it might be possible to extend my research appointment here another year? I thought the grant that Dr. Tennison announced this morning might create some additional openings that haven't been filled yet."

Humsinger studied Kat thoughtfully, tapping his fingertips together slowly. "You're very astute and have done some wonderful work here. And you are right about the need for additional staff, although I haven't really had time to take inventory of those needs."

Humsinger paused momentarily and then continued. "However, there is a delicate issue that I'm concerned with and I'm uncertain as to what to do about it."

Kat knew that legally Humsinger could not broach the subject of her marital status but she suspected that this was the 'delicate issue' he was concerned about.

"Dr. Humsinger. If you have any concerns about me and Nathan, please let me put those to rest." Kat sighed. Baring her soul to Humsinger seemed to finalize everything. "We have legally separated and I intend to file for divorce. Nathan will be leaving soon for an academic appointment in Utah and I won't be going with him. I have reconciled myself to the fact that our marriage was a mistake and I'm ready to get on with my career." Kat felt strangely drained after the speech and hoped the stress didn't show on her face. She fidgeted with her hands in her lap.

Humsinger, quiet for a moment, appeared to be mulling something over in his mind. The silence, no more than a few seconds, felt interminable.

"I'm sorry to hear about your personal misfortune, Mrs. Young, and I do appreciate your honesty." Humsinger stopped abruptly and raised an inquisitive eyebrow. "Should I continue to address you as Mrs. Young?"

It's odd how she hadn't considered the name change yet. "Abnaki. Kateri Abnaki." Her stomach began to grow queasy. Kateri Abnaki had a sense of finality about it. But it was final and she needed a job. Desperately. Maybe this meeting had served its purpose. Forcing her to recognize her situation and stop the denial.

It was over between her and Nathan.

"We will be short-handed until we can go through the proper channels and hire additional permanent staff." Humsinger tapped his fingers thoughtfully, "However, I have within my discretion the authority to add emergency personnel without going through the normal EEOC channels, particularly if I hire a minority. I could offer you a permanent position and expedite the process since you're a Native American and a woman. I must confess that our current permanent staff does not represent diversity and, as a result, our next permanent hire will almost certainly need to be a minority. You, Miss Abnaki, are already trained and have done exemplary work. Excuse me, Dr. Abnaki." Humsinger corrected himself. Kat had never heard him address one of the postdoctoral fellows as Dr. It seemed foreign to her.

"I think we can come up with an arrangement that is beneficial to both of us."

Humsinger tapped his fingers on his desk. "You mentioned an extension of your fellowship. Would you be interested in a permanent appointment instead?"

Kat's heart pounded so rapidly she feared it might be visibly moving her shirt. A mixture of emotions coursed through her mind. The finality of her marriage. A non-corporate research position offered. Sadness and joy within minutes. Humsinger waited for her response. She tried not to appear too eager.

"I would definitely be interested."

"Well, I'll have to obtain official approval but it's merely a formality. You realize the entry-level salary rate is pre-set by the government? The current pay scale for someone with a Ph.D. and two years work experience is $62,000 a year." Humsinger paused again, studying her reaction. "Is that amount acceptable, Dr. Abnaki?"

Kat could barely believe what was happening. She had scheduled this meeting to see if she could extend her fellowship one more year to give her time to find an academic appointment, and now she had been offered a permanent position doing something she truly enjoyed. And the money far surpassed her current $24,000 stipend. In fact, $62,000 was well above the average starting salary of anyone in archeology lucky enough to land a university or museum curator position.

"More than acceptable, Dr. Humsinger."

"Good. If we're in agreement, I'll start the paperwork. That will be one less issue that I'll have to worry with. Of course you realize that a large part of your job every fall will be to help train the newest crop of research fellows. After the first few months of every new group, you will be able to pursue your own research agenda. Within limits, of course. You will always be encouraged to pursue research venues that either further the use of remote sensing technology or use remote sensing technology in the actual research. Occasionally we will have priority projects that demand your attention or your particular area of expertise. In these instances, I will call upon you to put down the projects you are currently working on and give full attention to the priority project. And, as always, unless the project is sensitive, you will be expected to publish your research in refereed academic journals."

Humsinger looked at his watch. "I'm sorry Dr. Abnaki, but I have another engagement at two o'clock. Do you have any immediate questions?"

Kat, still trying to recover from shock, managed to croak. "No sir. I really appreciate this opportunity. Thank you very much."

Humsinger smiled. "One more thing. I would appreciate it if you did not tell the other fellows about our arrangement. It could create a hostile work environment for you over the next few days. I suspect something of this nature could create some jealousy."

Kat nodded her agreement. "I'll keep it confidential, Dr. Humsinger."

Humsinger started to say something and then stopped.

"Anything else, sir?"

"It's another issue, but I was wondering, how well do you know Harlin Rogers?"

"Fairly well. He and Nathan are great friends, and he's also the only other archeologist here."

"Does he have any history of family problems or anything you can think of that might make him just walk off the job?"

Kat thought about the question. "I guess I don't know him as well as I thought." She felt a little sheepish. "I know very little about his family. Most of our conversations were work related."

"Thank you, anyway, Dr. Abnaki." Kat turned to leave. "And, Dr. Abnaki?" Humsinger paused as Kat turned back to face him. He smiled broadly, "Congratulations."

Kat floated out of the office. The experience was surreal. To go in virtually begging for an extension and come out with a coveted job. Too bad she couldn't share the news with Nathan since job search pressures had caused a large portion of their conflict. He would find out soon enough.

Her thoughts turned to Harlin. How well did she know him?

A lot of people disappear for days at a time. Several years ago, a distant cousin of hers vanished. No one heard from him or saw him for over a month. Then one day he just reappeared, claiming that he needed some space and had to get away. He never mentioned where he'd been.

* * *

Kevin Croix bent over the pierced teenager lying passed out in the doorway and picked him up as if he weighed no more than a twenty-four pack of toilet paper. He reeked of the street smell and stale beer. The boy was new to the Quarter, obviously a runaway, and had yet to learn. Kevin hoped to spare him some of those hard lessons.

He carried the young man two blocks before entering one of the narrow brick corridors common to the French Quarter. The brick cobbled path, lined with azaleas, led to a small courtyard with a hammock suspended between two porch posts. Kevin deposited his burden in the hammock and stuffed a card in the boy's pocket with a twenty-dollar bill wrapped around it. Without a word, trying not to disturb the sleeping teen, he turned and left, exiting the same way he entered.

The boy opened one eye and watched Kevin's retreating back, one long braid of hair gently swaying as the big man walked. He cut his eyes to the left and right, and satisfied no one watched him, he took the card from his pocket and looked at it.

> *Kevin Croix*
> *Servant*
> *157 South Rampart*
> *Thursday nights at 7:00*

For a moment, he contemplated what "servant" might mean, before focusing on the twenty. It looked real. The boy, approached by gay men of every stripe for sexual favors since he landed in New Orleans, was even more curious now. The man didn't strike him as gay. The boy was curious now.

CHAPTER 6

Quin Laroche fingered the "Johnny the Conqueror" gris-gris suspended from a thin braided cord around his neck. A piece of lodestone felt heavy in his pocket. Both had helped in the past with the ladies, one for lady love and the other for lady luck. Johnny and the lodestone had been powerful gris-gris so far. Just last week he'd won $500 at the tables and that yellow skinned beauty had followed him home to his bed. He knew both potions were still powerful magic, but they just weren't designed for what he was up against now.

Quin needed something much stronger. Bad juju stalked him for taking the digging job. He knew it for gospel, and he also knew how difficult it was to put off.

He cursed himself for being so stupid.

Messing around with someone's grave was the best way to put a hex on them and he and Specky had somehow dug up an old hex. Quin wasn't sure just what it was, but he was glad he'd had "Johnny the Conqueror" with him. That stupid white boy Specky had always poked fun at him for being superstitious but his knowledge of the spirit realm had paid off again.

Which one of them was alive now? Darn sure wasn't Specky. "Johnny" had been powerful enough to save him for the moment but Quin feared it was only a temporary fix.

Quin glanced at his watch and waited a few more minutes. It wasn't quite midnight and Doctor John had been very specific. Sweat beaded Quin's forehead. South Rampart in the French Quarter at midnight was not the best neighborhood to be walking around, but that thought hadn't entered Quin's mind. The upcoming meeting with Doctor John terrified him.

Always before he'd gone to someone with lesser power. You could get a good potion or gris-gris from Madame Jean or

Madame Antoinette for a whole lot less money. But you got what you paid for. Quin slipped his hand in his pocket and felt the wad of bills he had placed there earlier. A thousand bucks was a lot of money, but cheap when he considered his life was at stake.

He looked at his watch again. It was almost time. At exactly midnight he stepped into the middle of South Rampart street and started taking purposeful strides backwards. After two blocks he stopped and made the sign of the cross before turning to face a narrow doorway. Quickly, before his courage completely evaporated, Quin walked through the now open door. Flickering candles dimly lit the narrow passage leading to a small courtyard. He focused on forcing each foot to place itself in front of the other. The candlelight shadows leaping off the walls were probably demons, and he knew enough to avoid eye contact.

As previously instructed, when reaching the courtyard he knelt before a small concrete cherub and placed the money in its open palm. His throat tightened and his heartbeat accelerated to the point where it felt like someone was thumping the inside of his chest with a paddle. He almost passed out when he heard the hissing. Quin knew it was the snake. Doctor John was said to have a thirty-foot snake.

"What need have you, little man?" The voice boomed from the darkness. Doctor John was said to have come directly from Senegal and his voice carried a peculiar sing song lilt.

"I messed up bad, sir. Uh, I mean Doctor, sir." Quin's sweat glands kicked into overdrive and bodily fluid ran from every pore like he'd turned on the kitchen faucet. He hoped it wasn't blood. "I took this job and . . . and . . . ."

The snake made its appearance, and Quin struggled to maintain some semblance of composure. The tears now welling up in his eyes threatened to spill over and run down his face. The snake, easily as big around as Quin's thigh, began coiling around his legs. He couldn't see its full length but it had to be thirty feet, maybe even fifty. Quin crossed himself again and made a desperate attempt to focus on something else.

Anything else.

"You have disturbed the Spirits." Quin wished he hadn't lost his voice and Doctor John hadn't finished that sentence. The voice slashed through the darkness of the courtyard and pierced Quin's mind. The snake terrified him less than the voice. Quin tried to refocus on the snake.

"I didn't mean them no harm." Quin pleaded, the fear threatening to stop his adrenaline pumped heart. Tears brimmed over and trickled down his cheeks.

Doctor John stalked forward. The moon and several candles provided the only light, but it was more than Quin needed. Still kneeling, Quin fell on his face. Doctor John grabbed a handful of Quin's hair and pulled him to his full height of six feet. He then placed a large finger under Quin's chin and forced his gaze upward.

Doctor John was another six to eight inches taller and massively built. His jet-black skin, unlike the lighter complexioned Quin, shimmered in the feeble light. The facial tattoos were easily visible in the moonlight. Quin gazed into Doctor John's eyes, open doors into the pit of hell. His knees weakened, but the finger under his chin kept him from falling.

"What have you done?" The voice coming from Doctor John resonated from afar giving Quin the sensation of floating above himself and watching the proceedings from a distance.

"I was helping a guy dig up some Indian stuff. Pots and arrowheads and junk." Quin wished he hadn't said junk. "We found some skeletons."

"You fool. You have disturbed the Old Ones." Doctor John hurled the words and then spit in Quin's face. Quin made no move to wipe the stream of spittle from his cheek. The spittle mingled with the tears and continued a salty procession down his cheek. Quin, scarcely aware of the viscous liquid sliding down his face, could feel himself losing the battle to remain conscious.

"What can I do? Can you fix it?" Quin pleaded. He knew he'd messed up big time. The look on Doctor John's face made Quin rephrase the last question, "I mean, will you fix it, Sir?"

Doctor John did not speak for a moment. "It will require much effort on my part." Doctor John plucked the $1,000 from the cherub's hand and threw the wad of bills across the small courtyard. "This pittance will not begin to pay my fee for such an act. You will not be able to afford my services."

Doctor John paused theatrically. "Make peace with your God and prepare your funeral arrangements."

Quin cried hysterically. Salty tears, Doctor John's spittle, and enough sweat to water the azaleas at the Audubon Zoo all competed for space on Quin's cheek. He felt a warm sensation move down his leg as his body relieved itself of other fluids. Quin had lost control of all of his faculties. "How much? How much? I can get the money. I promise. I'll make payments. Just fix it, please."

Quin grasped at the larger man's clothing, careful to avoid touching the shrunken head suspended from a gold chain around Doctor John's neck. The dark shriveled orifices, at one time the eyes, nose, and mouth of a living being were now stitched shut. Quin felt the shrunken head leering at him, pleased with his discomfort. His pleading grew more urgent. "Please, Dr. John. Please."

Doctor John glared at Quin until he released his grip. "Bring me ten thousand dollars, and I will talk to the Old Ones on your behalf." He laughed loudly. "Maybe I can at least postpone your death."

"Thank you, sir." Quin reached for Doctor John's large bejeweled hand to kiss it, "Thank you very much. I'll bring you the money."

Doctor John moved suddenly and blew a powder in Quin's face. Quin felt himself falling and tried to brace himself. He was falling towards the snake. Everything seemed to be in slow motion and then all went black.

* * *

The four-wheel drive was stuck; buried in the mud like it had been dropped from twenty feet above. Nathan had successfully navigated several previous mud holes but this one had claimed its prize. Yesterday, when he'd reserved a vehicle from the Stennis motor pool, the Humvee's were already booked, and he'd considered himself lucky to get any kind of four wheel drive vehicle since scheduling it so late. At the moment, he regretted not getting a two wheel drive. If he'd been driving a regular truck he would not have attempted those mud holes.

Mud blanketed the windshield to the point where neither he nor Humsinger could see out. Nathan opened his door, allowing the muddy water to run unimpeded into the floorboard of the truck's cab. He stole a glance at Dr. Humsinger, dressed like he'd just stepped off the pages of an L.L. Bean catalog, He was huddled on the front seat of the truck, glaring menacingly at Nathan.

"Any ideas, sir?"

"Call a wrecker and have them come and drag us out." Humsinger, almost fatherly acting yesterday, seemed to be back to his normal self. Or worse.

"I'll have to use your phone." Nathan noted thankfully that Humsinger had a small cell phone clipped to his belt.

Humsinger flipped the phone to Nathan who opened it only to read the flashing 'ns' in bright orange.

No signal.

They were too far from a tower. Without a word, he handed the open phone back to Humsinger who clipped it back on his belt.

"Well, we might as well get going, Mr. Young. We have a long walk ahead of us." Humsinger had called him Nathan earlier. Now he was back to Mr. Young.

"Sir, since we're this close, I'd like to walk on up to the site and look around." Nathan gestured ahead of them. "It can't be more than a few hundred yards."

Humsinger was already mad at him so what did he have to lose? Nathan saw him glance at his watch before replying. "I need to be back before two o'clock. We can take a few minutes to look around before heading back. I estimate it will take us at least two hours to hike to the nearest phone and have someone come and pick me up."

A derisive smile graced Humsinger's face. "You can take care of getting the truck freed from its current predicament after that."

Nathan rapidly approached a state of mind where he no longer cared what the mighty Dr. Brian Humsinger thought. He already had a job lined up and only a short while longer to work here. It would be nice to part on good terms with Humsinger since they were working on several research papers together, but it wasn't mandatory. He literally bit his tongue. It was a mind game and he intended to be the victor. Nathan felt Humsinger pushed people to their limits merely to find out where those limits were. His father had used similar mental tactics on him for years, so Nathan understood the game. All too well.

Nathan turned and leaped from the driver's side open door as far as he could, and still ended up in mud over his ankles. He had a good pair of boots on, so he didn't get water in them. It would be a miserable hike with wet feet. They should be able to skirt the previous mud holes on the way out since they were now on foot.

Humsinger did not fare as well in his quest for dry ground. When he landed, one foot slid under him and he teetered for a moment to regain his balance before falling to one knee in the muddy water.

Nathan winced.

The sight would be funny under other circumstances, but not when he would receive the bulk of the blame.

"It only gets better." Humsinger muttered loudly enough for Nathan to hear.

Without another word, he stood up and started in the direction of the dig site. Nathan plodded behind, an obedient dog following his master. Within minutes they reached the area.

A fairly extensive hole had been excavated in the side of an obvious burial mound. The mound, only about ten or twelve feet tall, towered over them when compared to the surrounding level terrain. Two shovels had been thrown haphazardly around the site.

Humsinger went directly to the hole and began looking around. He seemed to have forgotten his plight for the moment, always the academic.

"It doesn't look like they've reached the main burial chambers." Humsinger pointed at a thin black layer of soil visible in the bottom of the pit. "A layer of charcoal consistent with other sites. The main burial chamber should be another three or four feet below that."

Humsinger busied himself again. Several broken shards of pottery and some broken stone artifacts had been placed in a pan underneath a nearby tree. He began a studious examination of every artifact in the pan while Nathan looked elsewhere for any sign of Harlin.

Nathan surveyed the rest of the site, walking slowly. If Harlin came this far there had to be some sign of his presence. Nathan widened his search. Still he found nothing. Surely he'd made it to the site. He'd been so outraged last week.

Minutes later Nathan began to think there was a real possibility that Harlin hadn't made it to the site after all.

What could have happened to him?

Harlin's truck was gone from his apartment, but they hadn't found it here. Maybe he just got a call from family and had to leave suddenly. Nathan didn't know any of his family and Harlin rarely spoke about them.

Humsinger had finished with the pan of artifacts and was wandering around looking at the edge of the bayou. Nathan joined him, studying the water's edge.

"Well, here's where they've been fishing." Nathan picked up a beat up rod and reel he found laying on the bank. The reel, an expensive one that had seen its prime come and go, had someone's barely visible initials scratched on it. It appeared to be

Q-U-N. It definitely wasn't Harlin's gear.

Humsinger glanced at his watch. "I've got to get back, Nathan. And there doesn't appear to be any indication Harlin ever came here. I'm certain he wasn't the one doing the digging."

Nathan had to agree. But Harlin was missing. "I guess we'll need to notify the authorities when we get back."

Humsinger took another look around. "I'm afraid you're probably right, Nathan. We should contact the local law enforcement agencies."

At least he was back to being Nathan again. Humsinger's moods changed faster than Kat's moods when she had P.M.S. Like clockwork, every month Kat would turn into an emotional lunatic. Things that normally didn't bother her suddenly became intolerable. At times he expected to see her head rotate a full 360 degrees and to have to dodge projectile vomit. He often told her that he wondered if she had P.M.S. or was demon possessed.

Nathan took one last look around before they started back toward the main highway. However, he still couldn't shake the eerie feeling that someone was watching them. The hair stood up on the back of his neck.

* * *

James Bailey parked his Dad's old truck facing the mill pond with the moon's bright light shimmering off the surface. He liked this spot and he liked the full moon. The combination of the reflective water and moonlight made it almost as good as being in broad daylight, and he wanted to be able to see.

Megan, sitting beside him, snuggled closer and turned to face him. She tilted her head slightly and looked at him. James could tell she was ready. He slid his arm around her shoulders and turned a little in the seat.

"You look really hot tonight."

Megan flashed a coy smile. "So do you."

Her eyes twinkled in the moonlight as he bent to kiss her.

Megan's lips parted slightly, welcoming his, and her tongue probed his mouth.

A good sign.

His left hand, resting on her waist, moved cautiously up the front of her shirt. Megan did not react. The kissing continued and James chanced moving his hand a few inches higher. He was almost there. Another strategic move and his hand would be at the top button.

James's hand inched upward. Megan pulled back and, with practiced ease, fended off his hand with her elbow.

"Come on, Megan." James was not above begging. Some girls would give in if pursued long enough.

"I'm not ready."

"No one will know." James could see her face clearly. She looked ready to him. "Please!"

Megan slid to the passenger's side of the truck and opened the door. "Let's go for a walk in the moonlight."

James fumbled for the latch on his side of the truck and followed Megan. He slid his arm around her waist and walked her towards the old oak tree beside the swimming hole. Megan stopped and turned to face him and their lips met. This time she allowed his hand to stray a little farther.

She pulled back, her eyes twinkling. "Why don't we go for a swim?"

James smiled. "Skinny dipping. I like that idea."

Megan giggled, her hands on her hips. "I am not swimming naked with you, James Bailey." She batted her long eyelashes for effect. "Why, I don't think I could trust you. Now, close your eyes while I get ready."

James obeyed, closing his eyes until they were mere slits still allowing him to see. Megan stepped out of her summer sundress, revealing a leopard-print strapless bra with matching bikini panties. She draped her dress over a nearby bush to keep it from getting dirty.

"You're not peeking are you?"

James, scanning her body, lied. "No."

Megan approached him and stood on tiptoes in front of him, studying his face. James closed them the instant before she looked into his eyes. Her breast brushed against his arm.

"Keep them closed."

James felt her back away and allowed his eyes to open again. Megan walked away from him slowly, allowing him a long look at her backside. Her thin, gauzy undergarments left little to the imagination. She waded into the water up to her neck and then turned to face him. "Come on in. The water feels really good."

James raced out of his clothes, allowing them to fall where they landed, and headed toward the pond. Megan watched him unabashedly.

"I like your boxers."

Now ankle deep in the water, James stopped and looked down. "Now, don't make fun of my Scooby Doo drawers. These are my lucky drawers."

Megan giggled again. "Oh, I'm not making fun of you. I like Scooby Doo. I'd like to get a closer look at those drawers and see just how lucky they are."

James grinned as he moved closer. This night was getting better and better. "Anything to oblige. By the way, how come you didn't close your eyes?"

"You didn't close yours either."

"Busted. You look too good."

Megan, apparently flattered, smiled. "So do you, Scooby."

Megan turned as James reached her and began swimming away from him. "Let's race across the pond."

James gave chase and quickly overtook Megan before they reached deep water. He caught her, spun her around, and planted a deep kiss. Megan responded with passion, dropping one hand to his butt and pulling him closer.

His body felt electric with her warm body molded against him. James' right hand resumed its earlier exploration, while he fumbled with her bra clasp with his left hand. One quick twist and he'd be there.

Suddenly something large and abrasive brushed against his leg.

Megan felt it too. "What was that?"

James, uncertain and a little frightened, tried to remain calm. "I'm not sure. Why don't we get to the bank?"

Megan nodded and both started towards the shore about twenty feet away. They'd gone no more than a few feet when James heard something behind them. He turned and saw a v-shaped ripple moving their direction. Something large headed toward them. It was fast. Too fast!

Panic rose in his throat. "Hurry, Megan! Hurry!"

James stopped as Megan floundered toward shore. He refused to swim past her. Maybe it's just a beaver.

CHAPTER 7

Where was that blasted cow?

Two cows gone in one month, and he'd never lost one before. Dang things weren't bringing much at the sale barn, but he hated for them to just wander off. If nothing else, a body could butcher them and get some meat out of them. A few hundred pounds of hamburger beat a mouthful of nothing.

Luther should have mended that fence when the first one got out. But it wasn't like the cows were hurting anything. All they did was get into that buffer zone around Stennis and graze a little. Those government bigwigs claimed that 125,000-acre buffer zone was big enough to keep from bothering folks when they fired the test engines. Wasn't none of it true. Every time they fired one, his whole place shook like a 300 hundred pound belly dancer. Something always fell off a shelf or off the wall. Only thing that buffer zone was good for was grazing a few cattle and raising some pretty good buck deer every year.

The deer they just left alone, but they got real upset when they found you grazing cattle. But, the way he saw it, if they didn't find out, there was no harm done. All that land was just growing up in pine trees. Part of it was his anyway before the government made him sell it to them. And sell it for nearly nothing. He had just been getting some of his back.

He'd fix the fence for sure now. Free grass wasn't exactly free if the cows didn't come home. Luther kept a molasses wheel at the barn and they'd usually wander back in a day or two. If they didn't, he'd go find them. Most of the time they'd be mired down in the mud or maybe having problems calving and too sick to make it back. Only a couple of weeks ago, one had just disappeared. He'd spent two days combing the area and not found a trace. Coyotes or wild dogs may have run her deeper into the buffer zone but he sure couldn't find her. Of course he had to be cautious, no one was even supposed to be in there.

Luther was being careful now. He was a tad bit further inside the buffer zone than he normally went, and sure didn't need no headache from the government. The less he had to do with them, the better off he was.

Luther decided to make one more loop. He'd go a hundred yards further out and then circle back to the hole in the fence. He would patch it this afternoon, cow or no cow. He didn't have many cows and him and Ruby needed every one. It was nice to be able to sell one when the government check ran out before the month did. Over the years, the herd had dwindled considerably. He'd be seventy-four years old next month but his herd was down to thirty head, if he didn't find this one. Ten years ago, he'd had eighty head. Now he wondered if he'd outlive his herd.

For a man his age, he still got around pretty good. That last loop was a long one and he was halfway through it when he smelled the decay. He knew what it was before he saw it. The dead cow's rotting carcass.

Luther stopped and looked up, shading his eyes with his hand. He saw nothing. The vacant sky baffled him because the buzzards always pointed the way to dead livestock. But not today. Not a bird in the sky. Not even one way up there floating on the breeze.

He stepped up the pace, following his nose and still walked right past it. He was looking for the whole cow and didn't notice the one hind leg remaining. The odor got a little weaker and he turned back, retracing his steps. There it was on the edge of the little slough he used to coon hunt in. It was always good for one or two coons. A cloud of flies notified him he'd found it. Wasn't much left, just one hind leg from the knee joint down and a little bit of hide stringing out behind it like a kite's tail. The dogs or coyotes had gnawed it a little.

Luther nudged it with his toe. The crawling maggots reminded him of the little white grains of rice Ruby cooked for breakfast, except this rice was waving at him. He held his breath for a minute, not accustomed to the unbearable stench, while his stomach debated with his mind over whether to evict his breakfast.

Coyotes or dogs didn't do this. Only one thing he knew of and the thought scared him. Memories of years ago flashed through his mind. Vivid images of body parts, and not all of them cattle or dogs. His stomach won the eviction battle and he spewed the mornings' helping of rice over the mutilated leg.

Luther shuddered and his eyes darted around the area. There was too much cover here. The thick underbrush made it impossible to see very far, and that made him nervous.

No sense hanging around any longer.

He headed back for the hole in the fence. He'd fix it as soon as he got back, and tonight the house door would be locked for the first time in years.

He wasn't going to tell Ruby. All she needed to know was that another cow had wandered off.

* * *

Kat got out of bed and ran some cold water over her hands and splashed a little on her face. Her eyes started responding to the mental command to open. A few more handfuls of cold water and she could see the bronze visage gazing back at her from the mirror. She leaned closer to the mirror and stuck her tongue out, trying to look down her throat. It looked a little red.

Her eyes were a different story, they were still puffy from sleep and a maze of red blood vessels stood in stark contrast to the white sclera. They looked a lot red. It was official. The jury of one returned a guilty verdict. She looked as bad as she felt. Her head ached and her stomach twisted and turned like the scrambler at the county fair.

A hot shower and a bowl of cereal later she felt a little better. She needed to get dressed and get to work but she had a hard time willing herself to get up from the kitchen table and pad to the bedroom. In the not-too-distant past, Nathan would have still been in bed asleep. Every morning she'd call repeatedly for him to get up and get dressed. Every morning he'd ignore her and place a pillow over his head to block out the distraction. Five minutes before she walked out the door to go to work, Nathan would vault out of bed like a hyperactive preschooler and take a two-minute cold shower. Another minute to drag on his jeans and tee-shirt, brush his teeth and meet her at the door for the ten-minute drive to work.

There was only one way Nathan would alter that routine. Some mornings, fresh from her shower, she would slide into bed with him and wrap her arms around him and snuggle. Her nude body pressed against his never failed to remove the drowsiness. Wide awake, he would turn and they would make love until they almost missed work. She smiled at the thought. A few times they had been late. Six weeks had passed since he'd moved out, and she desperately missed him.

What happened to us?

Kat still didn't know. Life had a way of throwing roadblocks in your path and she and Nathan just hadn't been able to get around this one. Whatever it was. She had the blank divorce papers on the table and couldn't bring herself to fill them out.

What will I put for a reason?

Incompatible just seemed so childish.

How can two people be compatible one day and then incompatible a few weeks later?

Kat wiped a solitary tear from her cheek.

Without additional warning, her stomach informed her that breakfast had been a bad idea. She suppressed the urge long enough to make her way to the toilet. Minutes later, laying on the bathroom floor, the cool tile seemed to soothe her a little.

Probably a viral infection, she thought. Kat considered calling in sick, but banned the idea. Taking a sick day wouldn't fare well with Humsinger the day after he had informed her that she would receive a full time position. A few minutes of rest and she would be fine. She stood and stumbled to her bed, falling face forward into her goose down pillow. When the queasiness subsided, she would get dressed and go to work.

* * *

Nathan dialed the number for the Bay St. Louis police station. He hated to sound a false alarm but his gut told him that something bad had happened to Harlin. The phone rang several times and Nathan was about to hang up the receiver when someone finally answered.

"Bay St. Louis police. May I help you?" The woman's voice suffered from overexposure to caffeine and cigarettes. She'd rattled off the greeting so many times it sounded like one huge slurred word.

"Yes. I'd like to report a missing person."

"Just a moment, sir."

A local radio station, playing a several-year old Garth Brooks song, replaced the husky voice on the other end. Nathan waited for several minutes until he began to wonder if they had forgotten that he was on the line. Garth was long finished and Alan Jackson had almost crooned his way through another song when the husky voice returned. "I'm sorry to keep you waiting. We had a minor emergency."

"No problem." Nathan wondered what might constitute a minor emergency at the Bay St. Louis police station.

Probably a coffee spill.

"I'll need to get some information from you, sir. Please speak slowly so I can take all this down. Who do you want to report missing?"

"He's a friend of mine, Harlin Rogers."

"And how long has he been missing?"

Nathan glanced at his watch. It was five o'clock. "He didn't show up for work on Monday morning, so I guess it's been about thirty-six hours." As an afterthought he added. "But no one has seen him since last Friday."

"And where do you work?"

"Stennis. In the remote sensing lab."

"And Mr. Rogers works there too?"

How else would I know Harlin didn't show up? flashed through his mind, but came out as a simple, "Yes."

"Could I please get the actual mailing address?"

Nathan rattled it off. There was a long pause on the other end and Nathan wondered if she was having trouble writing it all down. A few seconds later the husky voice continued. "Does Mr. Rogers live in Bay St. Louis?

"He lives in Seabrook apartments. Down on the beach."

An audible sigh on the other end and then. "I'm sorry, sir, but that's outside the city limits. You'll need to call the Hancock County Sheriff and fill out a report with him."

Nathan bit his lip. Bureaucracies maddened him, and they surrounded his life. He currently worked for the federal government and would soon work for a state-supported university. Maybe he should go into the private sector. "Is there any way you can just transfer the information to them? You do cooperate with them, right?"

"Yes sir, we do, but at the moment we are very busy. The proper procedure is for you to file a formal report with them."

Nathan suppressed a snort when she said 'busy'. They probably had a new shipment of donuts down at Sarah's Kitchen. "Do you have their number?"

"Yes. It's 865-2234. You'll reach sheriff Neil Hawkins." The name sounded familiar to Nathan. "They call him Hawk."

"Thank you, ma'am." That was just great! Nathan remembered why the name was so familiar. Hawk was the same man who had driven out to Seabrook to settle his domestic dispute with Kat. He cradled the receiver, thinking. Maybe it would be best to give it one more day before he notified the authorities. Harlin could be anywhere and have a legitimate reason to be there. Something could have happened to one of his parents or another relative that forced him to leave on the spur of the moment. Of course Harlin should have notified someone, but how did they know he hadn't? Maybe a secretary had simply forgotten to give the message to Humsinger. It wouldn't be the first time that had happened. Nathan decided to wait one more day and then call sheriff Hawk.

* * *

Randy Bailey glanced at the digital display of the alarm. It was after midnight and James wasn't home. That was both good and bad. Good because James had taken Megan Kelley to the movies and the movie was over a long time ago. Bad because it was way past curfew and the old man would bust his tail when he got home. If he caught him. The half case of beer the old man had consumed before going to bed at ten might save James tonight.

Randy knew the pleasure would be worth the pain to James. He closed his eyes and tried to imagine what they were doing. James would give him play-by-play in due time, but for now he allowed his imagination to fill in crucial details. Megan was a hotty and was often sent to the office at school for wearing something too revealing, so it didn't take long to conjure up a wonderful visual image.

Hours later the picture grew dim, replaced with visions of James's wrecked '64 Chevy pickup and two mangled bodies. One of them had James's face, and the other his Mom's. Was James going to die like his Mom had? Bleeding to death while they tried to cut him out of the unrecognizable remains of a vehicle?

James would have to forgive him, but the new visual image tormented Randy until finally, at three o'clock, he woke the old man up.

CHAPTER 8

The entire ordeal had taken less than ten seconds, but Quin's mental video replayed it all in slow motion. It would last forever, indelibly tattooed in the deep recesses of his mind, as permanent as the bloody dagger tattooed on his bicep. The murky water of the slough parted and a white apparition emerged. It hurtled out of the water with the speed of a striking snake, soaking its prey with displaced water a fraction of a second before it engulfed them.

Huge jaws snapped closed with a sickening crunch and retreated back beneath the surface, dragging the screaming Specky and the stranger with them. He could still feel Specky's warm blood spray across his face. He could see Specky's legs flailing and hear his voice muffled by the cavernous throat of the white beast. The water roiled momentarily and then calmed, an ever-widening red stain on the water the only indication Specky had ever existed. Quin's terror-frozen synapses had thawed long enough to transmit the message to run. The lactic acid burn in his legs confirmed that the nightmare had been real.

He had survived and he intended to continue surviving and, if that meant getting Doctor John ten thousand dollars he would get it. But first he had to see Fat Frank. Frank's Place was a colorful bar at the end of South Rampart that attracted mostly locals, although Frank always welcomed the occasional tourist with plenty of cash to throw around. If a man knew the right words Fat Frank could get you almost anything. He was, after all, a businessman. And, in that constant celebration of human vices dubbed the French Quarter, business was always booming.

Quin stepped in the door and stood just inside for a minute to allow his eyes to adjust to the darkness. At three o'clock in the afternoon the place was already fairly busy but he found a vacant seat at the forty-foot long mahogany bar. He noted with satisfaction it was afternoon happy hour and beer was only two dollars a pitcher. For a moment or two he used the mirror behind the bar to survey the crowd. He saw several familiar faces even though it had been a while since he'd been here.

"What ya need, mister?" The speaker was new to Quin. A young kid with a bright green mohawk and a chrome stud through the bridge of his nose. Intricate tattoos covered both arms. A pretty ordinary kid in the French Quarter.

"Gimme a pitcher." Quin scooped a few pretzels from the dish beside him and waited on his beer. In a few seconds the kid slid his beer in front of him.

"That's two bucks."

Quin dug the two dollars out of his pocket. "Fat Frank around?"

The kid looked at him a minute and then yelled through the doorway behind the bar. "Frank! There's someone here to see you."

Frank soon rolled his considerable girth through the doorway while the kid parked himself out of hearing at the end of the long bar. Fat Frank came by his nickname honestly. He wasn't a tall man but weighed close to four hundred pounds. His legs had long since ceased to support his bulk and he'd been confined to a wheelchair for as long as Quin had known him.

"Quin. How you been?" Frank was genuinely glad to see him.

"Not too good, Frank." Quin looked around to make sure everyone was out of earshot. "I need a piece, and I ain't got much money. You got any specials this month?"

"I've got one the cops are looking for." Frank said. "But if you get caught with it you may get pinned for some stuff you didn't do. I've had it cooling for a while."

Frank rubbed the two-day growth on his face. "Since you're an old friend, I could let you have it for a couple a hundred. But you suffer from memory loss about where you got it if you get caught. Understand?"

"No problems." Quin was relieved. He'd only got a few hundred dollars when he sold the old junk truck he'd stolen to a wrecking yard that wasn't too picky about titles. "But it works both ways. You don't know nothing about selling me no gun if anyone comes asking."

"Done."

"Thanks, Frank." Quin dug the money out of his pocket, peeled off a couple of bills, and handed it to Frank. The transaction was so casual that any observer would think he was just paying his bar tab. "When can I get it?" He knew Frank wouldn't keep something like that around the bar.

"Come back around seven. I'll have it then."

Quin drained the last of his beer and poured himself another from the pitcher. He wouldn't need the gun before then anyway.

* * *

Doctor John closed his eyes and chanted, swaying rhythmically. He chanted louder as the thirty-foot python moved its undulating coils closer. The snake's tongue kept time with the chant, easing ever closer until it lay touching Doctor John's massive thigh.

Soon. He would know soon. Vodu would reveal the secret in due time. Maybe tonight. Maybe ten nights from now. For now he was content to worship and be patient. Tonight he would visit the spirit realm and he would listen.

He increased the pace of his chant and slowly laid back until he was prone on the ground beside the snake. Minutes passed and the chanting decreased in volume. To a casual observer, it would appear that Doctor John had ceased chanting. However, at closer inspection one would notice that Doctor John's voice instead sounded more like one would if he were moving farther away.

Doctor John's large supine body moved. Slowly, very slowly, it started to rise. More minutes passed. He chanted almost inaudibly now. A slight background noise at best. His body rose further until the snake, sensing Doctor John no longer rested his thigh against it, started moving again. The serpent searched for Doctor John's presence, it's tongue flicking in and out testing the surroundings. Not finding him, the snake coiled its massive body directly under Doctor John. The witch doctor's body now levitated over five feet in the air while his mind traveled in the spirit realm.

Tonight Doctor John visited a place he'd never been. A place that appeared fuzzy and indistinct at first, but then became rapidly clearer, like an oncoming automobile on a foggy night. A place where four shaman, each uniquely-attired, prayed and chanted in a strange tongue. A place both new and yet familiar. A place where he felt welcomed as a visitor, and yet at home.

He hovered unseen above the shamans in a tiny smoke-filled room. Tonight he would watch and learn from the Old Ones. Tonight they would reveal many secrets to Doctor John.

The Old Ones were seated around a small fire in the center of the hut. The walls of the hut were circular and slanted inward until they formed an almost perfect half sphere with a tiny hole at the apex. They appeared to be made of mud and straw. Doctor John reached out to touch them but could not reach them. They remained just beyond his grasp. Four small vividly-painted pockets in the room's walls contained tiny carvings. Doctor John focused on the carvings but could not tell what they were, only that they were important.

The Old Ones prayed and chanted fervently as a lit pipe passed between them. He felt the heat as the pipe smoke and fire smoke blended together and rose to exit the small hole directly above him. The pungent odor permeated his being. It clung to him much like an old friend that hadn't been seen in many years. The smoke's odor mingled with his sweat, the scent of the python, and the unique smell of shamans.

Doctor John spoke to them, trying to communicate with them. They knew the secret and would convey it to him. One of them looked up and fixed his eyes on him. The shaman's eyes were vacant pools of dark water. Searching. Probing. Not finding what he sought.

The shaman spoke, uttering something unintelligible to Doctor John. Doctor John tried to tell him he did not understand. The shaman did not hear. Doctor John reached out to the shaman and spoke. The shaman still did not hear.

Now the Old Ones moved away from him. They faded as the fog thickened and Doctor John found himself lying on the ground. The snake hissed, its forked tongue flicking out and touching his cheek. He could hear New Orleans street sounds in the distance. He could smell his city.

Doctor John rose to his feet. The spirit realm was troubled. Another had entered. One not welcomed by the Old Ones. One that was his enemy. One that complicated matters and intervened before the Old Ones could reveal the full secret. But they had revealed part. He didn't know how, but nevertheless he knew. Someone would help him locate the goat without horns. But Doctor John knew there was more. Much more.

Doctor John laughed his manic laugh and the streets of New Orleans heard. Many of those who heard made the sign of the cross on their chest. Others merely trembled and waited for the morning light. Somehow they felt safer in the light.

CHAPTER 9

"Now calm down and tell me the whole story." Hawk had been trying for the last few minutes to get some idea of what had happened. Angie Kelley had called 911 for some reason, and he still didn't know why. She was an old friend though, so he waited patiently.

Angie managed to control her sobbing enough to speak. "It's Megan. She's gone."

Hawk sighed and handed her his handkerchief. Angie accepted it gratefully and made an attempt to dry her eyes. Her body shuddered as another sob ran through her thin frame. Hawk held his silence for a moment. Angie needed time to vent. This would probably be a delicate issue. He'd seen Megan out running around a lot lately. Her father was gone most of the time, and Angie couldn't control her. He'd overheard a couple of the kids refer to her as the town bicycle; anybody that wanted to could ride her.

"I'm sure she'll show up, Angie. Was she out with somebody?"

Angie's sobs subsided as she struggled to regain her composure. She wiped her face with his handkerchief and turned her bloodshot eyes on Hawk. "I think so. But I don't know who it was. She just said she was going to the movies with some friends."

A slow flow of tears continued to roll down her cheeks. "I haven't been a good mother, Hawk, but this is the first time she's stayed out all night."

Hawk spoke in a gentle tone. "Do you remember her saying which movie she was going to see?" If they could locate the right theater, it would save some time. Of course Hawk felt like she'd probably show up from her all-nighter before they expended too much manpower on the search.

"She just said the movies." Angie's eyes searched Hawk's face, pleading for reassurance.

Hawk felt compelled to pat her on the back. Even though he knew Megan would most likely show up unharmed, Angie wasn't as convinced of that fact.

"Will she be alright, Hawk?"

"Yeah, everything will be fine. I'll call it in."

"Have you got a cigarette?" Hawk tapped two low-tar cigarettes out of the pack and offered one to Angie. He lit Angie's and watched the tip turn red as she took a deep drag.

How could something so calming be so deadly?

For the moment his remained unlit. He had cut his ration down to five cigarettes a day, and it was too early in the morning for him to smoke the second one. Angie didn't appear to notice.

Hawk took the opportunity to call the dispatcher and let them know to be on the lookout for Megan. He couldn't put out a full-blown missing persons alert because Megan had only been gone a few hours. But everyone could keep their eyes and ears open for any news. He returned to Angie, still seated on the front steps of her house.

"Angie, are you going to be OK?"

"I'm worried. I just have a bad feeling." Angie paused long enough to take another deep drag on the cigarette. "I know Megan hasn't been an angel lately, but I guess she's had a bad example."

Angie studied Hawk's face, trying to read his expression. Searching for some sign of absolution. "Phil's been gone a lot lately, and I've . . . ."

"Angie, you don't have to tell me any of this."
Hawk cut her off. Her confession made him nervous. It was a small town, and as a member of local law enforcement, he already knew she'd been running around on Phil.

"What did I expect my daughter to do? She's not blind." She took another drag on the cigarette. "Like mother, like daughter." The bitterness in her voice was almost thick enough to see.

"Hawk?" The dispatcher's voice squawked over the radio, rescuing him from an uncomfortable situation.

Hawk trotted back to his cruiser and snatched the microphone. "What's up?"

A few sketchy details later Hawk walked back up to the house to tell Angie he had to leave. "She'll be okay, Angie."

"Thanks, Hawk." Her tears were almost gone now but had left visible trails in her make-up. She stood up and threw her cigarette stub on the sidewalk and rubbed it out with a slippered foot. Angie started to go in the house and then turned back to face him. "Hawk? Please find her for me."

* * *

Quin felt better after his visit with Madam Jean. She'd read his palm and said his life line told her he wasn't going to die any time soon, and then she gave him a dragon blood stick dipped in candle wax. Everybody knew that was real good luck. And all that for only a hundred dollars.

That hundred dollars was the last of his money, but Quin didn't mind. He needed the good luck for what he was about to do. He would get that ten thousand dollars for Doctor John the only way he knew how. And without getting caught this time. If he did, it would violate his parole and he'd be gone for good. The last time he'd done five years, but he'd been lucky. He'd been sentenced to serve fifteen, but prison overcrowding graced him with a ticket home after five.

Quin thought about that time. He'd been out now for a couple of years and had no desire to go back. But he didn't have a choice. He'd have to chance it. Angola was hell, but it wasn't the real hell. If Doctor John wanted ten grand, he'd have ten grand. Quin would risk going back to the pen to get shut of the mess he was in.

You couldn't screw around with the spirits like he'd done, and expect to get off without some powerful magic. He'd been stupid, letting that ignorant redneck Specky talk him into digging up those graves. He'd known better the whole time. Now he was paying for it.

Thinking about the whole nightmare again made the hair stand up on the back of his neck. Quin felt like someone was watching him. He looked around, craning his neck to look directly behind him. He couldn't see anything but it was pretty dark and he still felt uneasy. The dark shadows under the trees would be good places to hide and that made him nervous. He couldn't imagine what might be hiding there, but it couldn't be good.

He slid his hand in his pocket and wrapped his fingers around the gun. The cold steel usually had a calming effect, but not tonight. You couldn't shoot it if it wasn't flesh and bone. Spirits and ghosts couldn't be shot, he didn't think. Bullets just went right through them. At least that's what he'd heard, and it made sense.

Howcouldyoukillthemifthey'realreadydead? Quin glanced back again, certain that something was back there. Huddling in the dark didn't help. He looked at the house one more time and then decided to move. He'd been waiting for the car out front to leave but sitting out here in the dark was too dangerous. He could feel the haunts out tonight and maybe the dragon's blood stick wasn't working. Regardless, he wasn't about to take any more chances.

Quin pulled the gun out of his pocket and waited a minute longer before he pulled the ski mask over his face and approached the back door. He was thankful they didn't have a dog. He peeked in the back window first and didn't see anybody. Carefully he tested the knob, expecting it to be locked. Luckily it turned in his hand.

Maybe he was getting something for his hundred bucks.

He eased the door open a crack and peeked inside. Still nothing he could see except a washer and dryer and a basket full of dirty clothes. He opened the door the rest of the way and stepped inside, leaving the door ajar behind him. Several voices drifted through the laundry room doorway. It sounded like they were arguing about something. Quin stepped a little closer and tried to get a look into the other room.

He could see some lab equipment set up. At least he had the right house. These boys were supposed to be cooking meth but sometimes folks could give you the wrong information. Things were going his way so far. He stuck his head a little farther into the doorway. He could see the men now. There were three of them gathered around a small table but they couldn't see him in the darkened laundry room. He glanced around the room to make sure no one else was there and then one of the men moved slightly. Quin's eyes widened. Sitting in plain view on the table was a small satchel of money. Easily the ten thousand Quin needed and these boys probably wouldn't report it stolen. But, if they caught him, they would take care of his sentence themselves. He'd rather face them than Doctor John and the spirits though.

He adjusted his mask and stepped around the corner. "Get your hands where I can see them and back over against the bar."

Stunned, the three men just looked at him.

"Move." Quin gestured with the gun. "I'll put a hole in you your Mama can't sew up."

The big burly one with a mass of blonde curls spoke up. "There's three of us and only one of you." His lip curled up in a sneer. "You can't shoot all of us before we get to you."

Quin didn't say a word. He'd been in similar situations before so he just shot the blonde in the thigh and gestured with the gun again. The other two men rapidly complied with his earlier spoken request. "Now, that's more like it."

The big man had fallen to the floor and was doubled over, holding his bleeding leg and whimpering. To his credit, he wasn't crying.

Quin stepped forward to the table. Several bags of meth were neatly rowed up on the table beside the satchel of money. Quin casually rifled through the money, trying to get a quick count. It would definitely be enough.

He gestured with the gun again. "Throw me the keys to your car and then get Curly there and drag him to the bathroom."

The men silently did his bidding. Quin checked the bathroom for a window and found none and herded them inside. He knew the police would be here soon checking on the gunshot so he had to hurry. Quickly he shut the door and pressed his shoulder against it until he'd created enough space to wedge several quarters between the door and the jam. The quarters kept enough pressure on the door latch to make it impossible for his prisoners to turn the knob. They would bust out soon but he'd be long gone.

"The first one that comes out of there I'll shoot." Quin's threat would hold them a few more seconds, while they waited until they were sure he was gone. He backed off, picked up the satchel and walked out the front door. The car was an older Ford, but nice enough. Quin pitched the satchel in the front seat and backed the car out into the street. He'd ditch it a few blocks from here and catch a cab. He still felt like someone was watching him. He pulled the satchel closer and drove on.

Now to see Doctor John.

CHAPTER 10

Hawk eased his cruiser down the rutted road to the old sawmill. Millpond number two was another few hundred yards ahead but he could already see Ed's car, the lights still flashing, parked close to the trail. He'd passed Miss Ella's house a few yards back. She'd found the body this morning on her walk. Eighty-five years old and she walked two miles a day.

A few minutes later he pulled up behind Ed's car and got out. Three more police cruisers, a local ambulance and a '64 Chevy pickup were already there. A Bay St. Louis officer stood guard at the path leading to the pond.

"Good morning, Jermaine." Hawk greeted him as he approached.

"It ain't a good one, Hawk."

"Who was it?" Hawk paused to finally light his second cigarette while he visited with Jermaine.

"They haven't identified him yet." Jermaine wore a haunted expression on his face.

"Stranger, huh?" Hawk drew deeply on the cigarette, savoring the moment, knowing it would end all too soon.

"We don't know who he is. Ain't enough left to tell for sure."

The news stunned Hawk. "What do you mean?"

"I mean part of him's missing. Ain't nothing left but the lower half of a body." Jermaine gestured towards the '64 Chevy. "That truck over there is registered to Ned Bailey though."

Hawk's stomach churned as he covered the remaining distance to the actual crime scene. Billy Blanchert was still in jail swearing his innocence. Maybe he was telling the truth.

But who else could be dismembering people on the coast?

On most days Mill Pond number two looked like it had been stripped from a scenic postcard and transplanted to Bay St. Louis.

Sometime early in the twentieth century a logging operation had created a series of four large mill ponds that now offered some decent fishing, a swimming hole and a favorite picnic spot. The ponds were surrounded with some good-sized trees--uncut since the logging company left--that provided a welcome shade during the summer.

Today the pond looked far different from an idyllic postcard scene. Yellow police tape cordoned off the area from curious onlookers and attempted to protect the crime scene. Several officers searched the surrounding patch of trees for clues. Hawk saw his friend standing just inside the ribbon.

"What's it look like, Ed?"

"It's bad, Hawk." He nodded toward the pond bank where a tarp covered something bulky on the ground. "We've got the lower half of a nude male and Randy Bailey didn't come home last night. That's his daddy's truck parked out there."

"Somebody cut him in two?"

"Don't know yet." Ed looked pale and ragged. "But it's not a clean wound."

"Where'd Miss Ella find him?"

Ed pointed at the tarp. "Just a few feet beyond that tarp. He was floating in the water and we brought him to the bank."

Hawk and Ed had been moving toward the tarp as they talked. "Take a look for yourself." Hawk noticed that Ed averted his eyes when he lifted the corner of the tarp.

Hawk did his best to view the gruesome remains in a clinical manner, instead of as the dead body of someone who only hours before had been the star quarterback of the Bay St. Louis Tigers and the living, breathing son of Ned Bailey. The wound told Hawk little. The turtles had been at work and the millponds were full of them. They'd been especially aggressive where the body had been severed. There wasn't much to be gained from additional scrutiny, so after a few seconds he dropped the tarp.

Hawk reached for his third cigarette, but had trouble lighting it because he couldn't steady his trembling hands. After a conscious effort, he managed to light up. Ed pretended he didn't notice.

"What could have done that, Ed?"

"I don't know. Jermaine says it looks like that body they found over in Lafourche about ten years ago. The one that psycho killed and then dumped his body in the marsh. The turtles ate him too."

"But turtles can't eat bone, Ed. Where's the rest of him?"

"I don't know yet." Ed nodded towards the pond. "We've got some flatbottoms on the way. We'll drag the pond for the rest of the body."

"I hope we don't have a trend here. You don't reckon this is related to Lou Blanchert's disappearance, do you Ed?"

"I don't see how it could be. Billy's still in jail. He can't make bail."

Ed thought for a minute. "Unless he's telling the truth and someone else killed Lou."

"What would the kid be doing down here by himself?"

"He wasn't alone." Ed gestured toward some nearby bushes. "We've already bagged them, but we found two sets of clothes. The boy's clothes were over there, and we found a dress hanging on that bush. And there's a pair of women's sandals in the old pickup."

Hawk's stomach churned even more. He could see Angie's tortured face from earlier that morning. "Ed? Angie Kelley's daughter, Megan, was out with someone last night and she's missing this morning. Was she dating the Bailey boy?"

"I don't know, but we'll find out. It looks like we've got a killer and now maybe a kidnapper. I'll get the ball rolling." Ed, his lips set tight, turned to walk away. "Maybe she's still alive."

Hawk's vision wandered to the tarp covering Randy Bailey's remains and then back to the millpond. Yesterday the millpond would have seemed peaceful and calm, a place where you brought your children for a picnic and some afternoon fishing. Today it seemed brooding and mournful and the Spanish moss draped from the big live oaks appeared ghostly.

Hawk shuddered involuntarily and then glanced around. Everyone was busy doing their assigned tasks yet he'd gotten the distinct impression somebody was watching him. He looked back at the pond. Somebody or some thing. His eyes searched the surface of the pond one more time and then the tree line on the far shore.

Nothing.

In his gut he knew they wouldn't find Megan alive. Whoever had killed James wouldn't hesitate to kill Megan.

Hawk turned to leave. Somebody had to tell Angie about Megan and James. The part of his job he hated the most. He didn't relish the task, but he knew it should be him. Somehow he had to give her a glimmer of hope. He'd never been good at lying. Maybe she wouldn't be able to read his eyes like everyone else could.

Hawk thought a moment about taking the sundress to have Angie identify it, but rejected that idea. That way Angie could still hope. Until they found the body.

* * *

Ella knew something was happening to her. Something strange. Something that had never happened before. Her right arm was numb to the point where it hung useless at her side. She focused all her mind on the arm, trying to will it to move. It was no use. Maybe it was because she hadn't had breakfast yet. She should get up and fix breakfast.

Why haven't I already had breakfast?

She should ask someone, like that nice young police officer in her living room.

Why is he here?

He was looking at her. Speaking to her but his words didn't make sense. She tried to focus on the policeman. On his voice. Ella noticed her vision was blurring too. The policeman crossed the room and stood beside her chair. He took long, slow strides, lifting his feet higher than was necessary. He looked funny, like the wooden puppets with their hands and feet attached to strings her daddy used to make for her.

She laughed.

Or tried to laugh. One half of her face didn't respond. There was a small puddle of spittle accumulating on her lap, and she could tell she was drooling on herself. She lifted her right arm to wipe her mouth, only the right arm didn't move. Ella stared blankly at the uncooperative arm.

That nice young policeman loomed over her and said something else. Ella tried to tell him to speak English or French. Or even a little of the ancient language her mother had taught her. She could understand those. But this man spoke in a foreign tongue.

She was tired. So very tired.

Although she rarely napped, today she might make an exception. Maybe she would just close her eyes for a minute or two.

She tried to hold her eyes open, but suddenly remembered what happened. The nightmare came back. Her daughter screamed and called her name. Suddenly, Miss Ella didn't want to sleep. She tried again to tell that young policeman what was happening, but she couldn't. Something was indeed wrong.

Am I dying?

She yelled at the young policeman, only nothing audible came out. Her head fell forward until her chin rested on her chest. The frantic young policeman stood over Miss Ella and held her head up, willing the ambulance to hurry and get there.

CHAPTER 11

Kat awoke with a start and glanced at the alarm clock. It was after ten o'clock and she was over three hours late for work. Frustrated at herself, she slammed her fist down on the bed. Her stomach felt fine, but she couldn't go to work. If she went now, looking and feeling fine, no one would believe she had been sick this morning. Kat picked up the phone and called the personnel office at Stennis.

She informed the man who answered the phone that she would be taking a sick day. He would notify the Remote Sensing Group. It irritated her to take a sick day even though she had at least two weeks of sick leave built up. After a point, you quit accumulating sick leave, and she was close to a full bank.

A long hot shower later and Kat felt refreshed enough to make another attempt at breakfast. She entered the kitchen, glancing at the spot where she'd had Nathan's possessions boxed up for so long. Now the boxes were gone. As long as they were there, it had seemed possible to reconcile. Yet she had nagged and pushed, until Nathan finally moved them. She could be such a fool sometimes. Why couldn't she just swallow her pride and admit that she still loved Nathan? He still loved her. He had told her many times that he did, even in some of their most heated arguments since the separation.

Why can't I just pick up the phone and call him?

For the first mouthful or two of milk and cereal she was tentative, uncertain as to how her stomach would react. Apparently she was fine now. The morning's bug seemed to have vanished as rapidly as it had arrived. It had managed to accomplish one thing though. Her mood was set for the day. She couldn't shake the sadness and despair.

Kat had always tried so hard to belong. All her life she had striven to rise above the poverty of her upbringing. She could still remember the stinging taunts of the other kids in her class. "Hey, Redskin." Or "Here's some wampum. Go buy a new deerskin dress." Kids could be so cruel.

Her struggle to leave all that behind had driven her to get her doctorate. A doctor, of any kind, was the ultimate status position. Ironically, she had always envisioned moving away from the coast. She'd graduated high school not too far from here and attended the University of Southern Mississippi for her undergraduate work. Several years in California to get her graduate degrees and then back to southern Mississippi for her post-doctoral appointment.

Life was funny that way.

She'd applied to several post-doctoral positions and been accepted to all of them, mostly because of her minority status she suspected, and then taken the one that brought her back home. Secretly the choice had been made so she could show everyone she'd made it. She was Dr. Kat Abnaki.

Until yesterday it looked like she wouldn't be able to find a job at all unless she went into industry. There were basically no academic jobs in archeology right now. Too many state budget cuts. And now, with her post-doctoral appointment nearing its end, she had accepted a full time position in southern Mississippi. It was all so strange. Maybe there was a greater reason she didn't know about.

Kat still felt empty. In spite of her academic success she wanted more from life. She wanted Nathan back. But would he take her back? She had been vicious and cruel and really couldn't explain why. How could she ever ask him to reconcile? She didn't want to swallow her pride and beg him back. More than enough humiliation had been dealt her as a child. A single tear rolled down her cheek and dropped into her half-eaten cereal. No longer hungry, she pushed back from the table and took the bowl to the sink.

Maybe he'll call.

She needed to occupy herself. Sitting around moping all day and waiting for Nathan to call would do her no good at all. She glanced around her tiny apartment and the total disarray. Clothes on the floor of the living room. Magazines and papers scattered everywhere. Dirty dishes overflowed the kitchen sink and cluttered the small countertop. She and Nathan had been too busy to clean the apartment and, since he'd moved out, she'd spent every waking moment at work.

The apartment was a daunting task but it had to be done sometime. She rolled up her sleeves and started on the dishes. The work made her feel better emotionally. Maybe she could busy herself with her work until the memories of Nathan were less painful. Kat wondered how long that would be. For the moment she tried to focus on the happy times.

Like the few times they had driven to New Orleans and spent the day strolling around the French Quarter admiring the architecture and the foreign feel of the city. Sometimes they would sit for hours feeding the pigeons in Jackson Square and people watching. She could taste the powdered sugar on the *beignets* and smell the *café au lait* from the Café DuMonde. She could see the portrait artists, the palm readers and the mimes all plying their trades on the cobbled streets.

Even though she'd grown up near New Orleans, her grandmother did not go to New Orleans, and she'd never allowed Kat to go. Grams always said it was an evil city. By the time Kat was old enough to drive, when most kids her age that lived in the area were sneaking off to see Bourbon Street, she sat home alone. Her poverty and Native American blood isolated her in the small town where she grew up. The ringing phone brought her back to the present.

Kat looked at it for a couple of rings while she dried her hands on a small towel. On the fourth ring, right before the answering machine kicked on, she picked up the receiver. Slowly, wondering if it was Nathan, she spoke. "Hello."

"Miss Young?" There it was again. The last name. The constant reminder of Nathan.

"Yes."

"Miss Young, I'm afraid I have some bad news." The voice paused and Kat tried to identify the background noise. "It's about your grandmother, Ella Abnaki. She's had a stroke."

Kat couldn't speak for a moment. Grams was so strong and vital. Even in her eighties. She had always been there and always would be. A fiery dried-up wisp of a woman who would fight a grown man over Kat. When Kat came home from school and cried over the cruelty of the other kids, Grams was there for her. The one solid non-wavering absolute in her life.

"Where is she?" Kat couldn't bring herself to ask if Grams had lived through the stroke.

"She's at Hancock County Memorial."

Now Kat knew Grams was alive. "I'll be there in ten minutes."

She hung up the phone and found some shoes. Before she went out the door she grabbed the phone and called Nathan. The shock of Grams having the stroke made her petty differences with Nathan feel as insignificant as bugs on the windshield. They were truly annoying but wouldn't keep you from driving the car.

With no hesitation in his voice, Nathan agreed to leave work and meet her at the hospital. She'd known he would come but was grateful to hear him confirm it. Kat needed Nathan to help her face this thing with Gram.

What if Grams dies?

Tears welled up in Kat's eyes and started rolling down her cheeks. She was overly emotional lately.

But who wouldn't be, given the circumstances?

* * *

"We've stabilized her, but she's not doing well." The young man briefing them seemed barely old enough to be a medical doctor. "Her right side is paralyzed and she can't speak. We'll be running some tests to determine the extent of the blockage once we're certain she can physically handle them."

Nathan held Kat, squeezing her shoulder with his right arm as the doctor delivered the news. He'd arrived before Kat and was waiting by the emergency room entrance when she pulled up.

"For the moment, we'll just have to watch her around the clock. I'm keeping her in ICU for at least a couple of days, until we can be certain she's not going to have another stroke."

"Can we see her?"

"For just a few minutes."

Kat entered the ICU cubicle assigned to Grams. Her tiny body, that recently appeared so wiry and strong, now seemed small and frail. She bristled with wires and tubes that monitored every conceivable vital sign. Kat gasped. She wasn't mentally prepared for the sight.

To Kat's knowledge, Grams had never been sick a day in her life. Not even the sniffles. She walked several miles a day and consumed all kinds of teas brewed from plants she collected on her walks. Grams swore by herbal medicine and Kat had never known her to take even so much as one aspirin.

While growing up, Kat had learned to hide her sickness from Grams if at all possible. If Grams caught her sniffling she would make her drink some noxious foul-tasting brew designed to conquer the ailment. And conquer it did. The thought of having to consume the concoction a second time was unusually homeopathic.

Kat reached out and stroked the part of Grams' hand that wasn't pierced with a needle. Grams had taken care of her so many times and lately she'd neglected her grandmother. Since her split with Nathan, Kat had stopped going by to see her the normal two times a week. Grams hadn't said anything, but Kat knew she disapproved of their breakup. The easiest way to keep from feeling guilty was to stop seeing Grams. It wasn't really a conscious decision, but rather a continual postponement of her visits. Maybe, if she hadn't been so selfish, she would have known Grams was not feeling well.

She had always known that Grams wouldn't live forever, but Kat had expected her to make a hundred. Longevity ran in their family. Kat's great-grandmother lived to be ninety years old. She died when Kat was nine. Kat's mother and aunt had been the exceptions. Both had died young when Kat was a baby; Kat's mother in a car wreck and her aunt had been murdered. She had no memory of either, just stories Grams had told of her daughters.

A nurse came and ran them out. Nathan still had not spoken. He just continued to hold her and lightly squeeze her shoulder.

"Are you all right?" His voice was soft and concerned.

"I'm fine." Kat wiped another pesky tear away. "I just need Grams to make it."

"She will, Kat. I've never known a stronger-willed woman." Nathan gave her a soft smile. "Well, maybe just one."

Kat curled up on one of the small sofas in the ICU waiting room and fell asleep. Nathan had never known Kat to take a nap. For her to sleep in the daytime she had to be past exhaustion or sick. He bent toward her and felt her forehead. Her skin felt cold.

She's probably just stressed out.

While Kat slept, Nathan consumed mass quantities of the free coffee provided by the candy stripers and read everything in the waiting room even remotely masculine. His reading choices were becoming very limited. It was either an article in *Cosmopolitan* on *What your man really wants* or *The Ladies Home Journal* article on gazebo placement in your backyard.

He nixed the gazebo article since he didn't even have a backyard and opted instead to discover his true desires, *Cosmopolitan*-style. He had read about half the article when Sheriff Hawkins appeared. Nathan sheepishly put down the magazine when the sheriff glanced at the cover before scanning the room. He and Kat were the only ones in there.

"Is anyone here for Miss Ella?"

Nathan stood up, noticing Kat stirring as well. "We both are." He gestured at Kat. "That's her granddaughter."

"I hope you two are getting along a little better." The sheriff stuck out his hand. "I'm Sheriff Hawkins. Call me Hawk. You probably remember me from last weekend."

Nathan felt his face flush. "How could I forget?"

Kat raised up and rubbed her eyes. "Is something wrong?"

"No ma'am." The sheriff removed his hat and ran his fingers through his unkempt hair. "I just came by to check on Miss Ella. If she gets better I need to speak to her."

"What about?"

"Miss Ella found a body this morning on her walk."

The news stunned both Nathan and Kat. No one had mentioned a body. Nathan recovered first. "Is that what triggered her stroke?"

"It's a possibility. But I'm no medical doctor."

"Was it a murder?"

"It looks that way." The sheriff watched them closely, gauging their reaction. "Miss Ella didn't exactly find a whole body. It was only the lower half."

Nathan recoiled.

No wonder she had a stroke.

Some butcher on the loose and she'd found the remains of one of his victims. Neither he nor Kat had anything to say. The sheriff seemed satisfied with the shock painted brazenly across their faces.

"Have you caught the killer?" Nathan asked.

The sheriff hesitated, apparently reluctant to divulge the details of an ongoing investigation. "We don't have any strong leads yet."

Nathan suddenly remembered Harlin. With all the excitement of Grams' stroke and Kat's unexpected phone call, Harlin's disappearance had slipped his mind.

"Sheriff, I have a friend who's been missing for a couple of days now. I don't know if it's connected in any way to this or not but I've been meaning to call you."

Hawk's brow furrowed. "Why haven't you reported it?"

The light rebuke stung. "I called the Bay St. Louis police station to report it and they said to call you." Nathan felt foolish about the next part. "I was going to wait another day to make sure he was missing because I was embarrassed about this weekend. You know, about the argument ......" Nathan's voice trailed off. He knew the excuse sounded lame.

Now how would he feel if Harlin had been murdered?

"Have you identified the victim?"

"Tentatively. It's a young man from the community."

Nathan's relief about Harlin was tempered with sadness for the unknown young man's family. Memories of the many funerals he'd attended as a child flooded back. His father, the pastor of a small non-denominational flock, had mumbled insincere words over numerous church members. Nathan could still remember the ashen faces of the dead, frozen in time, as they paraded past the open caskets for the viewing. He could see the faces of the grieving family, tears trailing down their faces, as they sought some comfort in his father's hypocritical words.

"Nathan? Nathan?" Kat gripped his hand, looking at him searchingly. "Are you okay?"

He realized he'd momentarily slipped away. Mentally revisiting a part of his youth he tried to forget. He hadn't seen his parents in over ten years. As far as he knew they were still fleecing, they called it pastoring, that same church. His father still preaching hellfire and brimstone sermons until the congregation felt sinful enough to throw more money into the offering plate to buy a bigger slice of forgiveness.

He smiled reassuringly at Kat. "I'm all right. Something reminded me of my parents."

Kat had never met his parents. She knew they had been upset with him when he majored in biology. They couldn't tolerate their son studying heretical doctrines in biology and bringing those ideas home to his siblings. Their harsh words had driven Nathan away for good. He functioned as someone whose parents had died. There were no Christmas cards or birthday phone calls. Only isolation. Orphaned in the name of God.

Hawk cleared his throat and spoke. "I'll need you to give me some more information on your friend. Have you got a few minutes?"

"Sure. What do you need?"

"I'll need an address and the name of someone I can talk to at work and anything else you can tell me that might help."

Nathan filled him in on the few details he knew about Harlin. Neither he nor Kat knew of anyone to contact. Hawk indicated he could obtain numbers of individuals to notify from Harlin's Stennis employment records.

"When was the last time you saw him?"

"Friday at work. But we were supposed to go check out a dig site on Saturday."

"So he didn't show up Saturday?"

Nathan again felt foolish. "Not exactly. I was supposed to meet him and didn't because Kat wanted me to come over and get my stuff out of her apartment."

Hawk looked at Kat. She nodded to verify Nathan's statement was accurate.

"So you did talk to him Saturday?" Hawk had taken out a small notebook and was jotting down some information.

"By the time I called him he was already gone."

"What time was that?"

"Between nine and ten in the morning."

"Do you think he went out to this site by himself?"

"Dr. Humsinger and I went out there Tuesday to see if we could find anything." Nathan noted Hawk's frown and knew that he'd made a stupid mistake by going out to the burial mound. "We thought Harlin might be hurt or something. It never occurred to me that there might be foul play."

"So you two Sherlocks have already tramped around this site." Hawk made no attempt to hide his irritation with Nathan. "Did you find anything?"

"No. But someone had definitely been digging." Nathan thought a moment. "They left a fishing pole and some shovels out there."

Hawk closed his small notebook after getting directions to the site. "I'll check out his apartment and the dig site. I'm going to have to ask you to stay in the area. I may need to ask you a few more questions."

Kat spoke up. "Sheriff. I have a key to his apartment at my place."

Nathan glanced at her. Why did she have a key to Harlin's apartment?

Kat caught the glance and explained. "He gave it to me to feed his cat when he was out of town last month."

"Did he mention going out of town this time, Miss Young?"

"No. He didn't say anything about it."

"I'd like to get that key from you if I could."

Kat looked at Nathan. "Would you go to my place and get the key? It's hanging on the nail by the fridge."

Nathan nodded. "Sure. When do you want it, Sheriff?"

Hawk glanced at his watch. "Meet me over there in about an hour."

The sheriff left with a promise from Kat and Nathan to call him if Grams woke up. Hawk needed to ask her some questions, if she recovered enough to talk.

Nathan sat next to Kat and settled in to wait for the next visit to ICU. Neither spoke. Nathan placed his arm around her and pulled her close. Maybe later, when Grams was out of danger, they could talk about some of the walls that had been built between them. For now the silence would do.

CHAPTER 12

Humsinger's house resembled his office. A comfortable home by almost any standard stuffed with a lifetime of exotic memorabilia from his globetrotting days when he worked as a field collector for several museums. Along the way he'd accumulated a modest collection of artifacts and specimens from locales that no longer invited Americans interested in their antiquities. Modest by yesterday's standards. By today's standards, of frowning on artifact collecting by private individuals, it was an enviable collection. Several of his pieces would easily bring thousands of dollars on the open market. But it had been a long time since he'd acquired anything new of that same quality.

His library contained several thousand volumes and was housed in his home office in floor-to-ceiling shelves. The classics—Hemingway, Faulkner and Dickens among others—shared shelf space beside popular fiction of Baldacci, Grisham and Rollins. Reference and non-fiction works about the sciences filled any remaining gaps. Humsinger read voraciously about geology, archeology, paleontology, anthropology and ancient history. As in his work office, in every conceivable vacant space rested an artifact or mineral specimen.

He was seated at his computer when the phone rang. Preoccupied, he picked up the receiver and mumbled his usual phone greeting. "Humsinger."

"Brian? Any progress?"

"We've had a little setback."

"What kind of setback? I just dropped twenty million on your little dog and pony show down there to keep from having setbacks." The irritation in Crawley's voice was palpable. Humsinger rubbed his temple and sighed.

Before he could respond, Crawley continued. "Is it that hot shot archeologist you hired? Is he poking around where he doesn't belong? I told you he was trouble."

"No. It's not him. He hasn't shown up for work in a few days, but even if he does I've solved that little problem. I've hired someone who isn't quite as nosy. For the moment, I can't locate my diggers."

"Get some more. I've sent you plenty of money besides the grant." Everything was a simple solution with Neil Crawley. Throw some more money at it.

"It's not that easy, Neil. How do you want me to find them? Run an ad in the paper asking for someone willing to commit a federal offense for a few thousand a week?"

"Have your boy find some more diggers."

"You haven't been listening. I just said I couldn't find my boy."

Neil didn't speak for a few seconds. "I'll send some people down there. You hook up with them and get them started."

"I'm sure they're trained in archeology and know exactly what they're looking for." Specky was many things, a number of them unflattering, but at least he'd worked a couple of legitimate digs so he had a rough idea of what to do. And what not to do. A person with no training at all could destroy several thousand dollars worth of artifacts through sheer ignorance.

"I'll find someone who has a little experience. But listen, Brian. Don't lose sight of the real goal here. I didn't drop that kind of coin on you to have a couple of arrowheads and a pot or two." Crawley paused for a moment, allowing his words to sink in. "I need some real goods. You better deliver. Your little theory better be right."

The corners of Humsinger's mouth turned slightly upward in the hint of a smile. In his right hand he rolled a small stone between his thumb and forefinger. "Don't worry about that, Crawley. Just send me some more diggers. Experienced ones."

"They'll be there. I'll call you and let you know where to meet them."

Humsinger hung up the phone and stared at the section of mastodon jawbone with three teeth still in place resting on his desk. Briefly he wondered if there could be a connection between the missing Specky and Harlin not showing up for work. Nathan seemed certain that Harlin had gone to the dig site.

Even though there was no evidence of that, it still made Humsinger nervous. Would Specky implicate him if Harlin had convinced him to go to the authorities?

Without a doubt.

He regretted letting this thing get so out of hand. But his current retirement account, while sufficient for most people, would fail to support the types of activities he had planned. His travels alone would cost far more than he had accumulated. Add that to his desire to acquire a few key pieces for his collection, and he would need a lot more money.

Brian Humsinger did not intend to spend his retirement playing bridge and eating at Shoney's buffet on senior citizen discount day. Life was to be lived. He intended to spend his retirement like he had his twenties and part of his thirties—traveling from one exotic forbidden locale to the next in search of specimens and adventure. Only this time for his own private collection. And all that was within his grasp. He looked at the small stone in his hand. Definitely within his grasp.

* * *

Quin hefted the satchel of money and then placed it on the bed. It was far more than the ten thousand dollars he needed for Doctor John. He held the dragon's blood stick he'd gotten from Madam Jean aloft and murmured a quiet prayer.

It had worked beautifully.

Only one shot fired, and he'd been far away by the time the cops responded. He suspected his victims had too. For the first time in several days Quin felt like his luck had changed. He wished he could read the stars and find out what was in store for him.

He dumped the money on the bed and counted it. A little over twenty thousand dollars and all of it in mixed-age twenty dollar bills. Quin spread the packets of money out on the bedspread and rolled on it. He'd never had that kind of money. He looked around the ratty hotel room. The place reeked of curry. How anyone could eat that stuff was beyond him. Well, this was his last night in a dump like this. With ten thousand dollars a man could start over.

Quin thought a little about his situation. With twenty thousand a man could really start over. If he left town he might get by without giving Doctor John that ten thousand dollars. But he knew that was dangerous. He'd seen people turned into zombies before and he knew Doctor John could do it. But did he actually owe Doctor John the money?

All he'd done was go to Doctor John and ask for his help. The witch doctor had told him he'd help him when he brought him the ten thousand dollars.

What if he just didn't take him the money? Would Doctor John put a hoodoo on him for not showing up? The whole spooky mess was beyond Quin's understanding.

But, ever since he'd gotten that dragon's blood stick, he'd felt like the curse was broken. And it had only cost him a hundred dollars. That was a good bit less than ten thousand dollars. He just wasn't sure though. If the curse still followed him, he'd gladly pay the ten thousand. He could still hear Specky screaming as the apparition dragged him underwater. The memory of Doctor John and his snake played in his head in vivid detail. That little shrunken head grinning at him.

Quin wrestled with the problem in his mind while he flipped the channels on the television. This place advertised the Playboy channel in big neon letters outside the office, but he couldn't find it. He gave up looking after flipping through two complete revolutions of the available channels. Maybe that was a sign. His good luck might be wearing out.

Quin made a decision. He stuffed one of the packets of money into his jeans and looked around the room for a place to stash the rest of it. His eyes wandered to the window unit air conditioner but he couldn't find a place big enough to hide all of the money. He knew better than to put it under the bed.

Quin was searching the bathroom when an idea hit him. He turned off the water to the toilet and flushed it, draining the last bit of water from the porcelain tank. Then he took the plastic liner out of the trashcan, dumped the money in it, and stuffed the whole package inside the toilet tank before replacing the lid. The empty satchel ended up in the closet where someone would think it was his luggage.

Satisfied that his money was safe, Quin left. Madam Jean would be open and he needed to ask her a few questions before he made his decision. He might be able to buy a few more dragon's blood sticks and keep the good luck flowing.

* * *

From his front porch rocking chair, Tommy Robideaux watched the sun ease lower on the western horizon. It would be a good night to go frog gigging. There would be a full moon and the big bullfrogs would be out in droves tonight, puffing up their cheeks like so many jazz musicians, trying to attract the lady frogs. He hadn't been gigging in a coon's age and for some reason he craved frog legs. The last batch he'd had was over at Waldo's Crab Shack and they hadn't been cooked right.

Cooking frog legs was fast becoming a lost art. You had to get the grease just the right temperature and then drop the legs in fresh cleaned, but rolled in beer batter. The legs would jump around in the grease like they was still attached to the frog. It wasn't a sight for the squeamish. If you froze them they didn't do that, and he was pretty sure that Waldo's cook had used frozen legs cause they'd tasted a bit freezer burned. That, or they'd been farm-raised frogs.

Tonight he'd get a good mess and bring them home and cook

them up. Tommy's mouth was watering already. He kicked back on the porch and waited. As soon as he heard the first one bellow he'd head out. He'd dug around in the closet and found his hip waders and his old three-prong gig was hanging from the rafters of the barn. The new six-volt battery for his headlamp was still sitting in the Wal-Mart sack on the kitchen table.

Three hours and a six-pack later he was standing waist deep in the bayou with two nice frogs already in the wet tow sack tied to his belt. He'd forgotten how much fun this was. After dodging a couple of snakes and missing the first frog of the night he'd gotten the hang of it again and had frog number three pinned to the bank with his light. As long as he shined their eyes with a powerful light, they wouldn't move and he could ease close enough to gig them with the six-foot long spear. If he got careless and moved too fast the frog would jump anyway. Kind of like women in some respects he thought. At least the ones he'd been after lately.

Tommy inched closer to the unsuspecting frog, keeping it pinned with the light in his left hand while he handled the gig with his right. He was almost close enough.

Now!

He jabbed the gig forward and missed the frog by less than an inch. The frog jumped and landed with a plop in the water. He cast the light over the surface trying to find the quick amphibian.

It was no use. He'd missed another one.

Tommy heard a noise behind him and slowly turned, expecting another frog or a snake. Maybe a gar rolling on the surface. He shined the light around, but didn't see anything. Must have been a fish, he thought. He shined the light directly on the water. It had a peculiar white sheen to it.

He took another step forward and something jerked his legs violently out from under him. His head sank below the surface before he had time to catch his breath and water poured into his open mouth. Tommy fought desperately to close his mouth but his lungs fought just as desperately to evacuate the water that had entered. Panic-stricken, he clawed for the bottom of the bayou when his hands found one of the many stumps of ancient cypress trees cut long ago.

Gratefully he pulled his head above water and tried to stand. An unfamiliar warm sensation came from his lower body. Tommy looked down, the light still in his left hand, and emitted a blood-curdling scream that originated in the pit of his stomach.

Both legs were gone and the bloody stumps pumped streams of crimson into the murky water of the bayou. Another fear-inspired scream pierced the night when one of Tommy's severed legs bobbed to the surface of the water. He crossed himself and tried to stop the flow of blood. He was dying, and he was afraid. Afraid it wouldn't be quick enough. Strangely, he felt no pain.

CHAPTER 13

Doctor John's graceful movements belied the weight of the burlap-wrapped burden he carried. To a bystander, he would appear to glide around the large courtyard with an effortlessness that reminded one of someone hang gliding. In due time he would reach his destination; the weed-choked swimming pool in the center. The ritual was as critical as the ultimate destination.

At one time this area had been the exercise courtyard and recreational facility for the old hotel he now owned and lived in. The old Mystic Inn that once housed sixty guests now provided ample room for his staff of four and his three wives. Otherwise, he was the sole occupant. The pool in the center, once teeming with bathers, was no longer used for swimming. The dingy water and dense mat of aquatic plants made the pool uninviting at best. At worst, Doctor John might catch them there.

The once neatly kept courtyard now resembled a jungle. Numerous tropical plants forested the space not occupied by the pool. Exotic birds flew from limb to limb, flashing colors normally seen only at Mardi Gras. Narrow paths, winding randomly, crisscrossed the area. In all four directions, small alcoves contained statues of the Virgin Mary ringed by lit candles. Leering human skulls watched over each statue, silent guardians that kept all but the most foolish from entering the courtyard. At closer look, one could see the skullcaps were removable and that small candles inside could be lit for special ceremonies. The courtyard was his private chapel.

Doctor John was troubled. He had read the bones this morning and the message was startling. Could it be possible he was wrong? He did not think so, but never, even in his many past lives, could he recall an event so momentous. For the first time in years, he was uncertain about how to proceed. Confusion was for the weak-minded and those unskilled in the ways. He was neither, but he must test the spirits and proceed with caution. The spirits had little patience for those who chose to be disrespectful.

For now, Vodu demanded he be tested and proven worthy. Doctor John followed the circuitous route without thinking and arrived at his destination unharmed. No one knew the path but him. The skulls of two others who had attempted the path now stood silent vigilance over the Virgin Mary on the south wall, the place where the offenders had breached his sanctuary. No one else had dared try. The streets of New Orleans sang a quiet song of warning. Locals, tolerant of many things that defied understanding, heeded the warning and kept their distance. Doctor John, the most powerful voodoo priest in the city, commanded respect in every walk of New Orleans society although it would be denied vehemently in public.

He gently placed his burden on a small altar located where the previous tenants had anchored a diving board. Ceremoniously he lit three candles and slowly stripped naked. His enormous framed rippled with muscle, pure bone covered with sinew. Even he was not aware of his full strength. When he had first arrived in New Orleans several years ago he had often earned money by betting on his strength. Many times he had easily lifted liquid-filled fifty-five gallon drums that weighed almost five hundred pounds over his head. Once he had picked up the front end of a small car and moved it several feet to win $100. The small burden he'd brought today weighed only 200 pounds.

From an opening beneath the altar he removed a tortoise shell made into a bowl. The wooden lid bore the carving of a cat. Doctor John passed his hands over the lid twice and muttered something known only to him. Gingerly he removed the lid and dipped his fingers into the gooey substance. He began to chant and apply the substance as one would apply sunscreen, rubbing it thoroughly over every square inch of his ebony body. The smell of decay from the grease engulfed him and he inhaled deeply, consuming the aroma as one would consume a glass of lemonade on a hot day. He had rendered the grease himself from the fat of several black cats for just this purpose.

His preparation complete, he unwrapped the burlap to reveal a full hindquarter of beef. From the odor, barely detectable over the smell of the rancid cat grease, it was properly aged. He placed the half-rotted beef hindquarter in front of him and called out in his booming voice.

"Rapma. Come to me."

His eyes searched the dark waters of the large pool until finally locating his quarry. Doctor John smiled, revealing a row of animal-like teeth filed to perfect points. The two canine teeth, longer and more pointed than the others, were both covered with gold caps.

"Rapma. You are needed."

A small ripple originated on the surface of the pool, spreading outward in concentric rings as something sank below the surface. Moments later, and twenty feet nearer, the water parted and a sixteen-foot bull alligator emerged, waddling onto the surface of the old pool deck. Two yellow reptilian eyes rotated toward Doctor John, studying him. Watching him.

"Rapma. You are needed," he repeated.

The alligator moved with a swiftness unimagined in a beast so large and apparently lethargic. It seized the hindquarter of beef in its prehistoric jaws and began to shake its head back and forth in the manner of a small dog shaking a sock. The big gator ripped off a large piece of the beef and quickly gulped it down. The massive throat distended to receive the fifty-pound chunk of flesh. Doctor John watched the reptile finish off the rest of the offering in like manner.

The beast then turned its attention to Doctor John. Slowly it waddled closer, its olfactory nerves testing the air, drawn to the smell of rancid cat grease covering the witch doctor's nude frame. Doctor John stared at the gator, mesmerized by its performance with the beef and the raw power of the beast.

The gator waddled still closer. Doctor John smiled when he

saw the reflection of his two glimmering gold-covered fangs in the gator's eyes. The beast stopped and tested the air again, much like a small dog would when a larger one marked its territory.

"Rapma. Your strength is needed. The bones tell of another one more powerful than even you."

Doctor John stood, stretching himself to his full height, and continued his one-sided conversation with the gator. "We must talk, Rapma."

Doctor John dove into the pool. The bull alligator followed, its considerable bulk sliding silently into the water.

* * *

Nathan found the key where Kat said it would be. Why hadn't Harlin asked him to feed his cat? Was Harlin trying to step in as Nathan faded out of Kat's life? The thought troubled him. Harlin knew they were having marital problems, but would he take advantage of that? When Nathan first left Kat he'd suggested that he move in with Harlin and Harlin had been adamant about living alone. In retrospect, that seemed a little odd. Why had he not wanted someone to share the expenses with him? Nathan had dismissed it as Harlin simply wanting his privacy, but had there been more to it than that?

Nathan scanned the small apartment, now cleansed of his presence. He noted the obvious voids in the living room previously occupied by sundry traces of his existence. The table lamps on each end of the sofa now sat on the floor, unlit reminders of a relationship in a similar state. The garage sale end tables, the former residence of those lamps, now gathered dust in the center of his small living room where he'd dumped them last weekend. The pictures on the wall above the sofa leered at him, a gap-tooth grin with every missing tooth a photographic record of their relationship.

Nathan could list every photo. A collage of their vacation to Florida last spring. A blown up photo of them both in the lab poring over the latest remote fly-over shots. A single wedding photo taken by the pimply faced son of the Justice of the Peace. When he closed his eyes, he could still see Kat in a simple white-cotton summer dress. He could see the light reflecting off her dark hair and the brilliant smile. He could even smell her fragrance.

Yet with eyes open, everything was gone. All physical evidence of the good times sterilized by removal from the wall. The irony was tangible. We photographically record the good times to remind us they happened, only to shove them in a box in the closet so that we can forget. It was all too easy. Disposable gloves, disposable diapers, disposable relationships. All designed to do the same thing. To keep you from having to deal with the crap. It was too easy to move on and leave the difficult things behind.

Was that what he was doing with Kat?

After all, hadn't he done the same thing with his parents?

When things get rocky, just move your end tables and a few photographs and pick up the next link in the chain of life. Ten years later and you wonder how they are. Are they healthy? Are they financially okay? Are they lonely?

Would he wonder the same things about Kat ten years from now? How many more times would he move the end tables and pack away the photographs? How many more disposable relationships would he have?

The knock on the door rescued him from his demons. Nathan wasn't ready to move on to the next link, at least not alone. He looked at the key to Harlin's apartment in his hand. Nathan sure didn't intend for Kat's next link to involve Harlin. He opened the door and stepped outside where Hawk waited.

"Did you find the key, or do I need to round up the apartment manager?"

Nathan handed the key to Hawk. "Do you need anything else from me?"

"Have you been in Harlin's apartment before?"

"Several times when we brought work home."

"Could I get you to come with me and see if you notice anything different, like something missing or out of place?"

"No problem." Nathan checked his watch. "I want to get back to ICU in time to go in with Kat to see Grams. Kat needs me right now."

"I'll just get you to look around a few minutes." They had covered the few doors to Harlin's apartment while they talked and now Hawk paused at the door. "I'm going to ask you to not touch anything in case this ends up as another disappearance."

Nathan nodded. "That's fine."

Hawk opened the door and entered the small apartment. It was identical in design to Kat's apartment. They had taken only a few steps when Harlin's cat came yowling into the room. The big male Siamese was a gregarious cat, always in the middle of everything. If they spread out a map on the kitchen table, the cat would lay on it. If you watched television, the cat would be in your lap. The cat was always friendly, but rarely vocal.

The foul smell of a litter box, badly in need of refreshing, assaulted Nathan's nasal passages. Hawk, a frown on his face and his nostrils wrinkling, looked at Nathan. By way of explanation Nathan offered. "It's the litter box."

Hawk nodded. "Good. I was a little worried."

The cat rubbed against Hawk's legs, meowing loudly.

"Do you mind if I feed him? I don't think he's eaten lately."

"Please do. Maybe it will shut him up."

Hawk started a quick visual inspection of the apartment while Nathan entered the kitchen in search of cat food. Two cabinet doors later he found the cat's treasure trove and popped a lid of some concoction labeled turkey giblets. The ravenous cat attacked the can with vigor and rewarded the intruders with silence. Nathan noted the bowl where Harlin normally kept out some dry food and the cat's water bowl were both empty. He picked up the sack of dry cat food to refill the bowl. The sack looked nearly full but was surprisingly light. He peered inside and saw a sea of small dried food pellets. A ten-pound bag just didn't feel as heavy as he thought it should.

Nathan dismissed the stray thought and tried to pour the cat a generous helping of dry food. Very little food came out causing Nathan to once again peer into the bag. This time he saw something other than food. A blue-denim cloth bag rested in the cat food sack. Nathan carefully removed the bag and laid it on the kitchen countertop.

"What have you found?" Hawk had finished his casual search of the apartment and returned to the kitchen/living area.

"This bag was inside the cat food sack." Nathan looked at Hawk. "That strikes me as a little odd."

"That's a lot odd." Hawk came over. "I asked you not to touch anything."

"I just pulled it out." Nathan held his hands up and backed away from the bag. "I haven't opened it."

"Good." Hawk seemed satisfied. "Let me see what's in it."

The bag was fashioned from one leg of a pair of denim jeans that had been sewn shut on one end, and tied closed with a strong cord on the other. Hawk gingerly opened the bag. Cautiously, he peered inside before inserting his hand and removing four small parcels wrapped in old newspaper. He carefully unwrapped each object, and placed it on the bar, until the sack's contents lay spread before both men.

Nathan couldn't believe it.

Was Harlin robbing burial mounds?

Each object was obviously an artifact. He'd seen enough artifacts with Kat when they'd taken a pilgrimage to the Field Museum in Chicago last year. There were two finely chipped flint arrowheads, a small white stone carving of a lizard and a turtle effigy bowl of pottery. Nathan knew they were all quite valuable. Particularly the bowl and the carving.

"What is this stuff?"

Nathan cleared his throat, hesitant to inform on Harlin without first seeking an explanation. "They're artifacts."

"I can see that." Hawk gave him a blistering look. "I mean why would he have them in a cat food sack?"

"They would bring several dollars at auction. Maybe he was just trying to hide his collection."

Hawk was no fool. "Either that or he's stolen them from somewhere."

Nathan shrugged. His gut told him Hawk was right, but he hoped he was wrong. Maybe Kat would know what was going on. After all, she did have a key to Harlin's apartment.

CHAPTER 14

Madam Jean's place of business alternated between a small nondescript house on South Villere near the cemetery known as St. Louis Number One, and a more high-traffic location on Jackson Square. Her regular customers preferred the South Villere location because the proximity to the dead made it easier to follow some of her instructions. It also had easy interstate access.

Several of Madam Jean's most requested potions required the purchaser to conduct some ritual in the cemetery. A woman desiring a husband had to knock three times on the burial vault containing the remains of Marie Laveau and speak her wish out loud. Then she typically penciled a cross on the vault and left a penny laying on top of it. The South Villere location made those tasks easier to perform while the customer was still confident enough to enter the cemetery. If a person waited as much as fifteen minutes after their visit with Madam Jean they usually discovered their fear of the cemetery overpowered their need for a husband. The Jackson Square location catered to the tourists. During Mardi Gras, and on weekends, Madam Jean could be found plying her trade among the jugglers, portrait artists, assorted musicians and other street performers. Palm readings and pre-made love potions were her best sellers, although she would sell a few magic powders (talcum mixed with blue or pink chalk and perfume) and an occasional Johnny. Her limited market research favored a location closer to Café DuMonde.

It was Wednesday so Quin knocked on the door at South Villere. Even this late in the evening the oppressive heat enveloped him like a wool overcoat as he waited patiently for the door to open. Her normal business hours were over but Quin knew she'd see him if he had money. His hand fondled the roll of bills in his pocket. Madam Jean would be more than ready to do business.

Madam Jean answered the door. She looked the part of fortune teller or palm reader: A small rotund woman with an olive face that had more wrinkles than New Orleans had streets. A brightly colored scarf wrapped around her head and covered her thin hair. Several large gold loops dangled from each ear. She had discovered early in her career that if you dressed the part you were much more financially successful. Madam Jean was an astute woman and had done quite well in her career. She also respected those in her profession that had real power. Of one she was afraid and that one wanted this man on her stoop.

"Come in, Quin Laroche." Madam Jean turned and entered the small parlor, its walls lined with overstuffed chairs and two small sofas. Low light emitted from several large candles placed in sconces on the walls. Sculptures of multicolored wax formed beneath each one giving the impression that the candles had been burning for centuries.

Quin obediently followed instructions as Madam Jean seated herself on one of the sofas and gestured for him to sit beside her. She clapped her hands twice and a small girl appeared, probably not over twelve or thirteen years old.

"Bring us some tea, Cherub."

Her apprentice wordlessly exited and returned in minutes with a tray and two cups of a steaming foul-smelling brew optimistically identified as tea. She then bowed slightly and again exited the room.

The child had an errand to run.

With the nimbleness and agility of youth and the speed of fear the small girl ran through the streets of New Orleans that grown men feared to walk at night. Quin sipped his tea and waited. Madam Jean sipped her tea and stalled.

"I sense a troubled spirit tonight, Quin Laroche." She used the full name to create a sense of formality and seriousness. Often she adopted that technique when the customer had a spirit of negativity or foreboding. Over the years she'd learned that a person's attitude dictated the circumstances they would soon face. Or maybe it was their interpretation of the circumstances as good or bad. In either case, repeat business was her bread and butter, and if her prognostications came true, good or bad, it generated repeat business.

In Quin's case it wasn't difficult. If Doctor John looked for a person it was rarely good and probably didn't bode well for repeat business from Quin. However, if he had opportunity to spread the word about her forecasts before his misfortunes befell him, his story would go far to convince others of her abilities.

"I need some more good luck." He pulled the wad of bills from his pocket to show her he could pay. Madam Jean nodded in approval.

I "Good. Let me see your hand."

Quin placed his hand, still holding the money, in her outstretched arthritic claw. Madam Jean palmed the entire roll and the money disappeared as she caressed the hand and slowly traced the lines on his palm with a crooked index finger. She closed her eyes and studied the hand as a blind person reading Braille.

Minutes passed and Quin's fear grew. He remembered the beast devouring Specky and wondered if his fate demanded he end up in the beast's belly. He remembered the shrunken head adorning Doctor John's necklace and wondered if his own head would soon reside there. He closed his eyes and tried to think about something else. Anything else.

Madam Jean continued her reading, but now she was humming. He recognized the tune but could not place it. Quin opened one eye. Everything else appeared to be the same. The old woman continued to grip his hand with one bony claw and trace a pattern with the other. He tried to discern the pattern. It was a cross.

Footsteps on the front porch sounded and the humming grew in volume. Now Quin recognized the song. He remembered it from his youth. A far away time when his Mama would carry him to the tiny community church. The song was an old hymn. Quin fixed his eyes on the opening front door. Doctor John's immense frame filled the entrance and Madam Jean released his hand. She continued to hum.

Quin knelt on the floor and clasped his hands together. "Please, Doctor John. I was coming to see you."

Doctor John's cloak billowed around him as a puff of wind caught the light fabric. His eyes fixed on Quin like a pin holding a bug to an entomologist's collection board. Quin trembled, again unable to control his fear. He would die tonight, he knew. No longer could he look at Doctor John. He tried to recall the words to the hymn but couldn't.

Doctor John stepped closer and took one immense finger and placed it under Quin's chin. He tilted Quin's head upward, until Quin was looking into those demonic eyes.

"I have need of you, little man. Rapma tells me you will lead me to the one I seek."

The pressure under Quin's chin increased and he stood to relieve it. Doctor John smiled, and Quin felt weak in the knees.

"You will come with me." Doctor John grabbed the much smaller man by the arm and left. He had not even acknowledged Madam Jean was in the room.

Madam Jean heard the back door close and the small girl appeared in the doorway. She was breathing hard from her run. Wide-eyed, she looked around the room. "He is on his way, Madam Jean."

Madam Jean continued to hum until, after several seconds, she finished the tune. Amazing Grace had always been one of her favorite songs.

"He's already come and gone, Cherub."

The child looked bewildered. "But I ran all the way. I promise I did."

"I know, Cherub. I know."

Madam Jean blew out the candles in the front parlor and beckoned to the child. "Let's go out and get something to eat tonight." Madam Jean appeared motherly. "Would you like that?"

* * *

Nathan shaking her shoulder startled Kat awake. The ICU waiting room still housed just the two of them. Nathan looked terrible. Large bags under his eyes and a day's beard stubble accented the rumpled clothes he'd slept in. Kat knew how important his sleep was to him yet he'd stayed awake most of the night talking to her about Grams. Neither had mentioned their separation and impending divorce, each unwilling to broach a subject that might reverse the current détente brought about by Grams' stroke. Both knew the subject would have to come up sooner or later but preferred later.

"It's eight o'clock. They'll let us go in again."

Kat sat up and rubbed her eyes. She knew she had to look as bad as Nathan. "Let me splash some water on my face."

She quickly washed her face so she could see Grams. Every four hours the ICU unit let them visit for a few minutes. So far, Grams had been the same. She seemed so peaceful lying there, although Kat wondered how anyone could rest, no matter how medicated, with the constant beeping and blinking of all those monitors. It made Kat fear that she would be comatose until she died, something Grams would never have wanted.

The shift change had occurred around seven, so Grams had a new group of nurses. They smiled reassuringly as she and Nathan passed the nurses' station. Kat wondered how they could be that optimistic surrounded by sudden death the way they were.

Grams looked the same. Kat approached the bed and gripped her hand, giving it a light squeeze. To Kat's surprise, Grams squeezed back and opened her eyes, a slight crooked smile playing across her face. Kat broke into a grin that Nathan hadn't seen in quite some time.

Grams tried to speak but couldn't form the words. She motioned with her hand for a pencil and paper. Kat rummaged through her purse for the notepad and pen she always carried and handed them to Grams. With her left hand she laboriously scrawled the words 'I love you' on the paper.

"I love you too, Grams." Kat felt ashamed. "I'm sorry I haven't been by more often."

Grams shook her head from left to right and managed a crooked smile. One side of her face failed to respond. In her own way she was telling Kat not to worry about it. She was always forgiving of anything Kat had done. What made her think Grams wouldn't forgive the divorce? In her heart Kat knew that the real reason she hadn't been to see Grams wasn't because she was afraid Grams wouldn't forgive her, but because she knew Grams disapproved. She'd loved Nathan from the beginning and adopted him as one of her own.

Grams scribbled something else on the pad. Watching her grandmother struggle so hard just to write a simple sentence filled Kat's eyes with tears.

How many times had she cried in the last two weeks?

Grams finished the sentence and settled back exhausted. The simple effort of writing the two sentences had taken its toll on Grams' weakened condition.

Kat picked up the pad and read out loud, "Bottom drawer of my dresser. Find Jake Lloyd."

Kat looked at Grams to verify the sentence. Her grandmother managed a slight affirmative nod and tried to open her mouth. She was trying to tell them something else. No words came out as Grams struggled to make a sound.

Kat looked at Nathan who shrugged his shoulders. "Are you hungry, Grams?"

Grams tried to reach for the notepad. Kat understood and was placing the pencil in Grams' hand when a nurse came in and saw the pad and pencil. She grimaced at Kat, and shot an equally disapproving look at Nathan.

"Okay you two, visitation's over. You should have called us when she woke up. She certainly doesn't need the strain of trying to write stuff down." The nurse busied herself with Grams. "She just needs to rest."

Kat had no idea what the note meant. She hoped Lloyd wasn't a lawyer who had drafted Grams' will. There was really no reason for that since Kat was the only living relative and Grams had no estate, just a few personal possessions and maybe enough money for a funeral.

Kat's stomach began to churn again as she left the room. The now-familiar feeling made her wonder if she had ulcers. She would have to make an appointment with the doctor soon.

CHAPTER 15

Specky's former home epitomized the stereotypical Mississippi residence. A mobile home, twelve feet wide and forty feet long, occupied a central spot in an area identified by a faded 1950s era sign as Jimbo's Trailer Park. The sign pre-dated the marketing campaign that turned trailers into mobile homes, but no one living in Jimbo's Trailer Park cared much what you called their multi-colored metal-sided home on wheels.

Most concerned themselves with more important issues like whether or not the Saints would ever have a winning season again, this week's winning six numbers, or making sure their deer rifles were sighted in properly before the next gun season opened. And, true to form, none cared much what was happening at Specky's trailer right now.

Quin parked his beat-up old pickup next to Specky's project car, a four-door 1957 Chevrolet currently resting on concrete blocks and covered with a faded blue tarp to keep the elements at bay. Quin had spent about as much time as Specky had working on that car, guzzling one beer after another, and swatting mosquitoes more aggressive and less particular than the Red Cross.

He got out of his pickup and patted the car nostalgically. Specky was gone and Quin missed him. Even though Specky had been a stupid redneck, and Quin had called him that on numerous occasions, they had still been fast friends. An unusual friendship, in fact the shrinks would have labeled it a dysfunctional relationship. One where they would fight and then avoid each other for months, but one that had outlasted any relationship Quin had ever had with a woman.

Quin squatted and felt under the fender of the '57 Chevy for the key to Specky's trailer. He found the magnetic key holder, removed the key, and unlocked the trailer door. Specky, a creature of habit, hadn't changed the hiding place in the last ten years. Nothing had changed in the few days since Quin had last been here. He stepped into the tiny living room, still littered with dirty laundry and beer cans. Empty chip bags and magazines hid the surface of the coffee table. A National Geographic Magazine seemed out of place next to the current issues of Playboy and Mississippi Hunting. Specky had been doing some reading on the different artifacts archeologists found in other parts of the world. He'd been convinced that some of the stuff he'd found was much more valuable than his boss told him.

Quin crossed the tiny room and flopped down on the decrepit couch, disturbing an inch-long cockroach in the process. He swatted at the scurrying insect and missed, stirring up enough dust to pot a small plant. Quin remembered when he helped tote the broken-down couch home from a roadside trash dumpster. The seat springs had collapsed, and two of the legs were broken completely off, but Specky insisted he could fix it right up. A piece of half-inch plywood under the cushions, and a few bricks to level it, and it was as good as new. Quin reached over to turn on the deer hoof lamp setting atop the wooden spool end table Specky had stolen from the phone company. He had to admit the couch did fit the rest of Specky's white trash décor. Jeff Foxworthy could find enough material for another book in this one room.

He walked to the refrigerator and found a six pack of cold beer waiting on him. Specky wouldn't need them anymore, so he popped a top and sat down in the stained overstuffed recliner positioned directly in front of the new nineteen-inch color television. He drank his beer and contemplated.

Where would Specky hide something valuable?

The search area was not that large, but the debris of Specky's life cluttered the small trailer and complicated any search. Quin knew he could find Specky's guns easily enough, but that was secondary. His primary goal was to make Doctor John happy.

He felt the spot on his head where Doctor John had snipped off some of his hair. It was a constant reminder not to attempt anything foolish again. Doctor John had taken the small hair sample and placed it on the head of a doll fashioned in Quin's likeness. He'd then taken a pin and pushed it into the doll's leg. Quin's leg still tingled from the excruciating pain that felt like he'd stepped in a bed of fire ants. Big fire ants.

Quin was a true believer in Doctor John's power now. After the voodoo doll episode, he'd promptly gone back to his motel room, retrieved his satchel of money, and given the entire sum to Doctor John. Doctor John could have all of it. Money meant nothing in the face of pain. Nothing compared to what Doctor John could do to him. Quin shuddered. Just thinking about Doctor John made him shake like a wet Chihuahua.

Quin looked around the squalid quarters. Specky Vore, the ignorant bushy-haired freckled redneck that Quin had called a friend, had left little behind. He'd passed unnoticed, like someone killing a spike buck. His life had been a non-event.

In fact, very little physical evidence even pointed to Specky Vore's existence. All that remained was a trashy little trailer with a grinning picture of Specky hanging on the wall above the television. It was a senior prom photo. Specky in a tuxedo with the finest female flesh he'd ever dated. A pimply-faced overweight girl from high school stuffed into a dress three sizes too small for her. Quin couldn't remember how many times he'd heard Specky recount the tale of getting that girl out of her dress.

Of course, considering some of Specky's other sexual conquests, the girl was a real beauty queen. Specky had shacked up with one girl for over a year that the mere sight of would make you lose your breakfast. Three hundred-plus pounds of flesh that quivered like gelatin squares in a serving bowl, topped with a mass of long blonde locks braided into dozens of tiny rivers of greasy hair, each one tipped with a multicolored bead. Most of the time she wore a halter top straining from the excess that offered a full twelve inches of cleavage, front and back, that would look more appropriate descending into the back of a refrigerator repairman's jeans. Quin used to call her Bovine Derek. But not to her face.

Quin finished his beer, crumpled up the can, and threw it at the senior prom picture. All the scheming Specky and Quin had done amounted to nothing. Nothing but trouble. Quin sighed and headed back to Specky's bedroom. Rummaging through memories wouldn't help him find the goods Doctor John wanted.

He started at one end of the trailer, in what Specky referred to as the master bedroom suite, with the goal of working to the other end. Quin leaned Specky's mattress against the wall. Nothing under there but a homemade pair of brass knuckles and a switchblade he'd loaned Specky ages ago. There was no need to look under the bed since the box springs were setting on the floor.

The closet came next, where Quin found Specky's deer rifle and shotgun leaning in the corner covered with an old sheet. He carried them both to the living room and started a pile of anything valuable he could find. Specky wouldn't need the stuff and Quin knew he could hock it for a few dollars. He was broke again after giving all his money to Doctor John.

He returned to the bedroom and began to systematically search every possible hiding place. Two hours later he'd ransacked the whole trailer with the exception of the kitchen. The pile he'd started with the two guns wasn't much bigger. He'd added a nine millimeter pistol found in the night stand drawer, and a couple of nice hunting knives he'd keep for himself. The new color television and a toolbox full of wrenches completed the small pile. Not much of a legacy for a man Specky's age. Forty-one years of accumulation that could fit in a decent-sized cardboard box.

The kitchen would take a little more time because he was looking for a phone number too. He'd told Doctor John everything he knew about the burial mounds and Specky. But Doctor John wanted to know who Specky was selling the stuff to and Quin knew there had to be a phone number somewhere. He went through the kitchen drawers one at a time. Other than a handful of loose change strewn among a few thousand dead roaches, he found nothing of value.

Under the sink, he struck pay dirt. In a shoebox wrapped in an old towel Quin found two miniature clay effigy bowls. One looked like a turtle and the other bore some resemblance to a lizard. Quin knew that Specky had probably stolen them from a previous dig. The few days that he'd been working with him they had found nothing except a few arrowheads and some broken pottery.

Where did Specky put the arrowheads?

Quin glanced around the kitchen again, trying to figure out where Specky might stash something. His eyes landed on the oven and he smiled. That oven hadn't worked in at least a couple of years. It would be the perfect place to hide something valuable. He opened the door and the sight of two more shoeboxes rewarded him. Pleased with himself, Quin removed the first shoebox and opened the lid to reveal twenty or thirty arrowheads thrown haphazardly into the bottom of the box. He spotted one on top that he remembered picking up a few days ago. It was unusual, or he wouldn't have remembered it. The arrowhead was fashioned out of quartz so it was almost perfectly clear, with one exception. The clear point had a vein of red running through it like a jagged lightening strike of blood.

The other box contained a few more arrowheads, a small slip of paper and an old jewelry box. Specky had scribbled the name Humsinger on the paper. Quin recognized the name. He'd heard Specky say it once, but had forgotten it. Now all he needed was a phone number to go with it. Struck with an idea, Quin walked over to the kitchen table and picked up a stack of mail. He quickly sorted through and found what he was looking for. Specky's unpaid telephone bill. Quin ripped it open and scanned the numbers.

That Specky sure was one horny white boy. He'd racked up a couple of hundred dollars last month on some 900 number, no doubt a phone sex hotline. Who ever said talk was cheap? Of course, in Specky's case it was free. Good luck collecting that money. They'd have to dun Specky in hell, cause he was likely fetching Satan some ice water about now.

Other than the 900 numbers, there were only a few possibilities. Quin grabbed the phone and started calling. Five calls later, he got the answering machine of one Dr. Brian Humsinger. He circled the number on the phone bill. Doctor John would be pleased. Quin had found Specky's contact person.

Quin returned to the kitchen countertop and picked up the small jewelry box, one that would normally house a necklace or pendant. Carefully he opened it and drew in a sharp breath. It was beautiful. The small green figurine inside appeared to be carved from a single large emerald. He picked it up and held it to the kitchen's flyspecked light. The transparent green figurine cast an eerie shadow on Quin's face as he studied it. Doctor John would definitely be pleased.

For a minute Quin considered running. Instinctively he knew this artifact was worth a small fortune if he could find the right buyer. No one would have ever believed there would be anything that valuable in this trash heap Specky called home. Gingerly he replaced the carved jewel in its padded box. He felt the sharp pain in his leg and steadied himself against the kitchen countertop. The pain subsided and his initial thought to flee left. Doctor John could follow him anywhere. Quin touched the dragon's blood stick in his pocket. Maybe Doctor John would allow him to live when he was finished with him.

Quin's mission was far from over though. Doctor John needed him for many things. Quin would be his emissary to those outside New Orleans. A priest of Doctor John's stature would have many to do his bidding. And now Quin was one of those. Pain shot through his leg again and the cold clammy hand of fear gripped his heart and squeezed. Quin stumbled to Specky's recliner. He could barely breathe.

CHAPTER 16

Doctor John's nimble fingers pulled the collection of feathers into shape and secured the creation with sinew. He had procured the sinew weeks ago from a three-legged black dog he'd found roaming the French Quarter at night. Instantly recognizing the true value of the creature as a gift from Vodu, he ritualistically sacrificed the animal, salvaging the hair, bones, and sinew to await his need of them. The dog's dried eyes hung from a thin cord worn around his wrist. Doctor John sang a hymn in Creole while he worked.

He was almost ready. The feather creation, now a remarkable likeness of a rooster, needed only a few finishing touches. Deftly he completed the task and laid the rooster aside to gather the remaining items. It was midnight, and time to go. A moment later he exited his compound carrying his macabre collection in a snakeskin bag. Another normal denizen among the drag queens and French Quarter regulars.

Once again the night belonged to him. The Quarter, still very much alive at midnight, welcomed him with its familiar odor. He glided over the streets as one acquainted with every brick. As always, the crowd parted to allow his passage. Tonight he had a purpose, other than to merely revel in the decadence and the celebration of flesh. Tonight he recruited help. Help that would be needed soon.

The Old Ones had revealed even more to him in his dream. Bit by bit, piece by piece, he learned more every day. Soon the pieces would all come together and he would have power beyond belief. Nothing would be outside of his reach after the sacrifice of this particular goat without horns. Vodu had chosen him, Doctor John, as the most worthy.

Doctor John's destination carried him to the outskirts of the

Quarter. He now walked streets the revelers feared to tread in the daylight. And rightly so. The area was dangerous to those who did not know the ways. Not too long ago, he had killed a wayward tourist in this area. One who grew too curious and followed him when he did not wish to be followed. It had been a simple task of biting through the man's jugular and watching him bleed to death while keeping a massive hand clamped over the fool's mouth and nose to keep him quiet.

Doctor John reached the house. All was quiet. Gingerly, he placed his snakeskin bag on the front porch and began removing his collection of items. He first placed a miniature black coffin on the porch, oriented with the head toward the north. Next, the feather sculpture of the rooster went inside the coffin. The witch doctor then lit a black candle and allowed the wax to drip on the front porch before seating the lit candle in the melted wax. He repeated this process until four lit black candles, one for each direction, surrounded the small coffin, and then he placed a bowl of *congris*, or black-eyed peas and rice cooked with sugar, in front of the door. The potion complete, Doctor John backed down the sidewalk to the street. The entire task had taken less than one minute.

Very soon, he would have more help.

* * *

Kat looked around the tiny living room of the house where Grams lived. The pictures on the wall, the wooden rocking chair where Grams sat, and the small black and white television all looked the same as they had three months ago. And yet so much had changed. Life tended to be more about accumulating possessions and less about living. Except for Grams. She had always lived so simple, so Spartan, and yet had always been happy.

Kat fondly remembered the day almost two years ago when she'd helped Grams move to this house. Kat had taken to mentally referring to that as the B.N., or before Nathan, period of her life. She and Grams had rented a pickup from the local car rental and moved everything themselves. Two small women, one old and one young, had loaded and unloaded that truck several times and laughed until they cried over some of the day's antics. It had been like two sorority sisters moving into an apartment.

Grams' eyesight had grown weak enough that she felt uncomfortable driving and Kat moved her nearer to Stennis, and close enough to town that she could walk to the store. She loved to walk and keep active. Kat rubbed the arm of the rocker, shiny and smooth from countless years of use, and wondered if Grams would ever walk again. Or talk again. Kat knew that walking again would be more important to Grams, because Grams' spirit would die if she continued to be imprisoned in an immobile body.

"Are you okay?" Nathan placed his hand on Kat's shoulder and squeezed. The tenderness in his voice loosed the tears welling up in Kat's eyes. She tried to dry them with the back of her hand before turning around. She hated feeling so vulnerable.

"I'm worried about Grams. What if she doesn't make it?"

"She's a strong woman, Kat." Nathan spun her around to face him and looked her in the eyes. He smiled reassuringly. "I'd place money on Grams recovering before I would most people half her age."

Nathan pulled her to him and wrapped his arms around her. She gave in and buried her head in his chest. She needed to be held right now. Things were falling apart so fast. Would she soon be in the A.N., after Nathan, period of her life and be there without Grams? She was afraid that she and Nathan wouldn't be able to work things out. He had instantly responded when she had called, but she knew love had never been the issue. She still loved him and thought he still loved her.

At one time, she'd thought love could work through all things. Now she didn't know. Whether it could or couldn't, she was grateful for his presence. She needed someone to help her through this nightmare with Grams.

"Thank you."

Nathan pulled her closer and rubbed her shoulder. His cheek

rested against her head. "For what?"

"For being here."

"It's where I'm supposed to be, Kat."

Kat was silent, thinking about everything. Maybe, when Grams was out of danger, they could sit down and talk. But now wasn't the time. Other attempts to reconcile had started agreeably enough and ended in shouting matches. She wasn't up to that today. Kat just didn't have the emotional resources in her to deal with one more confrontation. She wiped a stray tear with her hand and looked up at Nathan.

"We need to look in Gram's dresser and see what she was trying to tell us."

"I'm with you."

Nathan sighed his disappointment, but Kat knew better than to start something that had no chance of resulting in success. For now she was content to let their relationship remain the same. It was safer for her emotionally. Kat walked through the small kitchen and dining area to the back bedroom. Grams' old shaker-style dresser stood against the back wall. In the old house in the country where Kat had grown up, the dresser had been placed strategically below the attic access in the bedroom. She could remember countless times being scolded by Grams for standing on the dresser trying to reach the attic access.

The attic contained so many unknown treasures. Throughout her young life she'd watched Grams stow numerous items in the attic. By the time she'd grown tall enough to reach the access, she didn't care. Life was sometimes that way. When the time came that you could reach your goal, it no longer seemed as important. She thought about her Ph.D. She thought about her new job. Her material goals had grown to be far less important in the last few days. Kat ran her hand across the top of the dresser. The wood surface still bore the scars of those futile attic attempts.

Did she bear those same scars?

Kat knelt down and pulled open the bottom drawer, filled to capacity with a hodgepodge of items. The few remaining vestiges of her childhood. Kat picked up two packets of pictures. The visual images were mostly the proofs of school pictures that were sent home with the student. They had been too poor to buy the photo packages, even the cheap ones. Kat glanced through them. She had a gaunt, haunted look about her as a child. Nathan peered at them silently. Kat had never shown him any childhood pictures.

"You were a beautiful child."

"You'd tell anyone that." She put the pictures back. There was nothing to be gained by any of those memories. That was in her past and needed to stay there.

The two old stone axes that Kat had loved as a child were in the drawer too. She picked one up and studied it. She traced a finger around the full-groove axe. Just touching the cold, smooth stone brought comfort, along with a flood of memories. These axes once belonged to her ancestors. Grams had told of her mother receiving them from her grandfather. Kat had studied them for hours as a child and fantasized about where the axes had been. She knew those axes and the questions they posed about her past were largely responsible for her doctorate in archeology. The need to find out who she really was had started with those two stone tools. Somewhere in her quest for credentials that need had gotten lost. She didn't know exactly where but it had been buried. Hefting the two axes in her hands, the need resurfaced.

Who was she anyway? That old familiar, and overwhelming, sense of not belonging washed over her.

Carefully, she replaced the ancient tools and picked up a weathered scrapbook. She'd never seen this as a child. Grams must have kept it hidden. Kat opened the book and thumbed through the first few pages. There were several pictures of her mother and aunt that she had already seen. At one time Grams had kept those in an old cigar box. They'd both died when Kat was very young and she had no recollection of either. Grams had been her life.

The last two pages held what they were looking for. There were three newspaper clippings, yellowed with age. The first one was a clipping that bore an account of the auto accident that had killed Kat's mother. Her whole life condensed into one tiny paragraph.

LOCAL WOMAN KILLED IN HEAD-ON COLLISION

Twenty-two year old Anna Abnaki was pronounced dead at the scene of a horrific head-on collision. The driver of the other vehicle, thirty-six year old Larry Roge', is listed in critical condition at Bay St. Louis Medical Center. The only other passenger was Miss Abnaki's three-year old daughter, Kateri. The child emerged from the wreckage unscathed. Captain Sam Vickers of the state police said, "It's a miracle that kid lived through all that. She must be a special child." Vickers indicated the cause of the accident is still under investigation.

Kat had never seen the clipping and it intrigued her. Grams hadn't told her that she had been in the wreck that killed her mother. She read the account again and combed her memory for any vague recollection of the accident or her mother. Her mind drew a total blank, like a chalkboard freshly cleaned of all evidence of the lecture. She remembered Grams telling her that she lost her mother when she was a baby, but the article said she was three.

The other paper clipping was slightly longer and dealt with the death of Kat's aunt, Kateri Abnaki, her namesake. It was dated a little more than two years before the previous article.

GRUESOME REMAINS FOUND BY LOCAL FISHERMAN

Local authorities began an investigation today of a possible murder. Jim Taggart, a local fisherman, found what authorities will only identify as "part of a body." The remains have been flown to the state crime lab for testing and officials indicated no decision has been made as to whether the cause of death was accidental or will be ruled a homicide. Speculation runs rampant regarding any connection between the remains and several recent disappearances along the coast. The state police are cautioning area residents to report any unusual behavior or suspicious activity. Motorists have been advised to be especially cautious about picking up hitchhikers. Repeated attempts to contact Jim Taggart for an interview have been unsuccessful. Although the authorities reveal that they have few leads, our sources indicate that a National Space Technology Laboratories employee has been questioned regarding the girl's disappearance.

Kat knew the ending before reading the next clipping. The remains would ultimately be identified as her aunt, Kateri Abnaki. Kat scanned the article for any hint of Jake Lloyd. Nothing.

Kat was more puzzled now than ever. Why did Grams ask her to locate this man? And who was he?

"Is that all there is? No mention of Jake Lloyd?" Nathan reached over and took the photo album and thumbed through the pages.

"I don't see anything else." Kat looked in the drawer again. Nothing else remained except the piece of cardboard Grams placed in the bottom to keep stuff from falling through the cracks of the drawers' shrinking boards.

"You don't have any idea who this Jake Lloyd is?" Nathan had put down the album and was studying one of the stone axes.

"No. I wish I did."

Nathan peered into the drawer and lifted the piece of cardboard, revealing a letter underneath. Both he and Kat reached for it at the same time. Nathan withdrew his hand and allowed Kat to retrieve the letter.

The yellowed envelope held only one sheet of paper. Kat opened it and read the blocked print handwriting.

October 25, 1976

Dear Miss Ella,

I feel compelled to write and let you know that I loved your daughter dearly and always will. My stupidity stood in the way of our ultimate happiness and I'll regret that all my life.

Hopefully you didn't believe any of the rumors or false accusations about me. I realize I was dreadfully wrong about some things but I am not evil. If you ever need to talk to me about anything I would like that.

As you know, I have moved, but not too far. I'm still trying to sort some things out in my mind.

Sincerely,

Jake Lloyd
Rt. 1
Red's Bayou, Louisiana 32121

Neither Kat nor Nathan said anything as they tried to digest the letter. Finally Nathan spoke. "So what does it all mean?"

Kat shook her head. "I don't know. Maybe Grams wants to

tell him something. "

"What should we do?"

"Grams has never asked me to do anything, Nathan." Kat's intense gaze pierced Nathan. "Do you realize that?"

"I know she's an unusually self-reliant woman for her age."

Kat placed her hand on Nathan's knee. "Will you help me find him, Nathan?" Tears were welling up in Kat's eyes again. "What if Grams knows she's dying and this is a last request?"

Nathan pulled Kat toward him. He'd drive to Red's Bayou, Louisiana, or Tobacco Spit, Wyoming for that matter, if that's what Kat wanted him to do.

CHAPTER 17

Kevin Croix posted himself against the side wall of the room, his muscular tattooed arms crossed, with his back to the wall. An imposing figure, six feet six inches tall with a build that had made most of the other linebackers in the NFL jealous. Today, ten years later, he still looked fit. A long black mane, sprinkled with nature's own gray highlights, draped over the massive shoulders and spilled almost halfway down his back.

He stroked his full salt and pepper beard, the end falling well below his shirt pocket, as he studied the crowd. The large white letters stenciled on the black tee shirt, those not obscured by hair, identified him as a bouncer. His piercing green eyes missed nothing any patron of Kelly's Dance Hall and Saloon tried to do. Often, if Kevin could catch their eye, a glance and a simple nod of his head would bring them back in check if they got too rowdy.

Occasionally it would take more than that. Sometimes people consumed far too many rounds of their favorite alcoholic beverage to keep their wits about them. Usually, those rare instances only required him to walk over and suggest quietly that they reign in their celebration. His sheer size and physical proximity, coupled with a look into his eyes and the three blue ink teardrops falling from his left eye into the mass of facial hair, typically calmed even the most volatile free spirit.

On very rare occasions it would take a little stronger persuasion, but Kevin handled it so no one was ever hurt, except a couple of times when someone had pulled a knife. He was the non-chemical alternative to a sedative, and Kelly's was the most trouble free strip joint in the French Quarter. All the regulars knew about Kevin and most of the tourists quickly spotted him and used the part of their brain that still functioned.

Tonight promised to be a typical trouble-free night, with one exception. He was adept at identifying problems before they became problems and defusing potentially explosive situations. Kevin had already catalogued everyone and the only anticipated problem area was the booth in the corner where two men consumed ten-dollar a bottle beer faster than politicians could lie. If they were true to form, the men would start verbally assaulting the dancers like those same politicians in a heated political debate and Kevin would be forced to step in. If things worked out well, they would decide to leave for a place that allowed more customer leeway to engage the dancers in verbal sparring matches and other extracurricular activities.

Smoke rising, from a dozen or more lit cigarettes, invaded his nostrils and impaired his vision. The dim lights didn't help much either, but Kevin knew that dim lights sold more high-priced beer. He would have preferred they sold less beer. Less beer meant less trouble and his concern was the people. Patrons and employees.

Kevin glanced around the room again, ever watchful for trouble. So much hopelessness and despair emanated from the crowd. The four men at the front table, all dressed casually expensive, probably had wives and children back in Peoria or Seattle that loved them dearly. No doubt they were in town for a convention and had no inkling of the damage they were doing to themselves and ultimately those relationships. Just a fun-filled night on the town with the boys.

Another man at the back of the room, the one much too drunk to make it home safely, probably had no one to go home to. Kevin guessed him to be a blue-collar type—bricklayer, electrician, carpenter—probably a skilled trade to be able to throw down the money he was blowing. The fresh white line on his left-hand finger told the story. Divorce or death, Kevin couldn't tell, but the wedding band that had been there a long time was now gone. The man had come to forget and maybe he had for a few minutes. But come morning the memories would return with a mind-numbing headache and a sour stomach. Kevin had called a cab earlier and soon he would escort the man to the back seat for a safe trip home. The man didn't know that yet, but would be agreeable enough by the time Darius arrived. Darius, a driver he knew and trusted, would not take advantage of his people.

Several tables full of harmless college boys having one last summer fling before semester started, and several more tables of convention attendees, gleefully consumed mass quantities of high priced drinks and eye candy as the night wore on. The two drink minimum cover charge rarely mattered at Kelly's. Kelly's had a reputation as a no-nonsense strip club and attracted a more docile clientele as a result. Kevin worried about that some.

Was he turning people away?

The alternative would be to allow some things to go on that he could not tolerate, like drunken patrons badgering and abusing the girls.

Amy, Kelly's newest dancer, was on stage now. She was a beautiful girl, if you didn't look into her eyes. They were haunted by a past so terrible that now she was dancing topless around a chrome pole placed strategically on center stage. Soon she would be totally naked and mercifully her act would end and she could exit the stage to go throw up in the ladies dressing room. Minutes later she would paste a fake smile across her ashen face and partially dress to come and mingle with the customers, brazenly allowing them to stuff low denomination paper bills into her g-string or the cup of her gauzy bra.

She couldn't be more than seventeen but had a fake ID that claimed otherwise. Her story would unfold eventually and maybe Kevin could help. For now he had to win her trust. He could report her to the authorities but he'd long since learned that he might be sentencing her to a worse fate. A father who sexually abused her, or a mother who made her turn tricks for a few bucks to buy this week's lotto tickets or ration of meth. Human misery was alive and well in the USA. At least while she was dancing at Kelly's, Kevin could protect her from some of that. He knew it was a fine line, a balancing act that he'd come to grips with, but one that had few real winners.

Amy would have to realize on her own that other alternatives existed or she'd end up like so many of the others. Stripping until their physical attributes ceased to bring monetary reward except in the sleaziest perverted dives on Bourbon Street. Or until their purple veins absorbed too much chemical to allow their weakened hearts to continue to beat. All in an attempt to forget. The story still saddened Kevin, still drove him, even after several years.

Kevin's watchful eyes absorbed every facial tic, every cigarette lit, every roaming hand splayed across a dancer's butt or breast. His job was not to judge, but to keep the peace. All the people working here considered Kevin a friend. A true friend who would do anything to help them. And this was where he could help. The front lines. A place not isolated from the people he loved. He was down in the ditches but he loved every minute of it. Kevin never had to fret over whether he was just paddling furiously as life flowed by like a swift mountain stream. He was one of those fortunate few people who knew he was exactly where he was supposed to be. Kevin Croix would live until he died. Not many could say that.

The corner situation was heating up. Karyn, a large bosomed brunette who finished her act before Amy, had been summoned to the troublesome table with a waving twenty-dollar bill. One of the men stood and allowed Karyn to slide into the circular booth between them. The two men converged on Karyn like vultures on a dead rhino and began an intense game of flesh exploration. Some of those areas, though fully visible from stage, were off-limits to patrons and Karyn caught Kevin's eye.

That was the signal. Kevin glided through the crowd, surprisingly agile for someone his size, and towered over their table.

"That's enough, guys." Kevin had spoken in a normal tone but both men, intent on disrobing Karyn, instantly looked around.

"We're just having fun." The largest one, several inches shorter and several pounds lighter than Kevin, appeared to be designated spokes-idiot.

Kevin extended his hand to help him out of the booth. "Fun's over for tonight. You boys need to get on home."

The man eyed Kevin, taking in his appearance, before moving. Reluctantly he began to slide around the booth. Kevin knew the man would try something. He could always tell. As soon as the man stood, he produced an opened knife and lunged. Kevin, waiting for it, merely sidestepped the knife and slapped it away from his body. As the man's momentum carried him forward, Kevin extended a left leg and propelled him a little faster with a right hand on the back of his head.

The formula for floor familiarity worked and the man landed sprawled on his face several feet away. He awkwardly tried to break his fall with a left hand and succeeded in breaking his wrist. The hand was skewed at an odd angle. A knot, that Kevin knew to be the end of a bone almost breaking the skin's surface, appeared close to the man's watch. The now-forgotten knife had fallen from his grasp as the man adopted a fetal position and cradled his injured arm.

Kevin, always watchful, kept his eye on the other man. The other one, who seconds earlier had appeared belligerent, now appeared to be quite docile. "I don't want any trouble, man."

"Neither do I, so just ease out of that booth."

Happy to oblige, he slid around the booth, keeping his hands glued to the table in the process. The other man moaning in the background punctuated his resolve to be peaceful.

Kevin gestured to the man on the floor. "Take your buddy to the hospital and we won't file charges."

The man acknowledged Kevin's generosity. "Thanks, man. We won't be causing you no more trouble."

Kevin reached out and placed two business cards in the man's shirt pocket. "Give one of those to him when he sobers up."

He nodded his head in the direction of the door. "Now help

him up and get going."

The man complied, avoiding the knife on the floor as if it were a six-foot rattlesnake. In minutes another dancer appeared and the crowd glued its collective eye to the stage. They would all go home with a story to tell. A little excitement in their quest for distraction from life. Kevin picked up the knife and resumed his post against the wall. The remainder of the night would be uneventful.

CHAPTER 18

A pothole big enough to swallow an average size pony caused Nathan's head to slam into the roof of his new car. He rubbed the offended area briskly for only a second before he needed his hand back on the wheel. The road was rutted from abuse, probably weekenders from New Orleans playing in their four-wheel drives. Apparently it was also fairly low on the list for receiving maintenance. Of course, what road wasn't in Louisiana?

Nathan glanced at the odometer and wished he had thought to look at it when he left the main road. He felt certain he had already come at least five miles on this goat path. Probably an old logging road, he knew he'd be lucky to get his car out without serious damage. Stupidly, he'd driven the new Lexus. Several times it had dragged bottom. He could visualize all sorts of parts hanging loose from the undercarriage.

The redneck at the station must get a kick out of giving outsiders bogus directions. As soon as he got to a place he could turn around he would go back and get some accurate directions. He could pull the aerials and find the place himself, now that he knew generally where the house was located. This region was too sparsely populated for there to be very many houses around here. And the next time he would borrow a Jeep from the Stennis motor pool, even though the last fiasco with a motor pool vehicle hadn't left a good taste in his mouth.

Nathan rounded a bend and abruptly entered an area, not over an acre, where the underbrush had been cut away. A small, unpainted cabin, sitting six feet off the ground on poles, occupied the far corner. A raised walkway linked a similar stilt-raised structure to the cabin. A new Honda ATV and an old junker Ford truck were parked in front under the shade of a huge live oak. Nathan saw what appeared to be some type of swamp buggy protruding from behind the cabin.

Maybe he'd found the place after all. As he pulled closer he could see that both structures were backed up to a bayou. An assortment of boats, including an airboat, dotted the bank behind the cabin. Nathan killed the motor and stepped out of the car to assess the damage. He stooped to look under it. As expected, his muffler was hanging loose.

Nathan stood and shook his head. This was not his brightest moment. Destroying the first new vehicle he had ever owned to find someone whose name was scribbled on a piece of paper in the ICU ward.

What kind of wild goose chase was he on anyway? But Kat had asked him to help, and she could persuade him to do virtually anything.

It would be a miracle if the guy could speak English. This deep in the swamp, French was much more likely, and Nathan couldn't begin to understand French.

Nathan approached the front door, but before he could knock, it opened. Someone who he suspected to be Jake Lloyd stepped out and glared. Even with his hands full of equipment, he was an imposing figure. A little taller than Nathan's own six feet one inches and much broader in the shoulders. A long gray mane, gathered together in a pony tail, topped his head. A trimmed salt and pepper beard and piercing green eyes completed the picture.

The man's appearance left Nathan momentarily taken aback. The man had to be at least sixty, yet appeared to be in perfect physical condition. He wore shorts and a tank top, and looked toned for any age. Nathan realized the man was more physically fit than he was at many years his junior. He decided to start working out. Lab work had made him entirely too soft.

"I don't want any encyclopedias, insurance or cellular telephones." The man mentally ticked off his list, "And I'm not interested in converting to whatever religion you're selling today. Now, get off my property!"

Nathan, ruffled even more, hastily extended his hand. "I'm Dr. Nathan Young."

Jake Lloyd glanced at the proffered hand and then back to Nathan's face as if to emphasize Nathan's stupidity. His hands were full of paraphernalia, so he smiled patronizingly. "I'm sufficiently impressed. Now get out of my way. You know where your vehicle is."

He brushed past Nathan and threw his gear in the old Ford pickup. Nathan hurriedly followed him.

"Please let me explain." This man intimidated him, mentally and physically, and it irritated him. He felt like a school kid seeing the principal, or a first year doctoral student around his major professor. "I need your help."

"So does half the free world." He started to open the door of the old Ford when Nathan grasped his arm.

Before he could realize what happened, Nathan found himself flat on his back. The crazy old coot had one bare foot centered in his crotch, placing slight pressure on a very sensitive area. His hands still held all the equipment. Nathan tried to pull back and extricate himself from the uncomfortable position, but the lunatic added a little more pressure. He noticed that the man's heel had his baggy jeans pinned to the ground and to apply more pressure he just shifted more weight to the ball of his foot. He had somehow swept Nathan's legs out from under him with a roundhouse kick. Nathan was helpless and it enraged him. He was also astute enough to recognize that this man could just as easily have killed him. The old man just stood there smiling down at him.

"I don't like anyone to touch me."

"I'm sorry for that." Nathan felt like a fool. He could feel his face getting red with embarrassment and anger, but he had heard in these types of situations that you should just go along with the attacker.

Still holding Nathan pinned, the old guy stared at him. "What kind of doctor are you?"

"I have a Ph.D. in marine biology." Normally Nathan felt some pride when he made that announcement and usually people were impressed. Given the ludicrous position he was now in, and judging from the man's reaction, neither happened here. The old hippie seemed to be mulling the information over.

"Where did you go to school?"

Nathan wondered where this was leading, but he was also certain this man was insane. You could not assign rationality to someone lacking the ability to reason.

"UCLA." Nathan paused. "That's the University of California at Los Angeles."

The old man gave him a look that made him wish he hadn't elaborated. Somehow this crazy, probably flea-infested, refugee-from-the-sixties made him feel stupid.

"Oh, I see. Hanson sent you here."

"Professor Hanson?"

"Yes. How is the old fool?"

The man released his grip and stepped back. Nathan quickly stood and stepped back out of leg's reach, his curiosity over how this man knew Professor Hanson overcoming his fear. Nathan was aghast that anyone could talk about his mentor that way, particularly the aging Haight-Ashbury transplant in front of him.

"He's fine. Have you functioned as his guide before?"

The old hippie smiled to himself. "You might say that."

He abruptly turned and got in his truck, Nathan wisely making no attempt to stop him this time. Jake started the motor and looked at Nathan, a slight smile turning up the corners of his mouth.

"I was his dissertation chair."

Nathan, his mouth open, watched Jake drive off in the rusted 1956 Ford pickup. He saw Jake shake his head as he passed the new Lexus. Suddenly, it occurred to Nathan that he hadn't even mentioned the reason for his visit. Jake Lloyd had taken him so off guard that he'd forgotten to even mention Grams.

* * *

Nathan knew the number by heart, even though he rarely called it any more. He dialed the number with his thumb and punched the send key while he piloted his car down Interstate 10. Baffled by his recent exchange with Jake Lloyd, he hoped Professor Hanson could fill in some of the gaps. What did some burned out academic living in a Louisiana swamp, one who just happened to be his mentor's mentor, have to do with a little Indian woman living in coastal Mississippi who just happened to be his mother-in-law? Talk about a puzzle.

"Biology department. This is Maria. May I help you?" The department head's secretary, Maria, was a fantastic source of campus gossip. Nathan was glad she'd answered instead of one of the student workers.

"How have you been doing, Maria? This is Nathan."

"Couldn't be better. Are you excited about your new job?"

"Lately it seems I haven't had much time to think about it. It's crazy over here." Nathan realized his new appointment was fast approaching and he'd done little to prepare for it. The textbooks for his classes were still boxed up in his new living room, untouched before they went into the boxes and obviously still untouched. He had three new course preps to do and he needed to get started. But what was more important, new job or making every attempt to salvage a marriage?

"It's crazy everywhere, Nathan. You need to talk to Dr. Hanson?"

"Yeah. If he's available."

"Just a second. I'll buzz him."

A minute later and Nathan heard the familiar voice of his dissertation chair, Dr. Ralph Hanson. He was Hanson to everyone except the students, who called him Dr. Hanson or Professor Hanson. "Nathan, how are you? Did you get that article revision done?"

Just like Hanson. Always trying to get the next article published. Nathan was supposed to have been working on a revise and resubmit to a major journal, a paper co-authored with

Hanson out of Nathan's dissertation, but other things had occupied his time the last few months. "I'm still working on it, Sir. I'll try to get it finished in the next few weeks."

I'll have to get it started before I get it finished, ran through his mind, but not through his mouth. Hanson would berate him unmercifully if he knew Nathan had yet to start on the revision.

"So what is it you need? Fatherly advice on your new job? Publish or perish, Nathan. Finish that article. It doesn't matter whether you do a good job in the classroom or not. Teaching isn't rewarded, research is." Hanson paused a second. "Did I miss anything?"

"No sir. You covered everything." Nathan knew the speech by heart. Hanson offered it partially in jest, but Nathan knew there was a large kernel of truth in his entreaty.

"So tell me what's up, Nathan." The pleasantries now over with, Hanson was ready to listen.

"I ran across someone who knows you today and I was wondering if you could tell me about him."

"Who was it?"

"His name is Jake Lloyd. He says he was your dissertation chair."

Hanson exhaled audibly. "Where did you find him? He dropped off the face of the earth about twenty years ago."

"Was he really your chair?"

"Definitely. Probably the most brilliant man I've ever met. Before or since. But tell me where you found him."

"He lives in a shack in the swamp not too far from New Orleans. A place called Red's Bayou."

"How's he doing?"

"I assume he's okay. I didn't really have much of a conversation with him." Nathan briefed his professor on their meeting, leaving out nothing. He ended with, "What happened to him, Professor Hanson?

"I guess he lost touch with reality, Nathan. Back in the mid 70's, the local authorities questioned him about a girl's murder, and he took it very hard. He started espousing some crazy theories and the academic community ridiculed him for it."

Nathan's curiosity piqued, asked, "What was he doing down here?"

"Let me start at the beginning . The Navy relocated their Naval Oceanographic Program to Stennis Space Center. Of course back then it was called NSTL, the National Space Technology Laboratories. Dr. Lloyd was the new director for that program. He took the job shortly before my dissertation defense."

"He'd only been there a couple of years when he was questioned about the murder. Apparently he'd gotten involved with some local girl. I think he'd actually gotten her pregnant, and they suspected he killed her when he found out.

"After that, he went a little crazy. He proposed some weird theory about how the girl was killed." Hanson paused and Nathan heard him draw a deep breath. "He tried to link her death in some way to his discipline. I think he really lost it."

Hanson sighed. "I hated the whole thing, Nathan. This man was like a father to me. He wanted me to support him, and I couldn't patronize him that way. He'd gotten to the point where he couldn't separate myth from reality."

"The authorities never found enough evidence to try him for her murder but I think the whole community felt like he did it."

"What do you think, Professor Hanson? Did he do it?"

"The Jake Lloyd I knew was incapable of that. But the Jake Lloyd that surfaced during that entire period? Who knows? I really think he actually had a mental breakdown of some kind."

"Thanks for the information, Professor Hanson."

"Nathan? If you see him again, tell him I said hello." Nathan sensed the sadness in Hanson's voice. It was a tragic story. Mental illness striking down someone that brilliant in their prime. Maybe the old saying was true. There was a fine line between genius and insanity.

CHAPTER 19

The plush office occupied one corner of the top floor of the Amerind Building and served as the central hub for the vast holdings of Amerind Enterprises Incorporated. The office was over two thousand square feet of high dollar real estate furbished with a huge walnut desk and all the trappings of success that inheritance generates. Amerind Enterprises Inc. had been started with a generous endowment from the old man that had since been multiplied many times by its founder and chief executive officer, Neil Crawley.

Neil had grown up in a luxurious home and had always enjoyed the finer things in life. Neil's prosperous father, himself the benefactor of great grandfather's several million-acre land grab, had amply provided those luxuries. In the last ten years, Neil's tastes had moved from art to antiquities. He no longer collected the work of the great masters and had even shrewdly liquidated his own collection at the peak of the art market adding nearly a billion dollars to his own coffers in the process.

Now he collected antiquities of all types. Artifacts from almost any early civilization now remained the focus of his efforts. His office, and the top five floors of the Amerind building, reflected those tastes and housed maybe the finest private collection of artifacts in the United States, possibly the world. Buyers scoured the globe for new acquisitions with strict guidelines to purchase only the best specimens of any known type, regardless of country of origin and legal barriers. Third world officials could easily be convinced to look the other way when a particular national treasure piqued Neil's interest.

Money was no issue. He had amassed far more, via inheritance and shrewd business decisions, than he could ever spend. Neil Crawley stared at the Chicago skyline and contemplated his most recent investment. Money was not a problem, but he did expect to acquire something when he opened his checkbook. Several million dollars was a lot of money to pay for a promise, and a promise was about all he had from Humsinger.

He'd made a substantial donation to allow Humsinger to escalate operations and find those other stones, and very soon he wanted results. Something other than the few trinkets enclosed in the box on his desk. Something akin to the stone carving currently residing in the wall safe.

Neil crossed to the framed case containing thirty St. Charles blades, fifteen hundred-year-old stone knives from Illinois worth over a thousand dollars each, and swung the hinged frame away from the wall revealing a small safe. He spun the combination with the practiced ease of someone checking his daily mail and opened the door. A two-inch tall stack of hundred-dollar bills and a small felt-lined case containing miscellaneous artifacts greeted him. Gingerly, as a father handling a newborn child, Neil removed the case and carried it to his desk.

Neil opened the case and removed one particular stone artifact and held it up to the light. The light penetrated the brilliant red stone and cast a shadow over Neil's face. He'd had it certified by a gemologist. It was definitely a high-quality ruby and an exquisite carving by primitive standards. Neil felt the collector's rush all over again. If Humsinger could produce more artifacts like this one it would be well worth every penny of his investment.

But he was growing impatient. He'd sent the diggers down there and now Humsinger needed to produce something. And produce it soon.

* * *

Hawk studied the road. Those tracks looked fresh, definitely since the last rain. He checked the topographic map again, piled back into the county's new Chevrolet four-wheel drive, and headed down the road toward the burial mounds. According to that Stennis employee, Nathan Young, he was about three miles from the site.

It was futile to hope any evidence might remain at this site. Nathan Young and his boss had tramped around down here and, judging from the tracks on the road, possibly several other people. He would be lucky if he could find some shred of evidence that hadn't been destroyed or contaminated.

No one knew for certain that Harlin Rogers had even made it to this site. He could have been fed up at work and left town. Maybe he just needed a break from those two squabbling friends of his. Hawk could handle belligerent drunks, dope heads, and even thieves, but if he had to be around Nathan and Kat very long he'd run away too. Just get in the car and drive. Go somewhere. Anywhere.

Who hadn't wanted to do that at one time or another anyway? Harlin's vehicle still had not surfaced so flight was a definite possibility. Even though Ed and Hawk both suspected murder, they still had yet to come up with a body.

To date, only James Bailey's and Lou Blanchert's deaths had been confirmed. Harlin Rogers and Megan Kelley were still listed as missing. No bodies. No evidence. Nothing.

It was also possible that Rogers was somehow involved in the other disappearances. Rogers was an unknown and, judging from some of the stuff in his apartment, involved in something shady. Who hid something in a cat food bag that they had lawful ownership to?

He had a background check running on Rogers at the moment, but was doubtful anything would turn up. If Rogers was shady, he certainly was intelligent enough to be using a false identity. He made a mental note to lift some prints from Rogers' apartment and send them to the FBI crime lab.

Maybe Billy Blanchert was involved? Had Lou's death been faked? Hawk still didn't have a positive identification on the hand they'd found. He had assumed it was Lou, but it was possible the remains belonged to someone else. But what would be the motive?

Sure they were thugs, and Billy was definitely capable of murder, but not for pure fun. Money, anger, women, a simple argument; those were all possible motives for either Blanchert brother to be involved, but Hawk could find no common thread connecting the disappearances and the one murder to the Blancherts.

Earlier today, Ed had echoed his thoughts. Both men were at a loss to explain anything and the disappearances kept piling up. Two murders and four people missing in the span of a week. And they were sure to continue. Why stop when the authorities have no leads?

Hawk successfully navigated a sizable mud hole, all the while thanking the county for buying the four-wheel drive. He had to be close because Nathan had mentioned getting stuck in that same spot and that it was only a short distance from the burial mound. He rounded one last corner and could see a vehicle parked up ahead. Hawk unsnapped the thong holding his pistol in the holster and then reached for the radio. This could be the break in the case they were looking for. He slowed the pickup to a crawl and held the microphone to his mouth.

"Jasper?"

"I'm here, Hawk." The retired cop working as a part-time dispatcher answered.

"Get someone on the horn and tell them I'm checking out that burial mound Nathan Young told me about and there's another truck here ahead of me." Hawk paused for a minute as he slowed the truck almost to a stop. He was only a hundred feet or so from the site. "I don't see anybody, but I'm going to look around. If I don't check back in about ten minutes give me a call."

"Roger, Hawk. I'll do it."

"Thanks, Jasper." Hawk replaced the microphone and patted his gun reassuringly. An uneasy feeling washed over him. Something wasn't right about this situation.

He killed the truck's motor and opened the door as quietly as he could, leaving it open. For a moment he stood silently and scanned the surrounding area for movement. Nothing moved. For that matter, nothing made a noise either. No sound of shovels digging, no birds singing, no frogs croaking, no pine beetles munching. Total silence.

Hawk turned his attention back to the truck. As expected, mud obscured the license plates. Any vehicle making it through the previous mud hole would look the same. The truck blocked his view of the burial mound itself.

Satisfied no one was lurking in the woods, Hawk drew his pistol and quietly walked toward the truck. He searched for any sign of movement in his peripheral vision. He'd done enough deer hunting to know he could catch movement quicker that way. Not a single leaf stirred.

He could feel a bead of sweat grow large enough to no longer resist gravity and, like a snow skier, begin its downhill slalom in the middle of his back. It caused an involuntary shudder to course through him.

Hawk reached the truck and peered inside. Miscellaneous food wrappers and empty soda bottles greeted him. The keys were in the ignition, but he saw nothing else. Satisfied, he glanced toward the burial mound. He could tell there had been recent activity. Two screens on rocker legs were set up near the mound and the handles of a wheelbarrow protruded from the large hole in the mound. Several shovels were strewn haphazardly around.

Hawk stepped around the truck and walked quickly to the hole. It was the only place he couldn't see from his current vantage point. No one was there. He holstered his gun.

Where were they? Had they walked off and gotten lost, or would this turn out to be another disappearance?

He climbed to the top of the mound to get a better view and did a slow three hundred and sixty degree turn searching for any sign of the diggers. Maybe they'd heard his truck coming and ran off into the woods to keep from getting caught. In fact, the more he thought about it, that was likely what had happened. He should have parked and walked in, but it had never occurred to him he'd find anybody here.

Hawk walked to the edge of the bayou. Nathan had mentioned seeing a fishing pole somewhere. If he could find that he might be able to lift some prints and run them through the computer. The shovels and the wheelbarrow probably belonged to these new diggers and they were wood handled anyway. Weathered wood didn't hold good prints, but a fiberglass fishing rod would.

He didn't see the pole anywhere and turned to leave when he caught a glint of something shiny a few feet away in the mud. Hawk turned and walked over to retrieve it and was rewarded by the sight of a Gerber hunting knife. Carefully he picked up the knife with his handkerchief. He noted some dark spots on the handle and part of the blade that could be blood. Hawk raised the knife a little higher and turned to catch the sun's light a little better as it filtered through the dense canopy of limbs and leaves.

An ominous wind blew against his back. Hawk heard something in the water behind him and turned in time to see the jaws parting. He could see the ghostly pale skin. He could see the hungry blue eyes with his reflection in them. He could see shreds of decayed flesh hanging from several teeth.

The hot breath and the smell of carrion engulfed him microseconds before the jaws snapped shut. He heard the popping sound of his own bones crushing. He felt as if he were a detached observer witnessing his own death. Bile rose in his throat and spilled out, mixing with the blood already pouring out of his mouth. Oddly, the pain was not as excruciating as he would have thought.

As the fierce predator pulled Hawk under the water, a slight smile crossed his face. He had often wondered how he would die. This scenario had never entered his mind.

CHAPTER 20

Kat checked the time. It was after five o'clock in the afternoon and she'd meant to call Humsinger to personally explain what had happened to Grams. Her intentions didn't translate into action in time though, and now she would have to catch him at home. She debated a phone call, but decided a personal visit would be better.

That way she could gauge his reaction.

With her new promotion not yet through the paper work, she wanted to make sure that Dr. Humsinger understood her current circumstances and that she still much wanted the job.

She had time. Grams rested peacefully at the moment, and she couldn't go back in to the ICU ward for another three hours. She had enough time to run home, grab a quick shower, and drive over to Humsinger's house. The charge nurse had her cell phone number in case they needed to contact her.

One hour later, freshly showered and wearing clean clothes, she pulled into Humsinger's driveway. She'd only been here twice before to attend the annual Christmas party Humsinger hosted for the Remote Sensing Group. Both times she'd felt like a second-class citizen. Today, when she stepped out of her vehicle, she felt the same. She wondered if she would ever lose that feeling of inferiority. In the past, Humsinger certainly did little to relieve it. Maybe things would be different since he had tapped her for a full-time position.

Kat loved his house and dreamed of someday having one like it. The house was nothing really elaborate, just a one-story ranch style home built in the sixties. But it was well kept and roomy, and located in an established neighborhood with huge live oak trees shading the two-acre yard. She admired the home again as she approached the front door and lightly knocked. The door opened almost immediately. Humsinger answered so fast it startled her and she inhaled sharply.

"Kat? Is something wrong?"

"No sir." Kat replied before she thought. "Well, actually there is. May I come in for a second?"

Humsinger seemed reluctant to move out of the doorway but did so. "I just have a few minutes, Kat. I don't mean to be rude, but I'm expecting someone shortly."

Kat, feeling worse than she ever had at Humsinger's house, blushed as she followed him into the main living area. "I'm sorry, sir. I should have called."

"That's quite all right." Humsinger tried to smooth it over. "What seems to be the problem?"

"My Grandmother has had a stroke, and I've missed some work. I just wanted to make sure you understood that I wasn't merely shirking." Kat's throat constricted and she could feel tears welling up in her eyes. "My Grandmother raised me and she's more like my mother and father all rolled into one."

"I understand, Kat. Take all the time you need. I'm sure you've built up enough leave time so that it won't affect your pay."

Kat swallowed hard. Normally she wasn't this emotional. "I just felt like I should tell you in person. I'm still very excited about the job you talked with me about."

"And we're happy to have you on board, Kat." Humsinger held out his arm and guided her to the door. "I'm sorry I don't have more time to chat but I've got some preparation to do before my guest arrives."

Kat was doubly embarrassed now. Not only had she missed work, but now she'd been virtually thrown out of Humsinger's house. "I'm sorry to bother you, sir. I'll call next time."

"It was no bother, Kat. Don't worry about a thing. We'll take care of everything at work." Humsinger closed the door as he spoke. He stopped with the door slightly cracked. "And keep us posted on how your Grandmother is doing, Kat."

The door shut before she could reply. Kat turned and almost ran to her car. She could no longer hold back the tears that welled up in her eyes. Tears of embarrassment, tears of worry, tears of long pent-up emotions all cascaded down her cheek.

Hurriedly she started the car and pulled out into the street. She didn't want Humsinger to see her crying. She wiped as many tears away as possible with a shirt sleeve and drove on. Kat couldn't understand why she was she so emotional lately. She'd never been one to cry.

* * *

Humsinger pulled the blinds and leaned back against the wall. Kat was gone, fortunately before his other visitor arrived. He didn't want anyone to be able to connect him with this man, in case something went wrong. The phone call earlier in the day had both worried him and excited him.

The caller, identifying himself as a friend of Specky's, thought he had something Humsinger would be interested in. A short description of the stone garnered his attention. The main problem was the caller's insistence on meeting at Humsinger's house. He would have preferred meeting the man somewhere else.

Humsinger glanced at the clock and paced from the living room to the entry hall, stopping every trip to look out the small window in the front door. His hand dropped frequently to the pistol in his waistband. He'd carried a gun for years when working as a field collector and knew how to handle one. The cold steel pressed against his abdomen gave him strange comfort. Humsinger, usually under control of his emotions, felt uneasy.

It had been ten years since he'd felt this way. He could clearly remember the instance, and his recall didn't provide him with any comfort. Humsinger and four others were on a collecting trip in the Moroccan desert. A private collector funded the trip and Humsinger had used a month of accumulated vacation time to go. He'd been approached because of his previous museum collection experience and had jumped at the chance to get back into the field. Even for a short time.

Two weeks into the trip, in the middle of the night, Humsinger had suddenly awakened. The only light emanated from the few remaining campfire embers. Otherwise it was pitch black, with clouds covering the usually brilliant view of the stars. He had lain silently and listened to the night sounds, or lack thereof. It was strangely quiet, even for the desert.

Everyone else appeared to be asleep. He could hear snoring from two bedrolls, but something else had awakened him. As quietly as he could, he stood and pulled on his clothes and drew his nine-millimeter pistol from under his pillow.

He heard a noise. Something other than snoring. Something large moving out there in the darkness, outside the perimeter.

What could it be?

He mentally ran over all the possibilities and came up with nothing dangerous.

Probably a wild camel.

But that didn't explain his uneasiness. He'd learned to trust his instincts over the years. They rarely failed him. For a minute he considered waking his colleagues, but hesitated. What if it was nothing?

Humsinger mentally relived those next few minutes. He had stepped away from the camp to see if he could hear better. The weight of the pistol felt good in his hand. He had gone no more than thirty yards away from the camp and stopped to listen when he heard the scream.

It was Nettles, back in the camp.

A large man with a bass drum voice that you would never expect to hear scream. The sound unnerved Humsinger as he ran the few paces back the way he'd just traversed.

The screaming abruptly ceased.

Several flashlights clicked on and illuminated the area. Nettles was gone and nobody had seen anything. For a few minutes they probed the darkness with the flashlights and found nothing, before turning their attention back to camp. Blood covered Nettles' bedroll. Indefinite tracks in the sand passed within inches of Humsinger's sleeping bag, and moved to the next in line. Nettles. If Humsinger had been in his sleeping bag, it would have been him instead of Nettles. He knew it without a doubt.

After sunrise they searched for several hours for any sign of the missing man. Finally, several hundred yards from camp, they discovered the gruesome remains. Nettles had been partially consumed by some large carnivore. His intestines were gone, and most of the flesh from his thighs and buttocks had been torn away. One of his arms was missing, and the other had been gnawed until little remained but the fractured bone. Humsinger could still see his eyes, wide open, frozen with terror.

Nobody could explain what had happened and the trip was cut short. The Moroccan authorities ruled the death as accidental and refused to release the remains citing a health hazard. The authorities expeditiously cremated Nettles' remains, closed the case, and invited Humsinger and the remaining three team members to leave the country. None of them ever knew what actually happened to Nettles.

Humsinger shuddered as a chill ran down his spine. The memory was as vivid as the night it had happened. And now that same feeling had returned. That same uneasiness he'd felt that dark night in Morocco.

He glanced out the front door again. Still nothing. He padded back to the living area and sat in his recliner. The waiting was the worst. They'd waited long hours until daylight that night in the desert and tonight, in his own living room, the minutes ticked by with that same rapidity.

Humsinger thought he heard a car pull up in front and got up to check. He peered out the front window again. The only vehicle he could see was his own. No visitors yet. He went back to the living room and sat down before he saw the man in the corner.

Humsinger reached for the pistol in his belt as the man

approached. "Are you Specky's friend?"

"Yeah. I was." The black man was large. Around six feet tall, but with a lithe musculature. "Specky ain't with us no more."

He nodded toward the gun in Humsinger's hand. "Ain't no call to be dragging that thing out. I just got something to show you. Something I know you want to see."

Humsinger's uneasiness lingered. "Are you alone?"

Quin nodded. "Just me."

"Put the stone on the coffee table and then step back."

Quin took a small paper-wrapped bundle from his pocket, quietly laid it where Humsinger directed, and then stepped back a few feet.

Humsinger picked up the package and carefully unwrapped the object. It was larger than he expected and it was exquisite. This stone would definitely keep Crawley off his back. This one artifact would easily be worth the entire amount Crawley had paid.

Distracted by the stone, Humsinger didn't notice the other man until he stood an arm's length away. The man towered over the seated Humsinger who made a desperate grab for the gun laying beside him on the couch. His hand clasped comfortingly around the cold steel, only to have a much larger hand completely envelop his hand, gun and all.

The man had incredible strength. Humsinger's keyboard and executive chair toughened body was no match for the golden-fanged giant smiling down at him as he effortlessly placed the muzzle of the gun against Brain Humsinger's temple.

Humsinger's rational side took over and he relinquished control of the pistol, certain the man would not kill him. He could do nothing anyway. Continuing the struggle might cause the man to anger and these two wanted something or he'd already be dead.

"I'm listening." Humsinger's voice cracked, but he knew the sincerity was there. He was definitely listening.

The man still had not said a word. With the gun pressed to

Humsinger's head, Doctor John took his free hand and wrapped a long ebony finger around a thick clump of Humsinger's gray hair. Humsinger winced with pain when the dark giant jerked the locks from his head. A small seep of blood appeared where seconds before hair had been firmly attached.

The man pulled the gun from Humsinger's temple and tossed it to the other man, standing motionless during the entire episode. Deftly he snatched the flying weapon from the air and trained it back on Humsinger. The larger man glided around the couch with the grace and agility of an acrobat. Still silent, he stopped a few feet in front of Humsinger and busied himself with the task of tying the tuft of hair to a small doll. Humsinger had seen enough primitive cultures in various parts of the world to recognize that the man fancied himself a witch doctor or shaman. Maybe that would be his out. He could play along with the man and pretend that he was terrified and believed in his power. Humsinger had seen ignorant fearful tribesmen do hideous things under the so-called power of the shaman. Without a doubt, a shaman could control a limited intellect through suggestion and manipulation of the very real fear those primitive peoples had for the tribal witch doctor.

Of course he'd noted similar abilities to control here in the states. David Koresh and Jim Jones were two prime examples. Many leaders of small rural cult churches exhibited similar controls over their fearful congregations.

The man finished his task and spoke. "I am Doctor John." He motioned to the other man. "Return his weapon."

The other man hesitated, reluctant to obey that particular order. "Loaded?"

"Yes. He cannot use it against us."

Quin obeyed, but glanced around for the closest cover should Humsinger open fire. The weapon landed on the couch cushion beside Humsinger and he glanced at it, certain that the weapon had been unloaded while his attention focused elsewhere. He knew he was no match physically for either man, much less both of them, without a gun.

Doctor John nodded toward the gun. "Pick it up and check the load."

Humsinger, at first a little hesitant, obeyed. The gun's weight felt comforting again. The bullets were still chambered. Incredibly the man had given him back a loaded weapon and appeared to be himself unarmed.

"What prevents me from shooting you in the leg and calling the cops?"

The man smiled. His confidence unnerved Humsinger. Was there another man behind him that had yet to reveal his presence?

"You may try. Point the gun at me."

Somewhat apprehensive, Humsinger complied. The request baffled him, but slowly he moved the muzzle until it was almost trained on Doctor John. Another few inches and it would be pointed directly at the man's massive chest. Doctor John's fingers moved, wrenching the arm of the doll bearing the tuft of Humsinger's hair backward.

Humsinger's arm slammed back in unison with the doll.

He tried to move the arm, but could not. Fear gripped him. How could this happen? Some kind of pre-hypnotic suggestion? This man controlled his actions!

Humsinger's right arm, now an entity of its own, moved again. The muzzle turned slowly towards his temple as Doctor John manipulated the small doll. With all his physical strength, Humsinger struggled to resist the force.

Concentrate. It must be mental.

Still nothing. The gun muzzle came to rest against his temple. Humsinger felt his own finger tighten on the trigger. His death would be ruled a suicide.

"Wait. I'm ready to talk." Humsinger screamed the request. "What do you want?"

His finger ceased to tighten on the trigger, but kept the same tension. It was eerie how he could feel every muscle make every move, but had no control at all over his entire right arm.

"Where are the other stones?" Doctor John's melodic voice cut across the room, each word floating on its own current. Humsinger wondered if he was about to pass out. Unfortunately he did not. For a fleeting moment he thought about trying to lie. He knew what Doctor John wanted, but had no desire to give it to him. Maybe a quick death would be preferable to submitting to this man's will. The fleeting thought passed. Humsinger enjoyed life. At least up until now.

"One is in the top drawer of my desk in the study."

Doctor John nodded to Quin who complied with the unspoken command and retreated toward the back of the house. Obviously both men were familiar enough with Humsinger's house that they didn't have to ask where the study was. He wondered how long they had been there.

"And the others?" Doctor John toyed with the doll. Humsinger's left leg raised into the air of its own accord.

"The only other one I know of I sold to a collector in Chicago." He knew better than to keep anything from this man.

"You will retrieve it." Doctor John stated matter-of-factly.

"Are you crazy? That would be impossible." Humsinger regretted the voiced thought the second it left his mouth.

Of course the man was crazy!

Crazy and powerful. He needed to play along and maybe he would live. Humsinger had no doubt he could find someone capable of breaking this man's spell.

Doctor John smiled again and reached into his pocket and retrieved a small knife that he threw at Humsinger. He dropped the gun and caught the knife realizing that for the moment he could control his own body again. But only for a second. His left hand now moved of its volition until it rested palm down on the coffee table, fingers splayed out. His right hand, wielding the knife, moved until the knife rested on the first joint of his little finger. The razor sharp blade penetrated the skin, a small drop of blood welling up from the wound. He could not stop himself as he continued to exert pressure and surgically separated the finger at that joint. Humsinger held his breath and tried to block the intense pain. But to no avail.

Humsinger's left arm became his own again and he jerked it away from the table and pressed the throbbing bleeding member to his chest. His right hand laid the knife down and picked up the bloody one-inch stub and held the severed finger in his palm. A macabre offering to the witch doctor.

"You do not want to ignore my requests."

Quin had returned to the room at some point and handed the stone from Humsinger's desk to Doctor John. He then gathered the one that they had brought and handed it to him.

"Bring me his finger."

Quin, swallowing hard and obviously not happy about the request, complied. Horrified, Humsinger watched Doctor John pop the severed finger into his mouth and swallow all hope of reattaching the finger. The witch doctor moved toward the seated Humsinger. His fangs glistened when he spoke. "You are mine now and you will do my bidding."

Humsinger shuddered involuntarily.

The witch doctor stopped his approach and inhaled deeply. His nostrils flared as he drank in several more huge breaths. A faint trace of perfume lingered in the air. He threw back his head and laughed maniacally and then trained his eyes on Humsinger again.

"You are more important to me than I first thought." The black eyes bored into Humsinger.

Humsinger held his throbbing hand to his chest and remained silent. He could not argue with insanity.

"After you retrieve the other stone, you will lead me to the goat without horns."

Humsinger noticed Quin shudder as he stood in the corner and awaited his next instruction. He refused to look at Humsinger, opting instead for an in-depth study of the wood grain in the hardwood floor.

Brian Humsinger's keen mind whirled as he sorted through the events of the past few minutes. His finger pulsed, but at least the blood flow had slowed to a steady trickle. If he lived through this ordeal, he would take great pleasure in seeing this man rot in jail.

CHAPTER 21

Grams' insistence that Kat go with Nathan was so unlike her. She'd asked about Jake Lloyd the last time that they had seen her, and Nathan's report of finding him seemed to lift her spirits. However, a minute later she'd gotten agitated after hearing the whole story and scribbled, "Take Kat with you" on the notepad. Before they could find out what was so important about Jake Lloyd, the nurse monitoring Grams' vital signs kicked them out. Her heart rate had accelerated and the nurse blamed them.

Nathan, to keep from turning the rest of his new Lexus into a collection of miscellaneous auto parts, had rented a truck. Since both he and Kat had missed the last couple of days' work, he didn't feel right about trying to check a vehicle out of the motor pool for personal business.

Another few bends in the road and they'd be at Jake's palatial estate. Was this how a person with a doctorate in marine biology ended up? Your retirement villa a shack in the woods? Maybe it was better than his parents would do. Waiting on a handout from some wealthy member of the congregation to provide for their retirement. He wondered what had happened to them.

They bounced around the last bend in the road and Jake's shack appeared. Nathan looked at Kat who had gotten carsick. She was leaning forward with her face an inch away from the air vent. Earlier, she'd turned it on full blast. It was cold enough to hang meat in the cab of the truck. "Here it is, Kat. Our future."

"I'm not amused." She cast a sidelong glance his direction, her face pallid, but a shade more colorful than a few minutes earlier. "Besides. What would be so bad about this?"

The old Ford pickup was parked in front and the same collection of boats served as back yard ornaments. The backwoods version of a plastic pink flamingo.

Maybe the Woodstock refugee was home. A phone call could have made that same determination but they'd spent three hours in a rented truck for the information because Jake had no phone. A person never really realizes how simple technology changes our lives.

Nathan let the truck roll to a stop and killed the motor. His memory of the last encounter with Jake, someone he now knew had been accused of murder, was a little unsettling. He smiled at Kat. "Are you sure you want to go through with this?"

"Yes. It's important to Grams."

Kat seemed determined and Nathan knew better than to try to dissuade her. "Okay. Let's see if he's around."

Nathan had no more than uttered the words when Jake appeared around the edge of the shack. He looked no less intimidating than the previous day. "Speak of the devil. There he is."

"Wow! Look at that build." Nathan felt a pang of jealousy. Jake was a lot older than Nathan, but with a body that looked ten years younger. Kat's reaction irked him. He shot a glare her direction and got out of the truck to meet the approaching Lloyd.

"Dr. Lloyd, I'm sorry about yesterday. I'd like to start fresh."

Jake glanced at Kat, who had also gotten out of the truck. For a moment Jake looked stunned, but he quickly regained his normal demeanor. "I see you brought a date. How charming."

"This is Dr. Kat Young."

Jake extended his hand in a display of friendliness not yet shown Nathan. "Are you a real doctor? Or just a play doctor like your husband?"

Kat smiled a little, and Nathan fumed, wondering what she found so entertaining. "A play doctor. Archeology is my field."

Jake appeared impressed. "Oh, archeology? That's a fascinating field of study."

Nathan could sense Kat swell with pride, in spite of her 'play doctor' comment. She loved her work and was very proud of her degree.

Jake continued without a trace of a smile. "Did you minor in short order cooking so you could have a job when you're through living off the government dole?" He paused for a moment to enjoy watching Kat suck air.

Jake forged ahead with the assault, before Kat regained her composure to justify a response. "Or do you intend to wait tables at one of the casinos?" He smiled patronizingly at her when he finished.

Nathan intervened before Kat could recover and verbally attack. He, of all people, knew she wouldn't take the insult lying down. This time he intended to get to the point of the visit.

"We're actually here because Kat's grandmother wanted us to find you."

"Who's your grandmother?"

Kat still fumed but managed to control her tongue, even as her eyes uttered silent retorts more appropriate to a locker room discussion. "Ella Abnaki. Everybody calls her Miss Ella."

Jake's face betrayed his astonishment. He appeared winded and leaned on the hood of the truck before he spoke. "I should have known when I saw you. You reminded me of a ghost I know."

The man was certifiable. He belonged in a nuthouse. Nathan tried to catch Kat's eyes. It was time to go before he turned them into ghosts. Kat watched Jake, making a concerted effort to avoid eye contact with Nathan.

"I haven't heard from her in twenty years. What does she want?"

"We really don't know. She's had a stroke and can't talk." The grief and sense of loss in Kat's voice poured out with the words. "She can write a little if the charge nurse isn't watching. She's written two notes asking us to find you."

Nathan intervened. "Now, you tell us why she wants you."

For the first time in Nathan's brief history with the man, Jake seemed less than in total control. Miss Ella's plight had created a tiny crack in the masonry of the man, or at least in the brick veneer. Nathan thought he saw Jake's eyes grow moist.

"I would never have expected Miss Ella to have a stroke." Jake turned away from them both and faced his shanty. "She was always a tough old bird."

Kat's eyes were getting moist now so Nathan spoke up. "She had some extenuating circumstances. On her morning walk last Tuesday she found half of a body."

Jake spun around and faced Nathan, oblivious to the single tear that had trailed down one cheek. "Do you have any more detail?"

"Well, the sheriff said that she'd found the lower half of a nude male and they took her back to her house and she started doing crazy stuff."

"I'm talking about the body. About her morning walk. What do the police suspect?"

Nathan felt foolish. "All I know is there are several disappearances and another set of remains they've found. The body Miss Ella found belonged to some kid they think was parking with his girlfriend. They haven't found her yet."

"Were there teeth marks on the remains?"

"I don't know. I'm not involved with the investigation." Nathan was getting more perplexed by the second.

What does this have to do with Grams?

Kat intervened. "Maybe that's what she was trying to tell us, Nathan. You remember when we thought she was hungry? She was biting."

"I guess that's possible." Nathan was skeptical. Kat was reaching, trying to grasp at anything.

"Dear God! It's started again." Jake slumped against the hood of the rented truck. The hardened exterior shell of the man crumbled before their eyes. The man appeared vulnerable. "I knew it was only a matter of time. But I hoped and prayed I was wrong."

"What are you talking about?" Nathan tried to catch Kat's eye before she asked the question but didn't succeed. They needed to leave before Lloyd went nuts again, and from the looks of things he wasn't far from it.

Jake raised his head to look at them. "You really don't want to know."

CHAPTER 22

Quin waited, careful to make no sound and no sudden movements. A mockingbird landed in a nearby hickory tree and broadcast its presence to the world, declaring the beginning of another glorious day. A squirrel chattered from a few feet away, appearing to disagree with the bird's optimistic forecast. Quin agreed with the squirrel. He saw nothing good about this day.

The morning sun had yet to burn through the gauzy fog so typical of a Louisiana morning. The heat and humidity wrapped its long fingers around Quin's lungs and squeezed, threatening to wring all the oxygen from his system. Just like every other day lately, he was trapped doing the bidding of Doctor John.

He rued the day that Specky Vore came into his life. It was all Specky's fault. That ignorant redneck. Everybody knew messing with somebody's grave would disturb the spirits.

Why did I even go along with him? Me and Specky were close, that's why.

You did a lot of things for a friend you wouldn't do for anyone else. But look where it got him. Look where it got Specky. Although Specky was probably better off. At least he didn't have to contend with Doctor John. Quin would much rather be dead than to be owned by a madman. He never thought he'd be somebody's slave, but here he was. His every move controlled by the devil incarnate.

A twig snapped and Quin's head pivoted around to scan the woods behind him. He remembered his assignment. Fresh mud, applied as much for insect repellent as for camouflage, plastered his entire body. A primitive loincloth barely covered the necessary area while he perched on a live oak branch like some oversized parrot. All this with a closet full of camouflage clothes and a comfortable climbing deer stand at home. Quin prayed no one would see him.

The bow in his hand was no better than his attire. As far as Quin was concerned, it was a stick with a string on it. A good Martin compound hung on a peg on his back porch. He'd killed fifty deer with that bow and could hit an apple at forty yards. But today he hunted Doctor John style.

A primitive bow, hastily constructed from mock orange wood with a sinew string, hung on the stub of dead limb beside him. Three arrows, with shafts made from dried cane and tipped with stone points recovered from the dig where Specky died, completed his scanty arsenal.

Even his fear of Doctor John could not stave off the thought of how foolish he must look. A black Tarzan without his faithful chimpanzee. If anyone saw him they'd be after him with an oversized butterfly net, because there'd be no doubt he'd gotten loose from the funny farm.

Quin's eyes continued to scan the woods for the source of the breaking twig. He saw nothing. He could hear a faint rustling, but couldn't pinpoint the direction. Quin remained motionless, ten feet off the ground, out of the field of vision of his prey. The rustling noise continued, sounding nearer, but the fog was still too thick to see through any great distance. But Quin could wait. Hunting was all about patience. The sound grew nearer.

Careful to make no noise, Quin removed his bow from its resting place and nocked one of the primitive arrows. He waited, making very little movement. Fifteen minutes later he reaped his reward. A young deer, probably a yearling, eased into his field of vision. The fog faded as the sun grew higher. The deer browsed around a huge white oak with its nose to ground, searching for a missed acorn from last fall's crop.

It was within easy range of Quin's modern equipment back at home but still way too far for what he was using today. He could wait, perched as he was directly above the well-trod game trail that led to a small field in front of him. If the deer continued on its current course it would be under him soon and close enough for a good shot.

The fog continued to dissipate as the deer made its way toward him. Quin willed the deer to hurry. If he did not get a shot soon, the deer would scent him. A deer's keen sense of smell could be fooled with the right scent cover, but Quin hadn't been able to use any of his modern hunting equipment. He knew if the temperature got much warmer, his perspiration would begin to overpower the crushed jimson weed he'd rubbed over his body that morning.

About twenty yards away, the deer stopped and tested the air. Quin could see that his target was a young doe. She flicked her tongue over her nose to freshen the scent. The deer was still too far away for Quin to feel confident about shooting with his primitive equipment, but he had no choice. The young deer stamped a foot and snorted inquisitively. She would bolt soon.

Quin drew the bow and sighted down the arrow shaft, aiming a few inches behind the deer's front foreleg. He held a little high to compensate for the anticipated drop during the arrow's flight. Releasing the arrow, he mouthed a silent prayer, unconsciously reaching for the place where the dragon's blood stick normally resided. The arrow struck home with a thud and the deer spun and retreated at full run down the path it had just followed. Quin would allow the animal to bleed out before he trailed it up.

Thirty minutes later he found the dead deer and began the laborious task of skinning it with a stone knife provided by Doctor John. Thankfully, he hadn't been forced to chip his own flint blade. If so, he would have been out of luck. That was a skill he did not possess.

* * *

Brian Humsinger felt the cold steel tip of the blade in his jacket pocket. The bandage on his left arm and the missing end of his little finger reminded him of the pain and the power of the knife. Only hours ago, before the flight to Chicago, he'd tried to summon the courage to slit his wrist.

He'd failed.

Doctor John, a man who held powers over him he would never have believed possible, had somehow intervened. The knife had strayed and cut a five-inch gash down his bicep. Humsinger had bandaged the wound himself and tried to figure some way out of his nightmare.

How did a man come to this?

In his case he knew the answer. Greed. Humsinger was not a stupid man but he had allowed greed to fog his intelligence. Greed alone had created the Humsinger that was at this moment intent on recovering an artifact that he himself had obtained illegally and originally sold. And recover it at any cost.

All for what? To buy a few things in life he could not afford. Luxurious travel. Trinkets for his collection. Most people would gladly have changed places with him. An easy job that he didn't have to leave for another ten years and then a generous pension that would allow him to live well above the average retiree. But that hadn't been enough. And now it had come to this. A felon, weapon in hand, ready to commit crimes that two years ago he would not have dreamed he was capable of doing. Or two days ago.

And the path he'd traveled was clearly marked. Those forks in the road weren't ambiguous. He'd justified them as such probably in much the same way that every criminal did before treading down the wrong path. He remembered those decisions clearly because he frequently relived them.

The first time he'd caught Specky robbing a grave and noted the value of the small collection of artifacts Specky had recovered. The initial decision not to call the authorities if Specky turned those things over to him. The decision several weeks later to pinpoint sites for Specky and split the take. The decision later to market those items via his old contacts to bring a premium instead of the fraction of their value Specky got selling to some local collector.

None of those were gray areas. The procession was clear.

From keeping a few artifacts for his collection and looking the other way, to actively searching for artifacts to sell on the black market, to actually fencing stolen federal property, to what? That next step terrified him. The first three had been too easy to slip into. The fourth—he felt the cold steel in his pocket—armed robbery at the least; murder at the worst.

And Humsinger feared the worst. Could Doctor John's powers reach Chicago? Would Neil Crawley simply hand over the artifact when he walked in the door?

Humsinger felt certain he knew the answer to the first question. He feared he knew the answer to the second question as well. The gash on his arm gave him a constant and painful reminder of things beyond his understanding.

Very soon he would know those answers. The sixty-story glass and steel nightmare of the Amerind Building loomed in front of him. An unadorned testament to the power of man.

How little we know and how mighty we think we are!

At another place and another time he would have found the realization humorous. But not so today. Today was reality check time. His personal day of revelation.

Humsinger stood in front of the building and watched the foot traffic of Chicago bustle about oblivious to the drama unfolding in their midst. An attractive woman carrying a masculine briefcase hurried by intent on some legal briefing, or corporate meeting, that wouldn't matter to anyone next year. A young man, fresh out of college no doubt, scurried in the opposite direction with the same grim determination etched on his face that Humsinger had carried over thirty years ago. Both would likely make the same mark on the world that he had. Nothing. A life lived for work that would not be remembered the week after he stepped off this planet's merry-go-round.

The footprint in time that represented his life had the same permanence of the ones left by sun worshipers on the beach in Panama City, Florida. The next wave of water or life would erase them all. However, in the morning, there would be new ones made by the next group. The cycle would continue. Life would go on. With or without Dr. Brian Humsinger. And the glass of water that represented his world would appear no different after his finger was pulled out.

He eyed the revolving doors of the Amerind Building and thought about his quest. No one was here to force him to comply. Maybe all he had to do was get geographically far enough away from Doctor John so that his powers would be impotent. Could that be possible?

Maybe he was far enough away already. He'd felt nothing unusual since stepping off the plane at O'Hare. Humsinger turned from the building's entrance and strode away. He felt at peace now that he'd made a decision. Maybe all it required was a forceful decision from a determined mind. Doctor John's powers probably relied on mental weakness and he'd been in such a state because of guilt. But not any more. Today was a new day, and Brian Humsinger could simply disappear and start over. No one would miss him anyway.

* * *

Pork Rind swore and spat. A long stream of viscous tobacco juice trailed unnoticed into his unruly beard. He wiped a gnarled hand against his mouth and smeared the offensive liquid around, adding to the brown discoloration clearly visible against his wiry white facial hair.

He shined his light up into the tree and dipped the tobacco stained hand inside a bag of his namesake chips. Emerging with a handful of the deep-fried pig skins, he popped some in his mouth and began to crunch noisily. Incongruously, a diet cola appeared to wash down the dry chips. The dogs encircling the tree continued to bark, their staccato yelps puncturing the dark night.

The coon was up there. He just couldn't see it. Looked like an old den tree. He'd have to climb the tree and punch the coon out. No doubt about it. Pork Rind didn't relish the thought either. At his age, a man should stay out of trees. But, if he didn't poke that coon out, the dogs would quit hunting. Dogs were just like people. They needed a little affirmation every now and then. Pork Rind glanced up the tree again, playing the flashlight beam around, before closing the lid on his bottle. Might as well get to it.

"Boss Hogg. Daisy. Good job." He patted each of the black and tan coonhounds on the head. The dogs, named after characters on his favorite television show, wagged their tails in appreciation. Pork Rind would never understand why the Dukes of Hazard had been cancelled.

Hiking up his bib overalls, he attacked the massive live oak with a vigor envied by much younger men. The first part of the climb wasn't too bad. The tree's massive limbs, each a full two-feet thick, draped out and touched the ground. Pork Rind picked one with a nice gradual slope and walked up it. In seconds he was twenty feet off the ground. The dogs continued to bark ecstatically.

The climb increased in difficulty from this point. Far too experienced for his taste, Pork Rind used the flashlight to pick his path up the giant oak. Limb by limb he searched for the coon. Finally, ten minutes and forty feet higher, he saw the red eyes reflect the flashlight's beam. He flicked the light off, hoping the coon would stay put, and continued his climb. Pork Rind wrinkled his nose. Something smelled rotten.

The coon, barely visible in the scant moonlight, peered out over something white in the fork above him. The pesky animal scampered even higher up the tree as Pork Rind approached. He reached up, grasped the limb where the coon had been hiding, and pulled himself up. The stench, especially strong now, assaulted his nostrils. He flicked on the light and stared slack jawed at the source of the stench, the coon forgotten.

Hastily, Pork Rind scrambled back down the tree, his breathing coarse and ragged. He patted the dogs on the head and peered nervously into the night. It was four or five miles back to where he'd parked the truck. Carefully, he memorized some landmarks. He'd have to find this tree again in a few hours.

* * *

Ed Hebert's diminutive frame convulsed again with the dry heaves. There was nothing left to come up. Breakfast had departed almost thirty minutes ago when they first found what was left of Megan Kelley. Normally strong-stomached, even he was no match for the partially decayed human remains displayed in front of him. Everyone at the scene had added new contaminant in the same manner.

What was going on? Could anyone be that sadistic? He knew from his training and his study of societal pariahs that it was possible. But how could it happen in Bay St. Louis? A sleepy little fishing village on the Gulf of Mexico. He wiped his sweating brow and salivating mouth with a not-too-sanitary shirtsleeve and resumed his study of the body.

Megan's body had been found wedged in the fork of a huge live oak by a coon hunter. The birds had pecked her eyes out and ripped holes in her exposed flesh. Found wearing only her panties, that meant most of her body. The incessant ants had also found the gruesome smorgasbord and covered the rapidly decomposing body. Hundred-degree weather, and the myriad of bugs, meant flesh didn't last long in the swamp. She would have been hard to identify if not for her braces with the new multi-colored rubber bands. That, and one remaining earring that her mother Angie had identified as Megan's. The medical examiner would make a positive ID, but that was unnecessary. Ed hoped that she hadn't suffered.

He tried his best to block out the fact that she was a young girl in her prime. A young girl the same age as his daughter. One that went to the same football games and flirted with the same guys. One that didn't deserve to die. One that hadn't made those choices that should make her forfeit her right to live. He'd shed no tears over Lou Blanchert's disappearance, but the salty fluid welling up in his eyes found its way down his cheek for Megan. And for her mother, Angie.

Ed tried to focus. There was little to learn, but he wanted to make sure that he didn't miss anything on this one. This killer would not get by with this murder. Ed Hebert would do everything within his power to make sure of that.

Several minutes of study revealed nothing new. The crime scene photographer had managed to document everything after several prolonged leaves of absence. No one questioned where he'd been. The blood drained from his face told the tale. A nearby tree would verify the reason for his departures. No one mentioned it as they performed their various tasks.

Ed studied the ground around the tree. He felt reasonably certain that Megan had been killed elsewhere and her body moved here. They were at least a mile away from the mill pond where the Bailey boy's body had been found. The area was densely wooded with almost every square inch of ground covered in saw briers and vines. An occasional palmetto filled in any vacant spot.

Nothing. No clues at all. Three bodies now, a string of disappearances, and not a single clue.

What was he missing?

Serial killers were supposed to follow patterns, so he should be able to find some connection between the crimes. Mentally he ticked through what they knew so far.

Lou Blanchert falls out of a boat in the middle of the night and they find a severed hand. Randy Bailey and Megan Kelley are swimming at the millpond when they're killed. Harlin Rogers had disappeared, from either his house or some archeological site in the county, or anywhere in between. His vehicle was also missing.

Ed tried to think it all through. It was possible that Lou's murder was completely unrelated to the other three individuals. For that matter, it was possible that Harlin's disappearance was also unrelated to Lou Blanchert or Megan Kelley's murder. What was the old saying? Bad things come in threes. He just couldn't connect anything. Maybe Hawk could shed some light on it later.

Bouncing ideas off someone else always seemed to generate new possibilities.

Ed nodded to the county coroner to indicate that he could now move the body. He was perhaps the only one there who had not thrown up. What kind of job did he have that made him desensitized to carnage like that? The body would go straight to the state crime lab for autopsy. Maybe something would turn up, although he had yet to receive the report for the hand or Randy Bailey. Now, with parts of three bodies, they might speed the process along.

Ed placed his hand over his mouth and nose as the county coroner eased the remains into a body bag. The stench increased tenfold with the disturbance, but he wanted to check the ground under the tree again. He spent a few more minutes looking, to no avail.

The medical examiner, finished with his field study, walked over and Ed raised an inquisitive eyebrow. "Cause of death?"

"Can't tell yet. But all her wounds look superficial. None that I can see would cause death." The M.E. was silent a moment before offering. "Right now, I'd say exposure."

"Exposure to what?"

"The sun." The M.E. pointed up to the fork in the tree where Megan's body had been found. "Thirty-six hours up there without water would do it. In this heat."

Ed couldn't believe it. "Are you suggesting she was capable of climbing down that tree and didn't?"

The M.E. shrugged. "Maybe she was afraid of heights."

Ed stood and looked around the surrounding thicket. Or maybe something else. What could terrify someone so bad that they climbed a tree and stayed there until they died?

"Ed?" The voice startled him out of his thoughts. It was Wanda, another Bay St. Louis officer. Her face was screwed into a tight frown and her eyes appeared watery.

"What's up?"

"They found another body out in the county."

"Same MO?"

"Looks that way."

"Who was it? Anybody we know?"

Wanda stopped and placed a tender hand on Ed's arm. "It was Hawk."

CHAPTER 23

The night felt peculiar, even for New Orleans. The strippers and female impersonators were out in their usual numbers. The mimes, jugglers, musicians, dancers, artists, tarot card readers, palm readers, and everyone else trying to grab the tourist dollar were positioned in their regular spots. The multi-colored hair, chrome stud wearing runaways congregated under the same awnings. Jazz music trickled out of a dozen doorways and floated on the wind before mixing with ten different languages and resonating off the cobbled streets. It was all the same and yet something was wrong.

Kevin couldn't put his finger on why, but it affected his overall mood. Something ominous, dark and oppressing weighed heavily on his normal cheerful demeanor. Tonight was his night off from Kelley's Dance Hall and Saloon. On a typical night off he would roam the streets and talk to people, in order to acquaint himself with anyone new to the Quarter.

Not the tourists. There were hundreds of new ones every day. Gawking, probing, buying. The all-important buying. Dropping those dollars that were the life blood of the Quarter. No, Kevin didn't try to get acquainted with the tourists.

They weren't his people.

The locals were his people. Not the wealthy writers and lawyers who kept cozy apartments, or the ones who split time-share condos with fifty-one other couples, but the ones who really lived in the Quarter. The runaways and societal outcasts that found few places to accept them.

Those were his people.

The French Quarter welcomed them and people traveled thousands of miles to gawk at them. And Kevin welcomed them in. Humanity in all its ugly splendor.

Many of them slept in the streets, piled up in doorways to stay warm when the night chill fell. In the summer they could sleep anywhere they wouldn't be rousted. Those were the ones Kevin made the rounds to meet and greet. To see how all of his old friends were doing, and to make new friends. He had to be their friend first and then, and only then, could he expect them to listen to anything he had to say. Otherwise it was just so much drivel coming from another insincere preacher, and they'd heard all that before. In many cases, that's why they were here.

They were searching just like he had been. Searching for the truth and there was something about that quest for truth that made you discount anything uttered by someone living a less-than-truthful existence. Kevin's own philosophy dictated an in-your-face approach to the gospel and lifestyle that would be openly criticized by most pastors. The same ones who ended up having an affair with some member of the congregation, or embezzling money from the church and skipping town.

Truth had a ring to it, and it only rang clear if the delivery man walked in the truth himself. And Kevin did all he could to honor that philosophy. He worked, lived and talked with these people on a daily basis. He was their friend and normally made it by to visit with several of his acquaintances on his one night off.

But not tonight. Tonight was different somehow, and Kevin knew he needed to stay in and prepare. Soon he would be required to help someone in a unique way. A way he'd never dreamed of or thought possible. If anyone had asked how he knew he would not be able to tell them. It was a subtle tugging in his spirit, a sixth sense, a premonition, an inkling. Call it what you want, it was all the same thing and he'd learned to obey it long ago. Tonight he would obey. It was time to stay in and read and pray. He would be prepared when the time came that he would be called upon. And he would know when that time came. Soon he would be used.

Kevin entered his sparsely furnished bedroom to make ready. First he would spend some time in prayer. He eased his considerable bulk into the oversized specially constructed coffin and stretched out comfortably, pulling the lid shut over him. Total darkness and quiet surrounded him. He began his preparations.

* * *

Nathan tried to catch Kat's eye, but she was riveted on Jake. Seconds before the man had seemed invincible, a graying tribute to benefits of hard work. Now he appeared almost fragile, slumped over the hood of Nathan's rented truck.

"Please tell us what's going on?" Kat pleaded. Nathan wondered if her natural curiosity had taken over, or did she really need to know for Gram's sake?

Jake ignored them and Nathan was content to leave him alone. He wouldn't make the mistake of touching Jake again, but somehow he had to get him off the truck so they could leave. However, Kat had no intentions of leaving. Before Nathan could stop her, she had covered the few feet to Jake and placed a tentative hand on his back.

Nathan tensed, fearful he would be forced to try and protect Kat from Jake's 'if-you-touch-me-I'll-kill-you' phobia. Instead, Jake merely turned to meet Kat's concerned gaze.

"You wouldn't believe me. No one believed me the last time."

Jake was getting entirely too spooky for Nathan. He remembered Dr. Hanson's comments about the murders from years ago. The man was mentally unstable and he'd brought Kat back with him to place her in danger. "Kat? Let's get out of here and give Dr. Lloyd some time alone."

Jake turned to look at Nathan and smiled. "The traditional academic response, Nathan. You're as predictable as Pavlov's dogs. Deny anything that contradicts your myopic world view."

Jake's glare withered Nathan. "Hanson trained you well. Always accept any new evidence that supports a basic tenet of your field and ignore any evidence to the contrary. How refreshing that the academic process hasn't changed in twenty years." Kat didn't intend to allow the digression. "Let's get back to what you think is happening again, Dr. Lloyd."

Jake turned back to Kat and looked at her for a long moment before speaking. "I'll show you what is going on and then you still won't believe me, but at least you'll have all the facts."

"Follow me." Jake abruptly wheeled around and headed toward the back of the shack toward the well-used airboat pulled up to the bank. He hopped in the boat and seated himself on the raised platform in front of the large fan blades that would propel the boat over shallow water filled with weeds that prevented navigation using a conventional boat.

Kat didn't look at Nathan or hesitate for a second. She positioned herself below Jake's tower seat in the center of the boat. Irritated, and bewildered at Kat's complete disregard for their safety, Nathan stopped on the bank. He glared at Kat as he stepped into the boat.

What could she be thinking?

They were placing themselves at the mercy of someone known to be mentally unstable and who had been questioned in the past about a murder. Also, Nathan feared it wouldn't be too hard to dispose of a body in the swamp.

"Kat? Are you sure about this?"

"Get in, Nathan. We don't have to be back that soon."

"We should probably do this another time, Kat?" Nathan spoke through clenched teeth, trying to relay to Kat that they were making a big mistake.

Kat grimaced. "Don't be such a pansy, Nathan."

Nathan, inflamed, started to respond but Jake intervened.

"Is that all you two ever do is fight?" Jake glared at them both. "It's obvious you love each other. Get married and get it over with."

"We are married." Nathan, now mad at them both, continued. "But not for long. She's already filed for divorce."

Kat opened her mouth to speak but was cut off as Jake, out of his seat now and standing beside her in the boat, reached over and rapped on Nathan's head like a door. "Hello? Is anybody home?"

Nathan's face turned beet red. Partially because Jake embarrassed him, but mostly because Kat seemed to take such pleasure in the event. She snickered in the boat beside the old swamp hippie.

Her turn was coming though. Jake performed a similar drum roll on her head and then cupped his hand around his ear as if listening. "It's got the same hollow sound, Missy."

"Both of you are idiots. Make a commitment to each other and stick with it." Jake continued as both Nathan and Kat were too stunned to speak, "You better beg her back, Nathan. In spite of the fact that she's slow witted, you'll not find her ilk again."

Kat started to respond, but Jake put his hand over her mouth. "Shut up and listen. I'm not finished. Your soul mate comes along once in a lifetime. When you find that person you have to seize that opportunity and fight with everything that's in you to make it happen."

Jake gazed at them, a faraway look in his eyes. "Stay married. Make that commitment to make it happen. Let me say it for you slowly, Com-mit-ment." Jake drew out each syllable. "As long as you two keep convincing yourself you're incompatible, you'll always have just what you're looking for."

Jake was obviously on a soapbox. Nathan wondered what button they had pushed as the lunatic continued. "There's no permanence. That's what's wrong with this generation."

Nathan couldn't maintain his silence any longer. "This generation lacks permanence? What about your generation, Mr. Freelove? Excuse me. I mean Dr. Freelove."

"Point taken, whelp. But intelligent beings learn from the mistakes of others."

He scowled at them in disgust, "I remember now why I live as far away from people as possible." He snorted. "The search for intelligent life forms continues. Now, get in the boat and keep your mouth shut."

Frustrated, Nathan stepped in the boat because Kat refused to get out. She had no clear understanding of the danger they could be in and all he could do was blindly follow. There was a village somewhere missing their idiot.

Dejected, he seated himself beside Kat as Jake started the motor. The deafening noise thankfully drowned out any potential conversation. Nathan brooded as the boat skimmed through the swamp at reckless speeds, barely missing stumps and submerged logs that could easily rip the bottom out of the aluminum-hulled craft.

He watched Kat as her short hair whipped around her head, and he could tell that she loved every minute of it. Nathan felt a sharp pang of jealousy.

They were at the total mercy of a silver-maned geriatric lunatic suspected of a twenty-five-year-old murder, and Kat appeared oblivious to it all. He gripped the seat until his fingers were white and stole a glance at Jake as he piloted the boat. The man was completely at ease in this environment. Nathan settled in for the ride feeling more comfortable about the trip. The destination was another thing though.

What would Jake do when they arrived?

For over an hour they meandered through the swamp at high speed like a cat dodging cars on the freeway, until Jake finally banked the airboat on a small island. At first, Nathan tried to remember some landmark by every turn they made, but how many times could the landmark be a big cypress tree and still be distinct? It was impossible in the swamp to pick out anything else. If this situation turned bad, he and Kat would be hopelessly lost.

Jake hopped down from his perch on the platform seat and started toward the interior of the island. He turned and waved them on. "Do I need to hold your hands?"

Neither bothered with a verbal response although Nathan caught Kat flashing Jake an irritated glance. Obediently, like lemmings going over a cliff, they followed Jake deeper into the swamp for what Nathan hoped would be a better fate than the one that awaited the lemmings at their journey's end.

Minutes later, soaked with sweat, lacerated by palmettos and munched on by every small winged critter that could find a place to land, they came to an enclosure of some type. Nathan almost ran into it before he saw it. It was approximately five-feet tall and draped with a gauzy camouflage material.

Curiously Nathan peered over into the enclosure. There was a small building on the other side of the fifty-foot wide fenced off area. Nathan could see nothing else inside the fence.

"Nathan? Are you coming?" Kat had continued to follow Jake who was halfway around the pen. Nathan realized he should be following her more closely.

What if Lloyd decided to kill them?

Maybe he could create a diversion that would allow Kat to escape. Escape to what, or for how long, he could not answer.

"Let's go." He nudged past her to keep himself between her and Jake who fiddled with a padlock on the door of the shack. He opened it as they covered the few paces to reach him. He stood back and gestured for them to go inside. Warily, Nathan entered the building and stood still, allowing his eyes to adjust to the darkness. He could feel Kat behind him, pressing in to view whatever Jake had brought them out here for. Nathan could sense her excitement and wondered if she could sense his apprehension.

Jake pushed around them both and retrieved a flashlight from a shelf on the wall in front of them. He clicked it on and illuminated an enclosure, like a horse stall, on one side of the shack. Nathan and Kat peered inside.

Kat gasped. "It's beautiful."

Nathan did not echo the sentiment. That was far from his first thought.

* * *

The dilapidated house sat on a small knoll overlooking a

bitterweed-covered field. A few fat cows cropped mouthfuls of grass not yet strangled by the encroaching weeds. A weathered black man and woman sat on the front porch swing sipping iced tea as the sun poured heat over steamy south Mississippi. Ed, in spite of his mood, was struck with how much it looked like a scene from a Norman Rockwell lithograph. He eased the cruiser up the driveway and stopped outside a freshly-painted picket fence. The manicured lawn and well-maintained shrubs stood in stark contrast to the house in bad need of a coat of paint.

Ed eased his diminutive frame out of the car and addressed the couple. "Evening Luther. Ruby. How y'all doing?"

The wizened sun-dried face of the old man broke into a grin. "Why Ed Hebert, you sorry dog. Where have you been?"

Ed removed his hat and wiped the inside band with a handkerchief. The heat felt stifling. A guitar-callused finger slid between his collar and neck, tugging to obtain a little breathing room. Refusing to meet Luther's gaze, his eyes wandered to the old hound dog lying on the front porch.

"What's wrong, Ed?" Luther knew Ed's silence couldn't be a good thing.

Ed's eyes watered as he faced Luther. "It's Hawk. We found his body yesterday."

The old man said nothing, obviously hit hard by the news. Ruby buried her face in Luther's shirt and began to sob. Luther patted her shoulder and hugged her to him as her body convulsed with grief. Ed averted his eyes and studied the cattle in the field.

A few seconds passed before Luther spoke in a voice cracking with emotion. "You boys was always like my own sons. You know that, Ed." Luther wiped a tear that navigated a circuitous route down his wrinkled countenance before he continued. "Glen will take it hard."

Glen, Hawk, and Ed had been inseparable as boys, an interracial oddity in the recently integrated south where they were raised. Hawk had spent more time under Luther and Ruby's roof than he had his own. For months at a time, he lived with Luther and Ruby while his own father spent marathon lengths of time too drunk to even know Hawk existed.

Luther and Ruby would set another place at the table and Hawk would just spend the night with Glen. One night led to another, until he spent the bulk of his childhood at their house while his father slowly drank himself to death.

Ed, a social outcast due to his small size, ran with the modern-day Tom and Huck and had eaten his evening meal more times than he could remember at Luther and Ruby's house. Glen now lived in New York and worked in the financial services industry. Ed never really understood exactly what Glen's job involved, but he was manager of some division in one of the big brokerage firms. Ed hadn't seen him since last Christmas when he came to visit Luther and Ruby.

Luther's voice jolted Ed back to the present. "I mind the time you boys buried my old truck down at the Potter hole. I ain't never seen a truck so stuck, before or since." Luther chuckled. "Every one of you drunk as a skunk and afraid to tell me 'bout that truck. But you had no choice cuz you couldn't get it out."

Ed remembered that time clearly. Luther had taken a belt and whipped all three of them. They had needed it too.

Ruby continued to sob against Luther's chest. The old man was taking it hard too, tears now flowing openly down his face. He made no attempt to wipe them away.

"I'm sorry to tell you about this, Luther." Ed struggled to maintain his composure.

"What happened to him, Ed?"

"He was killed while working on a multiple murder case we've got going."

Luther nodded. "Shot?"

Ed shifted his feet and stared at the dog, trying to keep his eyes off Ruby. Her more visible display of emotion threatened to crumble his resolve to keep himself composed. "I don't know for sure." He paused for a moment and gazed at the cows in the pasture. "We didn't find his whole body."

"Dear God!" Luther, more visibly shaken than before, stood. He shot a glance at Ed. "Let me help Miss Ruby into the house."

Luther guided the still-sobbing Ruby through the front door, a tender hand on her arm. A minute later the new window unit air conditioner protruding from the bedroom window kicked on and began to whir. Luther rarely turned it on, even though Glen had the utility bills direct drafted from his own bank account. Luther did not want to be a burden on his son. He was a proud man.

Minutes later Luther closed the front door behind him and nodded to Ed. "I gave her one of my muscle relaxers. That should put her to sleep."

Ed nodded. "I probably shouldn't have told that about the body." He couldn't bring himself to call it Hawk's body.

"I needed to know, Ed." Luther descended the front porch and came out to the car where Ed now stood. "What do you think it is, Ed?"

"What do you mean, Luther?"

"What killed him?"

"I don't want you to spread this around, Luther. But I guess we've got some kind of psycho running loose. He's dismembering bodies and throwing them in the bayous. Most of them are so ate up by the turtles we can't tell much." Ed knew he shouldn't share that much information, but he also knew it would be public soon as the reporters started adding things up. And he owed that much to Luther.

Luther stood dazed, a faraway look in his eyes. "I lost a cow last week, son." He paused for a second, groping for the right words. "You know they sometimes wander over on Stennis. I just let 'em stay. They always come back in a day or two."

Ed was silent as Luther wiped another tear. "Only this one didn't. I found her though." Luther stared intently at Ed. "Or I found what was left of her. All I found was a leg."

"Luther, you know the coyotes and buzzards will clean up a carcass around here."

"It wasn't that, Ed." Luther's panicked eyes bored into him.

"Something's out there. Something that was here thirty years ago and now it's back."

Luther pointed an arthritic work-hardened finger at him. "You better be careful, Ed Hebert. You hear me?"

CHAPTER 24

His normal appointed time approached, but tonight he had a different objective. Ten times in as many days Doctor John had visited the Old Ones. Much had been revealed, but much remained a mystery. Piece by piece, bit by bit, Doctor John learned of the ritual needed to control the Chinchuba and grant him the incredible powers promised by Vodu. His spiritual power grew immensely with each journey into the realm of the Old Ones, but still he remained unsatisfied. The ultimate was within his grasp.

However, the journey required much energy and his physical resources were depleted. Even his great strength had been sapped and needed replenishing. Vodu deemed him worthy to wield the power, and he would not disappoint his god. Tonight he would restore his energy so that he might continue with the task Vodu had set before him. Tonight he would go out and sup. But first he would be properly groomed and attired.

Doctor John moved through the darkened corridors of his compound as one familiar with every nail, every board, and every macabre furnishing in the old hotel. His stride, though purposeful, made no sound as he maneuvered down the long third floor hallway. The decayed and time-stained wallpaper bore the images of primitive artwork in various reds and blacks. Leering faces, agonized visages, tormented bodies, and images of dismembered animals, lined the hall like the masters on display at the Louvre. At closer inspection one would be able to tell that most of the pigments contained an element of blood. Animal blood. Human blood. The ingredient list depended to a certain extent on availability.

Doctor John paused and listened at two of the doors, stooping over to press his ear against the top panel of each door. Satisfied all was well, he entered his sleeping chamber located at the hall's end. Black stenciling on the door proclaimed room 321 to be the presidential suite. His room. The room befitting his status.

He turned the unlocked knob and entered the room. The shades, always drawn, discouraged any stray sunrays from desecrating the room during the day. Now, late at night, flickering white candles barely illuminated the room's blackness. Large and sparsely furnished, an enormous bed conspicuously occupied most of the floor space. Actually, the bed was merely a collection of mattresses fastened together and laying directly on the floor. Huge custom bed sheets, handmade by his servants, covered the bed along with dozens of black and red pillows. Doctor John's huge frame dictated a large bed.

Doctor John moved through the bedroom and entered a cased opening leading into the bathroom. His bath, already drawn and now cooled to the appropriate temperature, awaited him. He disrobed and admired himself in the floor-to-ceiling mirror. A lithe ebony human predator, scarred from countless skirmishes in his home country, stared back at him. He smiled, revealing the gold-capped canine teeth. Tonight would be a good night he thought.

His nude figure crossed the room to an ornately carved armoire, this one displaying one prominent skull relief. He opened the door to reveal several bottles and canisters arranged in neat rows containing various spices, powders, and sundry biological and anatomical components. None were labeled. None needed to be. Doctor John knew by heart each container's contents.

Without hesitation he removed one small glass bottle filled with a powdery brown substance and poured a handful into his palm. Turning to his custom-made tub, a hand-tiled whirlpool bath, he dumped the powder into the water and turned on the jets. The aroma of cinnamon filled the room as he eased his massive frame into the water.

Doctor John lingered in the tub, allowing the hot water jets to massage his body. Ten minutes later he emerged, totally relaxed, and dressed. His black garments had been laid out during his bath. A silent servant doing his bidding.

Tonight's task relied on stealth and the cover of darkness. In the past he'd gone out nude, using his ebony skin as the perfect camouflage, but it was infinitely more difficult to traverse the streets without clothing, even in New Orleans.

Before exiting his compound he donned two additional items; one a tall top hat that added inches of height to his six foot eight inch frame; the other, one of his newest acquisitions--a necklace made of human teeth. The intimidation value of his total appearance increased the satisfaction Doctor John derived from the night's task.

The main streets buzzed with activity, forcing Doctor John to take the lessor known side streets to his destination. A window slammed shut from a balcony as he passed underneath. An orange tabby growled deep in its throat when he walked past, the cat's sixth sense warning it that a much larger predator prowled the streets.

He fast approached his destination, one of the more deserted cemeteries surrounding the French Quarter. During the day, the cemetery bustled with tourist activity as countless hordes flocked to see the famous above-ground vaults. Of particular interest were the many purported to harbor the remains of famous voodoo queens and kings. Marie Laveau's gravesite, in St. Louis Cemetery No. 1, was by far the most popular.

In earlier years, Doctor John had frequented that cemetery. Now the tourists had turned the site into a shrine, and it would no longer serve his purposes. For he came to hunt. To hunt and prey upon the hapless victim sent into the cemetery at night. In spite of the warnings not to enter the New Orleans cemeteries after dark, or even during the day when not with an organized group, many drunken revelers fell prey to the constant badgering of their equally inebriated colleagues. A dare was a dare.

Other nighttime visitors included those ordered to place a penny on various gravesites and knock three times on the gravestone. This second group represented the clientele of some of the charlatan voodoo queens and kings in the city. It was widely believed that many potions and spells required the customer to visit the cemeteries for one reason or another.

It mattered not to Doctor John why anyone would visit the cemetery at night, only that they did. He positioned himself immobile in the dark shadows of one of the lesser known, but still popular, shrines. The tomb of Madame Chaveneaux drew many visitors, and Doctor John knew the full moon would not disappoint him.

He did not have to wait long. His nose caught the presence of perfume long before the woman arrived. An expensive perfume, not the cheap fragrances used by the Bourbon Street whores, but one more befitting a woman of culture. Doctor John's saliva glands moistened the inside of his mouth in anticipation.

Curious, Doctor John watched her approach through the moonlight. Haltingly she made her way through the granite maze until she stood before the very tomb he was watching. A lighter flickered as she bent to read the inscription on the tombstone. With a piece of red brick she quickly scribbled three X's and a cross on the granite face, then took a stub of red candle and lit it, seating the candle in the center of the stone.

Doctor John remained motionless a few feet away. Watching. Waiting for the proper moment. The woman, finished with her task, turned to leave and stopped. He could tell she sensed something out of place.

"What do you want?" She spoke into the darkness, still not certain where he stood. He noted she was a petite woman, but obviously one with inner strength.

"How did you know I was here?" Doctor John's singsong lilt was curiously disarming without the visual effect of the man.

"I can smell cinnamon and I thought I heard you breathing."

The woman's keen senses impressed Doctor John. This woman would be a worthy conquest at another time. "Not many would have noticed."

"You still have not answered my question." The woman was slowly backing away. He knew she would attempt to run soon.

"I intend to kill you."

Again, to her credit, she did not scream or attempt to reason with him. She merely turned and ran. And ran swiftly. It was possible that under other circumstances he would have let her go. After all, the qualities she exhibited were worthy of perpetuating. It was a shame he would extinguish her seed tonight.

But he needed her strength. Vodu had sent him a worthy sacrifice.

The woman ran zigzag through the aboveground burial vaults, darting left and right to confuse anyone following. But Doctor John took a more direct route. He knew where she would go and he simply leapt from vault to vault, covering the distance much more rapidly than the diminutive woman. The cemetery, ringed with eight-foot walls, had only four gates and Doctor John's direct route placed him at the nearest gate several seconds before the woman's arrival.

He heard her coming. Her labored breathing and the pad of her footfalls excited him. The anticipation of the kill sent pulses of electric adrenaline coursing through his body. Doctor John stood motionless, hidden in the shadows. He was careful to control his breathing, however he could do nothing about the odor of cinnamon.

The woman, running fast and hard, darted toward the gate. Closer to him. Closer to her destiny. Doctor John stepped from the shadows into her path when she was a few feet away. Unable to stop in time, the woman ran headlong into his immense frame. With a flick of his finger, he cut the woman's throat and frothy blood poured out of the incision. He held the woman up while she bled to death in his arms. She did not struggle and could make no sound, but her eyes betrayed her knowledge of death. With a blood soaked hand she traced a symbol on Doctor John's scarred face. He could not tell what it was, but allowed her the last rite. She was braver than most.

To a casual observer it would appear he had killed her with a fingernail. However, a closer inspection would reveal a small metal casing slipped over his index finger that flattened out into a razor sharp knife. An elongated metal fingernail designed for just such tasks.

Doctor John laid the woman's body on the ground and licked the small metal blade clean of blood. He then removed a larger more sinister looking instrument from his boot and, with surgical precision, removed the woman's heart. With slightly more care than a grocer bagging vegetables, he placed the organ in a plastic bag.

Unceremoniously, he discarded the woman's remains, heaving the lifeless body into a nearby trash dumpster. She would be found, but it might take several days. The dumpsters in this area were emptied infrequently.

Minutes later Doctor John entered his compound with his prize and strode to one of the doors where he'd listened earlier. He threw the door open and entered the room. Three women, all aged, worked feverishly on his project. One, sitting alone in the corner, drew his attention. He moved toward her. She held a portion of deerskin in her hands and chewed slowly on the fresh sun-hardened skin. Her gums bled profusely and stained the hide dark as her agonized eyes followed Doctor John and the plastic bag swinging at his side.

He halted in front of the cowering woman, enjoying her obvious fear. His left hand caressed the necklace of human teeth around his neck. "Do you miss these?"

The old woman did not know how to respond. Her gums ached terribly, the sockets where her teeth had so recently resided were pools of abscessed blood and pus. She focused on her teeth around his neck and tentatively nodded.

Doctor John tossed the plastic bag containing the human heart in her lap.

"Cook this for my meal and maybe I'll give them back." He threw his head back and laughed while Madame Jean stared in horror. She recognized the organ as a human heart and cringed.

Madame Jean thought about the black coffin and the bowl of *congris* on her front porch. Both were the sign of death. Her tongue, heavy in her mouth, swished across her reddened gums swollen from the recently extracted teeth. Madame Jean's pain diminished. It could be a lot worse.

Doctor John left the room and Madame Jean said a silent prayer and crossed herself. She prayed that her end would soon come. Swift and painless. She glanced at the other three women in the room, each careful to keep their eyes averted, and said the same prayer for each of them. But a hurried prayer, because she had to go cook her master's meal.

CHAPTER 25

Brian Humsinger found himself on Michigan Avenue. The Miracle Mile bustled with activity. The summer wind blowing off Lake Michigan funneled through the concrete canyons and increased velocity with each city block. The wind tugged at him, pulling him in the wrong direction, back toward the Amerind Building. Back toward a destiny that he was trying desperately to avoid. Back toward the future he'd created through his greed.

Each step he fought with all his physical and mental strength but to no avail. He was a prisoner in someone else's body. If only he could concentrate. What had he learned in nearly sixty years that could help him? Surely there was something in those thousands of pages he'd read on primitive cultures that would enable him to break this spell. His body moved without direction from him as he raced down the corridors of his mind, madly pulling books off those mental shelves, leafing through them all. The Aborigines, Moari, Souix, Cheyenne, Mayan, Aztecs; he turned page after mental page searching for some overlooked possibility.

Nothing!

He screamed inside. Nothing came out audibly. To any observer, he was just another businessman on his lunch break or on his way to a meeting. He navigated Chicago's sidewalk maze like the native he'd once been until the Amerind Building again loomed before him. This time he did not stop. His detached body moved through the revolving doors until he stood before the elevators, waiting for the next car up. Humsinger felt himself smile and nod at a young lady waiting beside him, all while his internal struggle continued. Brian Humsinger was doomed to merely watch from afar. An innocent bystander witnessing his own flesh and bone body calmly commit a crime.

He'd never experienced such frustration and fear. The elevator opened and he stepped inside, watching as every floor ticked by, bringing him ever closer to a fate he feared. Minutes later the door opened on the floor housing the executive suite. He willed his feet to stay put, to ride the elevator back down, but still he had no control. Casually he approached the receptionist and he could hear himself making small talk with her.

Humsinger tried to warn her with his eyes. Could he communicate with his eyes? Or were they controlled by Doctor John too?

"Mr. Crawley will see you now." She smiled at him as she buzzed him in. He screamed. Don't let me in that room! Nothing came out.

"Thank you, Samantha." Humsinger heard his voice say. He'd even read her name tag and greeted her personally.

He strolled to the door as it magically opened in front of him. Neil Crawley rose from the desk at the other end of the room when he entered. The man's face revealed his excitement. Humsinger had promised him another incredible piece for his collection.

"Brian. I'm glad you're here." His enthusiasm was genuine.

"So am I." Humsinger felt the corners of his mouth turn up in a smile. "I'd forgotten how little I like to fly."

"Can I get you a drink?"

"Water is fine."

Neil turned to the wet bar and filled a glass with ice before pouring the bottled water. Humsinger struggled to reveal his true mission to Crawley, but could not. He was watching a movie from inside one of the actors. In spite of the fear and dread, he had a sense of awe.

"Did you bring it with you?" Pleasantries over with, Neil was a like a kid at Christmas. He couldn't wait to open the presents.

Humsinger pulled a small bundle from his briefcase and handed it to Crawley. "I'd like to look at the other one while I'm here. I think the two pieces together may give some indication of where we might find others."

"You mean like a map?"

"Not really. More like a visual stimulus to get my mind to work. If I have both pieces in front of me and a little quiet time I may be able to come up with more clues on where to dig next."

"Whatever it takes." Crawley opened the package and reverently placed the piece on his desk. His face lit up. The beautiful primitive carving had been cut from a single large emerald. Humsinger watched Neil and felt his insides constrict as he awaited his own next move.

"Wow." The single word conveyed Crawley's excitement. His investment had already paid off. Humsinger stood, his stomach churning, afraid for Crawley and what he himself might do next.

Neil looked up remembering the earlier request. "Let me get the other stone." He hesitated a moment. "Do you mind stepping into the bathroom over there? I hate to ask you, Brian, but I don't like anyone knowing where I keep my valuables."

"No problem. I need to visit the facilities anyway."

Humsinger tried to warn Neil but again nothing came out. He screamed inaudibly as he strolled into Neil's private bath and shut the door behind him. Moments later Crawley called out. "You can come back in now."

Humsinger opened the door and walked back to the desk. He tried to focus his mental energy to warn Neil of the danger. He could do nothing but observe. The two figurines on the desk, indeed rare and valuable artifacts, enthralled Neil Crawley. Brian Humsinger did not exist.

Horrified at his own actions, Humsinger felt his hand touch the steel blade in his pocket and wrap around the fake bone handle. Neil's back was toward him as he approached. He felt himself pull the knife from his pocket and hold it semi-concealed against his pant leg. Humsinger watched as he deftly caught Neil's hair in his left hand while his right hand reached across in front and neatly cut Neil's throat. He felt the warmth of Neil's blood as it pumped over his hand and down the front of the billionaire's shirt.

Humsinger held the artifact collector while he struggled weakly to turn and face his killer. It was no use. The struggle was short-lived and Crawley's life soon expired. Humsinger eased the limp body to the floor behind the huge desk and carefully wiped the blade on Crawley's pants. He made one more trip to the bathroom to scrub the blood off his own hands before slipping the knife back into his pocket.

Humsinger felt limp and wasted inside. He had just killed a man as casually as making a sandwich. However, his body continued its mission. Humsinger watched himself as he carefully wrapped the two artifacts and placed them back in his briefcase. Seconds later he was winking at the secretary on the way out.

"He asked me to tell you to hold his calls for a couple of hours." He smiled broadly at her. "I just brought him some new toys."

The young brunette nodded and grinned. She'd worked for Mr. Crawley for three years now. "I know what you mean. I won't disturb him the rest of the afternoon."

* * *

Luther's comment stuck with Ed.

What had been here thirty years ago?

Four hours of going through stacks of musty newspaper had failed to reveal anything so far. But he was far from done. Ed laid his reading glasses on the table and rubbed his eyes. He glanced at the remaining mountains of newspaper. Surely, if anything had happened thirty years ago there would be some mention of it somewhere.

He'd quizzed a few old timers and gotten the same response. Everyone had either been stricken with selective memory, or they'd simply clammed up. Ed never realized how superstitious this entire town seemed to be.

Or maybe nothing had happened.

Ed momentarily thought about abandoning the quest, but the memory of Hawk's butchered remains pushed him on. He stood and stretched his legs with a short walk to the water cooler before resuming his search. This task would be so much easier if the library kept records on microfilm. But the Bay St. Louis Times wasn't that advanced, so he turned page after yellowed page, inhaling long undisturbed dust mites with every issue.

Two hours later he found the first story, dated January 3, 1976.

GRUESOME REMAINS FOUND BY LOCAL FISHERMAN

Local authorities began an investigation today of a possible murder. Jim Taggart, a local fisherman, found what authorities will only identify as "part of a body." The remains have been flown to the state crime lab for testing and officials indicated no decision has been made as to whether the cause of death was accidental or will be ruled a homicide. Speculation runs rampant regarding any connection between the remains and several recent disappearances along the coast. The state police are cautioning area residents to report any unusual behavior or suspicious activity. Motorists have been advised to be especially cautious about picking up hitchhikers. Repeated attempts to contact Jim Taggart for an interview have been unsuccessful. Although the authorities reveal that they have few leads, our sources indicate that a National Space Technology Laboratories employee has been questioned regarding the girl's disappearance.

Ed knew that Luther had been referring to this story. But there must be others. He cursed the fact that the Bay St. Louis police station, and all the police records, had burned to the ground in 1987. The fire had caused him more than one problem in the recent past. Last year a convicted murderer had won an appeal because the fire destroyed some critical evidence. That was before his time on the force. Since the fire they kept duplicate computer records and stored them at a backup location.

An hour later, seven hours into his search, he found the second article dated February 21, 1976.

MURDER VICTIM IDENTIFIED AS KATERI ABNAKI; SUSPECT SOON TO BE NAMED

Sheriff Lance Dartez revealed today that the dismembered body found last month was the remains of Kateri Abnaki. Miss Abnaki, a twenty-one year old Bay St. Louis resident, disappeared almost two months ago. A local fisherman discovered her remains while bass fishing in the Turtle Creek area.

Dartez also indicated that charges will soon be filed in the case, now determined to be a homicide. One anonymous source revealed the chief suspect in the case is Dr. Jake Lloyd, a NASA scientist rumored to be romantically involved with Miss Abnaki. Miss Abnaki was also a former employee at the NASA project.

Dartez refused to comment on that development stating that we should "Wait and see." Miss Abnaki is survived by her mother, Ella Abnaki, and an older sister, Anna Abnaki. The funeral will be held Sunday at 2:00 PM at the Hinkle Funeral Home.

Ed made two quick copies of the articles. It shouldn't be too hard to find Dr. Jake Lloyd, as long as he still filed taxes. It would be easy enough to obtain his social security number and see if Dr. Lloyd still lived in the area. He carried the mountainous stack of newspapers back to its proper place in the archives. Ed knew better than to get on the librarian's bad side. Miss Leola could redefine grumpy when she wanted to. In her library, she had jurisdiction. Badge, or no badge.

CHAPTER 26

Nathan's scowl conveyed his true feelings about the day. He was angry with Kat, and furious with the crazed swamp hippie, Jake Lloyd.

Kat studiously gazed out the passenger side window at the natural scenery as Nathan navigated the dirt road back to civilization. Nathan could tell she wasn't really seeing anything, instead deep in thought. After several minutes, Nathan broke the silence.

"He's crazy, Kat." Kat's gullibility frustrated him. "He's been living out in this swamp for twenty-five years, all by himself and his imagination has concocted this story."

Kat turned to face Nathan, her dark brown eyes looking like two pools of midnight reading his innermost thoughts. "Is he really crazy, Nathan?"

She brushed a wisp of stray hair back out of her face. Tiny rivulets of dirt-stained sweat ran down her neck.

God, she's beautiful, thought Nathan.

Nathan tried to soften the blow with humor. "He's two D-cells short of a full battery pack, Kat."

"I'm not so sure he's crazy. It must be nice to have that built-in ability to be able to pigeon hole everyone."

"How can you believe his line of crap, Kat? You, of all people. You're supposed to be a scientist!"

"You can't explain everything scientifically, Nathan. How can you explain the disappearance of the Biloxi tribe? Lloyd's recount of the legend is true. Remember? My Ph.D. is in archeology."

Nathan searched for the words that wouldn't be offensive. "I don't doubt the Biloxi tribe disappeared 450 years ago. What I doubt is the reason."

"What about the legend of the Chinchuba, Nathan? Do you refuse to believe in that too?"

"No, Kat. I realize the legend exists. I just believe it's what the mainstream conventional wisdom thinks it was. Disease."

Nathan continued to make his case. He desperately needed to convince Kat that Jake was dangerous. "Think about it, Kat. You know the history. In 1539, a missionary documented the conversion of the Biloxi tribe. Ten years later, another missionary came through, and they had disappeared."

Nathan paused. He didn't want to push her. She knew all this already. Jake's theory, espoused to them earlier, had just enough truth in it to make it believable. But Nathan knew all about that technique. He'd been raised with it and watched his parents ply that trade for years. Use just enough fact with any ridiculous story, and it would become believable because most people are gullible and searching for something else.

Well, Nathan had news for all of them! This was it!

Nothing more. Nothing less. You better enjoy it, because it was all there was. Only now, it bothered him that Kat couldn't see this problem objectively.

He continued before she could reply. "That could only be one thing, Kat. The same thing that decimated most indigenous tribes during that period. Disease. The missionary no doubt brought in some disease that the Biloxi had no immunity to and it killed them. It's happened time and time again. The disease was introduced by a Spaniard, a white man. Over hundreds of years the disease became the *Chinchuba*, Kat. Doesn't that make sense?"

"I'm not stupid, Nathan. I'm aware of all that, but I still think we can entertain alternate theories. Or have you forgotten that's how science advances?"

Nathan felt stretched to call their current discussion science, but knew better than to express that thought. Nathan tightened his jaws to stifle a reply. He'd have to come up with another approach. This one obviously wasn't working.

Kat's eyes bored into him like black lasers now, waiting for his response. When it didn't come, she continued. "Explain the legend of the Singing River then, since you're on such a higher mental plane than I am."

Nathan knew Kat referred to the legend of the mass suicide of the Biloxi tribe's warriors by drowning. Jake's recent crazed lecture on the subject refreshed Nathan's foggy memory. His outlandish theory was based partially on historical fact and partially on local Indian lore.

The local Choctaw Indian tribes that remained after the Biloxi's disappearance told the tale that most of the tribe had marched into the river to appease the river god. The few surviving Biloxi tribe members, all female, eventually assimilated into other tribes.

In the 1500's, the Biloxi tribe lived on the banks of the Pascagoula River located between the present day cities of New Orleans, Louisiana and Biloxi, Mississippi. Legend tells of the tribe worshipping a merman-like sea god who lived at the bottom of the river. After the conversion to Christianity by the Spanish missionary, the Biloxi threw their idols into the river and tore down their temple.

The river god, in his fury, arose from the depths and commanded the tribe to join him. According to the legend, one by one, the members of the tribe marched into the murky depths and drowned upon hearing his command. Supposedly, even today you could hear a low humming noise coming from the river, hence the modern day name Singing River. Those inclined to believe such nonsense claimed it sounded like hundreds of voices chanting in unison from the bottom of the river.

Jake had somehow stumbled onto the one area where Kat could not be rational. Even though the Biloxi tribe vanished according to archeologists, Grams maintained that she was of Biloxi descent so Kat had been raised with the notion that she was some type of Biloxi princess. Nathan was committing heresy, but continued anyway.

"I'm sure there's a reasonable natural explanation for the

noise, Kat. I don't know what it is right now. But you know how these legends and myths start."

Exasperated, Nathan continued. "When the tribe disappeared, the local tribes made up some reason for them being gone and the lie perpetuated."

Nathan tried to gauge her reaction. Kat, her face stoic, revealed nothing.

"Surely you can't believe it's more than that?"

"What about the white crocodile?" Kat just wouldn't let it go. She referred to the creature in the pen. Jake's pet, and pet theory. Nathan had no doubt it was a scientific anomaly, a discovery that warranted attention, but it was far from an explanation of the recent deaths.

Jake had found and captured a luecistic crocodile. Luecistic creatures were fairly uncommon, but not unheard of in this region. In fact the Audubon Zoo in New Orleans had a nice specimen of a luecistic alligator, part of a nest of twelve that had been discovered about ten years ago. And, like the crocodile he'd just seen, unknown to science until that time. Luecistic creatures were not albinos, although often mistaken for them. The luecistic alligators had blue eyes, instead of the pink eyes characteristic of albinism. The crocodile found by Lloyd had blue eyes.

"A luecistic crocodile is an amazing find, Kat. In fact, a crocodile at all is an amazing find since there are only about 50 or so left in the wild in North America. But I doubt it's responsible for Harlin's disappearance and your grandmother's stroke."

"You can't explain everything." She looked at him, her eyes pleading. "I know he's telling the truth. Don't ask me to tell you how or why I know. I'm not sure I know myself. Is it so hard to at least entertain the thought?"

Nathan couldn't help but roll his eyes, in desperation more than anything else.

Kat's demeanor instantly changed and she spit out the words. "Just like Jake said, Nathan, you are the typical closed-minded academic."

"Why do you simply believe everything that comes out of his mouth, Kat? Have you lost you ability to think?"

Kat turned away from him again and looked out the window. He hated it when he couldn't see her eyes. "Maybe I connect with him, Nathan." She turned to face him. "Is that so strange?"

Nathan felt a sinking feeling in his stomach.

Could Kat be attracted to this man?

Kat studied his reaction to her statement and, in spite of her anger, felt compelled to expound. "It's some kind of spiritual kinship, Nathan. Not a physical attraction."

They rode in silence for several minutes, leaving Nathan alone with his thoughts. Something nagged at his consciousness. Something he couldn't quite put his finger on. Something related to all of this fiasco.

What was it?

He mentally recounted the whirlwind events of the past week and then it hit him.

The artifact in Harlin's apartment!

It was a miniature of the luecistic crocodile. Earlier he'd thought it was an alligator. Now he realized it was a croc. Longer snout. Thinner body. And it was carved from a white stone!

Kat's voice, now gentle, intruded on his thoughts. "I have something to tell you, Nathan."

"What?"

Kat fidgeted with her seatbelt. "I think I'm pregnant." Hurriedly, she continued, "I've wanted to tell you for some time, but the timing didn't seem right."

Nathan was so stunned, and Kat so intent on his reaction that neither noticed the approaching car until the two vehicles nearly collided.

"Look out!" Kat screamed and grabbed the steering wheel, jerking hard to the right to miss the oncoming car. Nathan overcompensated when they nearly ran off the gravel road and into the ditch by jerking the wheel back to the left. The rented truck fishtailed in the loose gravel before Nathan regained control. The other vehicle was now obscured by dust in the rearview mirror.

The driver of the other car slid to a stop and got out to check his tires. He'd cut the wheels so hard that one tire had rolled completely off the rim. He stared back through the dust and tried to get a plate number of the rogue pickup, but it was already out of sight.

Dr. Jake Lloyd had better shed some light on this case, or he would have gone to a lot of trouble for nothing. Ed Hebert sighed, slammed the door shut, and rolled up his sleeves. Time to change the tire.

CHAPTER 27

Brian Humsinger paced his living room, a wreck of his former self. His hair, normally meticulously combed, was an unwashed tangled mass of dingy gray. Large bags under his eyes made him look ten years older than he had last week. Two dirty bloodstained bandages, one on his forearm and the other wrapped around the stub of his little finger, bore mute testimony to the current state of his life. He was a ruined man. Physically and mentally.

His hands trembled as he sipped the once-black coffee now diluted with a stiff jolt of bourbon. The brownish liquid burned his throat when he swallowed. Somehow the pain soothed him.

Five times in the past twenty-four hours he'd tried to call the police.

But what could he tell them? That he'd killed a man because he'd been controlled by a witch doctor from New Orleans?

There was no point in contacting anybody. No one could help him. It was too late. Soon the authorities would know he had murdered Crawley in cold blood. His face would be on the surveillance camera going into Crawley's office. His flight, booked using his platinum credit card, clearly indicated he'd been to Chicago. Crawley's secretary could easily identify him. Even though he'd made the appointment with Crawley under an assumed name, it was only a matter of time before the cops discovered his identity. He expected them to storm his house at any given moment. He could do nothing but sit and wait for the inevitable knock on the door.

Humsinger walked over to the liquor cabinet and poured another generous helping of bourbon into his coffee cup. He gulped the amber liquid, nearly all bourbon now, and studied the snub-nosed .38 caliber pistol on the cabinet top. He picked it up and turned it over in his hand. The gun was loaded, but he couldn't use it. An earlier attempt to shoot himself in the head only left a bullet embedded in his bedroom wall.

He sat down on the leather sofa and buried his face in his hands, massaging his temples, trying to chase away the memory of Neil Crawley's bloody corpse. The coffee table in front of him still bore the bloodstain from when he'd severed his own finger. His eyes rested on the crimson stained wood. He couldn't escape the blood. What was the point of cleaning it up?

Humsinger didn't hear the door open, yet he could tell someone had entered the room. His house. His room.

Not that it mattered any more!

Tentatively, he raised his head and looked around. No one was there. Humsinger gulped another shot of bourbon coffee and dropped his head back into his hands.

He was a defeated man. There would be no way to recover any semblance of his past life. If the crazed witch doctor allowed him to live, he would go to jail.

"Was your journey successful?" The now-familiar singsong lilt emanated from the furthest corner of the room, where no one had been just seconds before. Doctor John stood motionless, his towering dark frame blending into the rich tones of the walnut paneling.

"I got the stones." Humsinger couldn't bring himself to voice the fact that he'd killed Crawley.

"Good." Doctor John smiled, revealing the two gold covered fangs. "Did you feel the power when you killed your friend?"

Humsinger did not respond. In two quick silent strides Doctor John stood before him and grasped him by his greasy gray locks and lifted him to his feet. Another hand encircled his throat and lifted Humsinger off the floor. The man's inhuman strength bothered Humsinger more than anything. The bourbon, mixed with a couple of nerve pills, dulled his senses enough to numb the pain. But his fear was palpable. He needed more bourbon

What was Doctor John? Not who, but what?

"I do not like to be ignored." Doctor John spoke calmly as Humsinger's feet found the sofa. Doctor John allowed him to relieve the pressure on his neck enough to speak.

"No." He managed a hoarse croak. Doctor John smelled of cinnamon and stale sweat.

The witch doctor appeared amused. "You should enjoy the moment, Dr. Humsinger. Killing is the rare pleasure I most enjoy. A luxury that pleases me greatly."

He released his grip on Humsinger and strolled to the liquor cabinet. The gun lay in plain sight. He picked it up, engulfing the weapon in his huge hand. "Surely, you do not intend to use this?"

Humsinger prayed to die. Never before had he wanted to die. But in the last two days he had tried to commit suicide several times and now he prayed for Doctor John to shoot him. To let him go on and put him out of his misery.

He knew better than to remain silent this time. "I tried to kill myself."

Doctor John studied him appraisingly. "My magic is powerful. You will not be successful until I allow it, and I am not finished with you."

"What else do you want from me?" Humsinger's throat constricted more.

"The stones, and then one more simple task."

"The artifacts are in my bag." Humsinger finished the last few drops of bourbon in the cup, trying to erase the taste of stomach acid from his mouth. "I'll get them for you."

He retrieved the carvings and handed them to Doctor John, waiting silently while the witch doctor studied the two miniature stone figurines. Humsinger averted his eyes. Those stones had been his downfall. Worth a fortune, they had stimulated his greed.

He had uncovered the legend by chance. One of his diggers, a local man hired by Specky, mentioned the curse of the four stones when the first one had been found. Further prodding revealed the legend of the Chinchuba and something about four stones used in an ancient ritual. The man knew little else. But Humsinger had known that legend was often based on fact. That first stone only served to whet his appetite.

Brian Humsinger found himself in possession of an artifact worth millions on the black market. Chance dealt him another blow when Neil Crawley bought the stone. Crawley asked him about the possibility of any other artifacts of this quality and he'd mentioned the legend of the four stones. Crawley's enthusiasm, expressed in dollar signs, was contagious and Humsinger started plundering burial mounds with greater fervor, systematically searching for the other stones. That had been a little over a year ago. His only problem to date had been to keep that nosy Harlin Radkin at a distance. His disappearance was at first a blessing. Now apparently a curse.

Humsinger looked at Doctor John, still entranced by the stones. Two years ago he'd started down a path that led to this man. Now he was a cold-blooded killer.

"Where is the other stone?" Doctor John's gaze bored into him again.

"It hasn't been found."

Doctor John knew the stone's resting place had been disturbed. The Old Ones revealed it to him in a dream. He had yet to learn its whereabouts.

"You are wrong my friend." Doctor John paused, whether reading his reaction or reading his thoughts, Humsinger did not know. "It has been released from its earthen prison. Now you must find it for me."

"But how?"

"You will be resourceful."

"And if I don't find it?" Humsinger no longer feared death. In fact, he welcomed it as a sweet release from the present. Doctor John sensed this fact and approached him. He cupped a large hand around Humsinger's chin and pushed up until their eyes met. Humsinger felt the man's long sharpened fingernails digging into his cheeks.

"Do not underestimate my talents, Dr. Humsinger." He smiled, those hypnotic gold fangs only inches from Humsinger's face. "I can make you beg for death and keep you alive for years."

Humsinger's resolve to get Doctor John angry enough to kill him, moments before so rock solid, instantly evaporated. He averted his eyes, unable to meet Doctor John's gaze any longer.

Doctor John released his grip and stepped back. Intently, he watched Humsinger. An entomologist studying a new specimen now pinned to the collection board. "Now you will help me find the child."

Humsinger's stomach churned.

A child?

"The goat without horns has been in your house, Dr. Humsinger." Doctor John's nostrils flared and he inhaled. Something feral entered his eyes. "I can smell it."

* * *

Kat's eyes fluttered open. Something moved in her room. For a moment, she lay motionless.

Watching. Straining to see while waiting for her eyes to focus.

A faint stirring drew her attention to the window. The curtain billowed with a puff of wind.

Had she left the window open?

She couldn't remember. Kat listened for the slightest noise and heard nothing. The red digital display on her alarm clock blinked through several numbers. Ten minutes passed and still she felt uneasy. The curtain swayed with the night breeze.

Kat, now wide awake, decided to get up and call Nathan. She hated to admit her fear, but she knew he would come immediately. In spite of her stubbornness and his quick tempter, they were making some progress. Still far from perfect, but progress was progress. Kat's possible pregnancy forced them to iron out some differences they had been unwilling to address previously. The pregnancy, and of all things, the sanctimonious lecture from Jake Lloyd. Com-mit-ment. Kat could still see Jake mouth the word in his 'let-me-speak-slowly-for-you-stupid-people' manner. The truth stung, but it needed to be said. And she needed to hear it.

Glancing one last time around the room, Kat threw the covers back and placed her feet on the floor. Nothing jumped out at her and she began to feel a little foolish. She tiptoed to the bathroom, her eyes probing the darkness for any sign of an intruder. The pregnancy had caused her bladder to shrink to the size of a peanut. Yesterday, on the way home from Jake's, she'd made Nathan stop three times at places she would shun under normal conditions. In fact, her screaming bladder was probably what had awakened her.

Kat, a morning person, knew she would not be able to go back to sleep. She had way too much on her mind anyway. Nathan, their marriage, motherhood, Grams, Harlin missing. The list got longer every day.

She pondered her earlier conversation with Nathan. After recovering from the news that he might soon be a father, and nearly wrecking the truck, he'd told her about the artifacts found in Harlin's apartment. A white stone carving bearing an uncanny resemblance to the luecistic croc in Jake's pen. Was there any significance?

Kat came back to her bedroom and picked up the phone, hitting the dial button for Nathan's preprogrammed number. Feeling suddenly alone, she needed to hear Nathan's voice. Maybe it was time for him to move back home. She hadn't slept well since he'd moved out.

The phone rang and rang and rang. Fortunately Nathan didn't own an answering machine or he would never pick up the telephone. Finally, after seven rings, Nathan answered. "Yeah."

His voice slurred from sleep. Kat looked at the clock. It was 3:20 am. "Good morning, sleepyhead."

"Kat?" Nathan instantly sounded alert. "Is everything all right?"

"Yes. I just woke up and needed to hear your voice."

"Good. I . . . ." Nathan's voice ceased as the line went dead.

"Nathan? Nathan?" They'd been cut off. Kat pushed the phone button to get a new dial tone. Nothing. The comforting drone of the dial tone did not appear.

Kat cradled the receiver and nervously peered around her bedroom. She noticed the breeze stir the curtain again. Cautiously, she crept over and shut the window. Her cell phone, in her purse in the living room, began to ring. Kat hurried to get the phone when the dark giant stepped in front of her. Out of nowhere. He appeared almost inhuman, enormous and more frightening than any man Kat had ever seen. She stood frozen, unable to breathe, hoping he was part of a nightmare.

He moved toward her and Kat, regaining her voice, screamed with all her might. The man, unfazed by the piercing howl lingering in Kat's throat, held out his palm and blew a fine white powder in her face. She felt herself falling, the man thankfully fading out of her vision, as unconsciousness rescued her from the terrifying image.

She heard the phone still ringing. Ringing . . . .

CHAPTER 28

Madame Jean's trembling fingers turned the knob and eased the door open. Slowly, she poked her head into the hallway and stole a glance both directions. She'd heard the master leave much earlier, but fear kept her locked in the room with the other women. Tentatively, as if expecting a bullet to come at any time, she stepped into the hall. But Madame Jean wasn't afraid of a bullet. In fact she would welcome one. Gripped by a tormenting fear of Doctor John, and what he could do to her, Madame Jean had decided to take control of her destiny. Today, she alone would choose her fate.

Undetected with the first step, she moved with greater purpose to the room at the end of the hall. Doctor John's room. She tried the door, found it unlocked, and entered the darkened suite. Madame Jean knew his cabinet of ingredients would be in here somewhere, and she was desperate for relief.

Her tongue, as bloody and swollen as her gums from chewing on the hide, filled her mouth like a piece of raw liver. Her head throbbed from malnutrition and dehydration. She'd been allowed just enough food and water to keep her alive the past few days.

As quickly as her feeble body would allow, she searched the room. Nothing but wardrobe items in the main room. She entered the bath next and struck pay dirt. The armoire contained all the ingredients she needed and many she did not recognize.

Madame Jean pulled an orange peel from her pocket and laid it on the vanity top. The rind, stolen two days ago from the garbage, wouldn't work as well as a grapefruit halve, but she had to make do with what was available. A small stub of red candle, lit with a wooden match, joined the orange peel. Stopping only occasionally to listen, she sorted through the unlabeled jars and canisters looking for the right ingredients. Soon she found what she was looking for and sprinkled a pinch of cayenne pepper, garlic powder, and some steel dust over the tiny candle flame and dripped the melted wax onto the orange peel. With a knife she scraped a piece of snakeroot until she had a handful of shavings to add to the orange peel concoction.

Madame Jean retrieved a small mortar and pestle and a quart glass jar containing dried puffer fish. She then seated herself on the bathroom floor with her legs folded under her body and crossed herself, reciting the Lord's Prayer three times.

Sighing, a teardrop spilling from her saddened eyes, she opened the jar and removed two of the prickly fish and dropped them in the stone mortar. With efficiency borne from much practice, she ground the fish to powder, and poured the dusty remains into a glass of warm tap water.

Madame Jean raised the glass, a toast to the four directions, and tapped her foot three times on the floor before consuming the cloudy liquid. A warm sensation spread through her body when the toxins hit her bloodstream. Within minutes her vision blurred. Her spell would work. Soon she would be free from Doctor John. Never again would she do his bidding.

* * *

Kevin Croix, several blocks away, felt a sudden heaviness in his spirit. He'd lain awake most of the night, the coffin lid closed over him. Praying in the total darkness. Praying fervently for lost souls. The battle had gone to the enemy tonight. He said another prayer for the battles to come and closed his eyes. Sleep would be a welcome respite from the cares of this day.

* * *

Ed Hebert rolled the police cruiser to a silent stop in front of the Windsurf Apartment complex and loosened the strap on his gun. He'd turned the car's lights off before he entered the complex. Something unnerved him about this call. No lightning bolts or voices from a bush appeared, but the hair on the back of his arms stood at attention when he turned into the driveway.

Normally he would be home in bed while one of the younger cops took the night watch. Tonight, however, he'd volunteered to take Thane Arvil's watch. Thane had some personal business to take care of. Ed and everyone else knew Thane's business, but pretended otherwise. Thane's wife was making a run at the record books to see how many men, other than her husband, she could bed in a year's time. Or so it seemed. Ed, at times like this grateful his marriage didn't last, volunteered to take Thane's shift.

He really couldn't sleep anyway, so the decision was a simple one.

The night shift usually gave a person plenty of time to think and Ed needed some time to think. And tonight had been just like most nights. Until now. A few minutes ago someone called in and reported a woman's scream. More than likely another domestic disturbance, but he intended to check it out. The apartments were actually outside the city limits, but he always responded to emergency calls if they were close.

Apartment 262, in the building in front of him, was totally dark. He glanced at the nightlight in the parking lot and made a mental note to get the electric company out here to fix it. The cloud covered night sky didn't help matters. Only a couple of apartments showed feeble light escaping from curtained windows, but the night quickly devoured the faint glimmer.

He retrieved his flashlight from the car seat, but didn't turn it on. All was quiet as he got out of the car. He shut the police cruiser door and ascended the steps to the apartment's front door, careful to make no sound. Before he reached the door, a light came on in the apartment. He gripped the butt of his gun, trying to squelch the ominous feeling.

The door, slightly ajar, allowed him free entry. He sidestepped through the jamb and froze against the wall, electing not to announce his presence. His eyes, already adjusted to the darkness, scanned the small living area. Nothing seemed out of place.

Satisfied no one was in the living and kitchen area, he focused his attention on the bedroom door. The light he'd seen flicker on moments before was the bedroom light.

"Kat? What's happened?" A man's voice, a low moan of agony, interrupted the silence. Ed pulled his pistol from the hip holster and assumed a two handed grip, muzzle slightly down and pointed forward, as he crept toward the bedroom doorway. He froze in mid stride when a man erupted from the room.

"Hold it right there! Hands where I can see them." The man jumped at Ed's voice, obviously startled, and then appeared reassured when he saw the sheen off Ed's badge.

"Please help me!" The man looked vaguely familiar. Ed rifled through his mental file cabinet, searching for a visual match. "Something's happened to my wife."

"Is this your apartment?"

"No. It belongs to my wife, Kat." The man paused, realizing that sounded strange. "But something has happened to her."

"I heard you, buddy." Ed motioned with the barrel of his gun. "Step back into the bedroom so I can see if we're alone. Just keep your hands in plain sight at all times."

The man obeyed, opening the door wide, before entering. Ed followed, his eyes scanning the room. He backed over to the darkened bathroom and peered inside. It too was empty. He holstered his gun.

"Alright. Tell me what's going on. Start with your name."

"Nathan Young. My wife is Kat Young."

The name stimulated Ed's memory and he realized where he'd seen Nathan Young before. Yesterday afternoon on the way to see Jake Lloyd, the man had nearly ran him off the road. He could now clearly see the man's face through the window of the truck.

"Was that your wife with you at Jake Lloyd's yesterday?" Ed studied Nathan's reaction, taking his measure. Noting the shocked reaction.

Nathan's brow furrowed. "Yes."

"Where is she now?"

"That's just it. I don't know." Nathan waved his hands in the air and appeared near tears. "I was on the phone with her and the line went dead." He snapped his fingers in the air. "Just like that."

"So then what did you do?"

"I came over here." He gestured towards Biloxi. "I just live down the road."

"I thought you said she was your wife?" Ed tried to gauge the man's emotions. He was a hard read. "Are you separated?"

"It's a long story, but, yeah, we are." Nathan's hands rubbed his eyes. "But that's not important right now. I tell you, something's happened to her."

"Who were you talking to in the room earlier?"

Nathan's brow furrowed and then relaxed with realization. "Oh. Myself I guess."

"How do you two know Dr. Lloyd?"

"We went to see him because Kat's grandmother wanted us to find him." He stood up from the bed and raised his forearms, palms up. "Look officer, how is this helping you find Kat?"

"Humor me. If she's missing, and we haven't determined that, then we can put out a description."

Nathan glanced around the room. "She's not here, is she? How do you define missing?"

"For all I know she stepped outside for a cigarette." Ed decided to play a little of his hand. He'd recently read all Hawk's file notes for some clue about who Hawk thought the killer might be and Nathan Young's name appeared more than once.

"I also know last week there was an officer dispatched here to handle a domestic disturbance between you and your wife." Ed held his hand up and started counting off fingers with his other hand. "And here's another little tidbit. Within a week's time, Harlin Radkin, Sheriff Hawkins, and now your wife, are either missing or dead. And all of them have a connection to you."

The man's quickness surprised Ed. Nathan launched himself

from his position beside the unmade bed and hit Ed with a football forearm in the left temple. Ed, much smaller than Nathan, felt his head slam back against the doorjamb and the room started spiraling out. That slow-motion fade out where it takes minutes to hit the floor, when in reality it was only seconds. A comforting blackness engulfed him as Nathan stepped over him into the living room.

Nathan, shaken from what he'd just done, stopped to take a few deep breaths to keep from hyperventilating.

Kat had disappeared and he'd just assaulted a police officer! But he couldn't afford to be in jail right now and that was clearly where Ed intended to put him. Kat needed him NOW! Not tomorrow. Not next week or when he'd cleared his name or made bail. Now.

Nathan had to find her. There had to be some clue as to what had happened. He resumed his search of the apartment, stealing a glance at Ed. The man remained motionless. Worried, Nathan walked over and felt for a pulse. Thankfully he found one. As an afterthought, he removed the gun from its holster and stuck it in his waistband. He was already in deep trouble anyway and he might need it when he found Kat.

He could find nothing in the apartment and started to exit.

What would he do now?

And then he saw it. Painted on the wall above Kat's front entrance. Primitive symbols. It was a peculiar design. Some type of prehistoric looking pictograph.

The red paint, still fresh, stood in stark contrast to the white wall. He touched one of the images with an index finger and withdrew his hand. The paint, still fresh, stuck to his finger. He sniffed it. Odorless. Tentatively, he stuck his finger to his tongue, afraid of what he was about to uncover. His fears, now justified, overwhelmed him. Nathan felt faint. The salty taste confirmed it. Blood!

Was it Kat's blood?

CHAPTER 29

Kevin glanced at his watch. He'd be a few minutes late now, but it really didn't matter. They wouldn't start without him, after all he was the star attraction.

The warehouse teemed with activity. He could hear the buzz of a few hundred voices, all gabbing at once, before he opened the door.

"Hey, Kevin. You gonna win today?" The speaker, a fifty-something wisp of a man, monitored the door. Coming or going, you had to pass Lynn's inspection.

"Of course I am, Lynn." Kevin clapped him on the back and winked. "Don't I always?"

Lynn grinned, revealing two missing front teeth. "I've got a hundred on you, Kevin."

"I'll try not to let you down. See you Thursday?"

"Yeah, I'll be there."

"I'll be looking for you."

Kevin moved on past Lynn toward the buzzing crowd gathered in the center of the otherwise empty cavernous building. A number of people called his name and waved at his arrival.

He did his best to smile or nod, in some small way acknowledge every one of them. To let them know he knew they existed and cared.

The crowd, comprised of every conceivable shape, size, color and social status, parted to allow his passage. Most of them he knew. A very few, he did not.

The opponent's supporters represented most of the new faces. The work hardened, sun darkened faces fresh off one of the shipping vessels docked in New Orleans. Only rarely would a local fight him any more.

But, fortunately for Kevin's wallet, every merchant vessel on the high seas had their fighter. Nearly all thought their man was invincible, and they'd back it up with a month's wages, or more.

Bouncing at the bar didn't pay the bills. He had the place on Rampart that he rented every Thursday night, and he'd lost count of the money that he handed out on a weekly basis.

Fighting allowed him to do what he really wanted to do. Kevin considered fighting his tent making. The apostle Paul made tents. Kevin fought. He believed you focused on your strengths and did everything to the best of your ability.

When he got too old or too slow to fight, he didn't know what he would do. Tomorrow's battles were best fought tomorrow. Today he would worry about today's battle.

And today's battle looked challenging enough. Kevin, standing on the edge of a thirty-foot square chalked on the concrete, eyed his opponent. He was big. The man had at least three inches on Kevin's six foot six inch frame, and probably 50 pounds. Kevin noticed the man was a knuckle dragger and made a mental note to watch that wingspan. Reach could win or lose a fight.

Kevin peeled off his shirt and stretched a little. The betting began in earnest now that both fighters were at ringside. The odds, posted on a portable dry erase board, had Kevin at two to one, even with the size differential. The odds maker knew Kevin, he didn't know the challenger, listed ironically as Goliath.

"How's it going, Kevin?" Gene Lavreaux always set up these little events. How he located the fighters, Kevin didn't know.

"Good. I'm feeling my oats." Kevin nodded in Goliath's direction. "Where'd you get this guy?"

"He's from that German freighter docked across the river." Gene raised an eyebrow his direction. "They say he's never been beat."

Kevin shrugged. "There's always a first time."

"Have you looked at him? He's a monster, man."

Kevin studied the German, watching him strip to the waist. The man's long beefy arms appeared carved out of wood. "He looks a little soft to me."

Gene glanced around and then back to Kevin. "Are we looking at the same man?"

Kevin smiled. "Don't worry, Gene. I need the money and hunger always wins out."

A few minutes later, all initial bets placed, the two men squared off and listened to Gene recite the rules. Bare knuckles free-for-all with the winner the last man standing. No biting or eye gouging allowed. Everything else was fair game.

"Everybody understand the rules?"

Both men nodded and the match began.

"I crush you, little man." Goliath's thick accent screamed Eastern Europe.

Mind games. Always about the mental battle. Kevin responded in kind as he danced lightly on his feet with his hands in front, slightly raised. "Goliath? Call me David."

Kevin followed the statement with a combination. Two right jabs to the nose, to make the man think he was left handed, and a swift kick to the ribs that Goliath partially deflected. The two punches to the nose connected and a trickle of blood seeped out of Goliath's left nostril.

Kevin backed up a little, his hands low, baiting the man. Goliath moved toward him, a little quicker than Kevin would have guessed, and threw a flurry of roundhouse punches each designed to drop a mule in its tracks if it connected. He managed to get out of the way of most of them, but a stray left caught him in the ribcage. It sounded and felt like a hundred-pound feed sack falling on a ripe melon. Kevin felt a rib snap and tried not to betray the pain with his expression. Never show a weakness.

But Goliath knew it. He felt the rib give and came back hard and fast. Kevin met him blow for blow, and then dropped to the floor landing on one hand. With his right leg he made a sweeping kick that caught Goliath just above the ankles and swept both of his feet out from under him.

The big man knew how to fall though, and slapped the concrete floor hard with both hands to break his momentum.

However, Kevin didn't give him time to recover. He swung a kick at the bigger man's head. Goliath anticipated the action and moved his head just enough to make the kick miss, and then came off the ground pushing Kevin's leg upward.

Kevin knew better than to resist. He allowed his momentum to carry him forward and follow the leg. Like an acrobat, he performed a perfect back flip, and landed lightly on the balls of his feet. Before Goliath could adjust, Kevin whipped his head in a sharp circle and the long braid draped down his back lashed the giant across the face. A red lash appeared on Goliath's cheek like he'd been hit with a riding crop.

Kevin didn't stop there. He needed to finish this fast. The broken rib was a sign. This man could beat him if a lengthy brawl ensued. Goliath's hands were hung at his sides, so Kevin went for the lantern jaw. Five times, in as many seconds, he struck the big man in the face. Each time he exhaled sharply and twisted his fist just before the punch connected.

The sixth punch finished the match. The first five blows battered the man's head around until, by punch number six, Goliath faced ninety degrees to the right. Kevin threw everything into it and felt the man's jaw give under his hand. A collective moan erupted from the crowd as Goliath wilted to the floor unconscious.

The German shipmates stared at Kevin slack jawed. Incredulous that their champion succumbed to the smaller man.

Gene appeared with a bottle of water and a towel. "Man, that was fast."

Kevin pulled a watch from his pocket. Three minutes had elapsed since the fight started.

"I didn't have much choice, Gene. If I'd strung that one out, big boy could have whipped me."

Gene clapped him on the back and shoved a thick wad of bills into his left hand. "That's over three thousand bucks a minute, Kevin. But you earned it."

The money in his hand was a means to an end. That's all.

Otherwise it was merely worthless pieces of colored paper. Battles lost and battles won. All over the very paper in his hand. Wars lost and wars won, over the same thing.

Kevin closed his hand around the bills. His knuckles, cut and bleeding, would soon swell to the point where the hand wouldn't close. He'd soak his hands in brine tonight.

But first he'd go buy the sword.

* * *

"I don't know where else to turn." Nathan, frantic over Kat, stood on Jake's front porch like a school kid in the principal's office. Pleading his case. Telling his side of the story. "Will you help me find her?"

"I'll help you." That was it. No argument. No lecture. Nothing. "Tell me about everything, in detail. One more time."

Jake, without his normal contemptuous attitude, appeared almost human. Gone was the mushroom tea swilling I-know-it-all old hippie from the day before. The transformation shocked Nathan. He'd come prepared to beg and grovel if necessary. Anything to find Kat.

He gave Jake an abbreviated version of Kat's disappearance finishing with cold-cocking the cop in Kat's apartment and the finding the bloody drawing above her door.

"Can you reproduce it? The drawing?"

Nathan would never forget the primitive image. He shuddered at what Kat might be going through. Nathan focused. He couldn't help Kat if he fell apart. "Easy. Get me a pencil and paper."

Jake complied and Nathan sketched the few brief lines while Jake paced the front porch. He soon had a passable likeness of the bloody drawing on paper and handed it to Jake.

Jake spent almost no time studying the copy. Nathan watched Jake's reaction as he collapsed in thought into a nearby rocking chair.

"What is it?"

"I'm not sure."

"Well, what do you think it is?"

Jake, gazing into the swamp, turned to face him. "I'm pretty sure it has something to do with voodoo." He waved the paper Nathan's direction. "Are you sure it was blood?"

"Yes." Nathan felt a tightness constricting his throat.

Silence engulfed the front porch as both men lapsed into their own thoughts. Nathan heard the vehicle about the same time Jake did and glanced toward the rocker.

"I forgot to tell you. That cop knew Kat and I came to see you." Nathan, dejected, looked at his hands. "That's probably them looking for me."

Jake wasted no time. "Let's go."

"Where?"

"We've got to find Kat, and I've been down this road before. *Déjà vu.* They accused me years ago of Kat's aunt's murder and they intend to accuse you of killing your buddy and the other cop."

Jake heard the vehicle better now. He knew they still had a couple of minutes before its arrival. "They'll probably attempt to rope me in somehow too."

"What can we do?"

"We'll take the air boat. I'll disable the other boats so they can't follow us."

"But how will we find her?"

"Quit yapping and get in the boat." The truck sounded like it rounded the last corner before Jake's yard. "I know someone who might help us."

CHAPTER 30

Kat cringed when Doctor John entered the room. She could move very little with her arms and feet tied to the metal bedposts. The witch doctor spoke, revealing the gold-capped fangs she'd noticed last night.

"Ah, finally awake."

Kat ignored the man, focusing on the farthest corner of the ceiling, trying to choke back her fear. She could see him approach her bedside. The index finger of his right hand, tipped with some type of metal blade, caressed her face. A whimper escaped her lips.

"Do not fear, little one. Your time is not yet here." Kat's tensed body remained stiff as the metal finger blade slid under the collar of her nightshirt and slit the entire front open, exposing her chest and stomach. Tears welled up in her eyes, but she tried to remain focused on the now-blurry corner.

Ignoring her nudity, Doctor John laid his head on her stomach, facing toward her feet. Motionless, he listened. Kat felt her heartbeat accelerate. Seconds passed. Minutes passed. Doctor John's head remained glued to her abdomen. Kat choked back the bile rising in her throat.

What is he doing?

After what seemed like hours, in reality only minutes, Kat felt her stomach convulse like it had so many times in recent days. The baby moved in her womb and Doctor John raised his head and smiled at her.

"The 'goat without horns' knows its master."

Kat moaned. She'd heard her grandmother mention that phrase many years ago when a newborn baby turned up missing from the local hospital. The child, never found, simply vanished. Kat heard Grams mumble that phrase and then cross herself. She feared she now knew what it meant.

"Please! Please don't hurt my baby!" Kat trained her eyes on his scarred face and choked back the tears. "I'll do anything you want."

Doctor John again caressed her cheek, using his left hand this time. A faraway look made his eyes appear glazed. The pleasant odor of cinnamon filled the room. "I know you will, mon cheri. I know you will."

He glanced around the room and for the first time Kat noticed the tiny alcoves set in the four walls. All four contained candles, each one a different color. Three burned, while one remained unlit. Doctor John's gaze rested on the unlit one. A white one.

"Soon." He promised. "But the time is not yet here. Vodu must provide the remaining piece."

He returned his gaze to Kat's abdomen. "But Vodu will provide."

Doctor John wheeled and left the room, the door clicking softly closed behind him.

Kat's tears brimmed over as she raised her head to study the alcoves. They contained something besides the candles. Her eyes focused on the one nearest to her. The green candle. Behind it, resting on a small raised platform, sat a tiny stone carving. Another time and Kat would have been fascinated by the artifact. But not today. Terrified, she raised her head as much as possible and peered at the other two alcoves containing lit candles.

They all housed different color versions of the same thing. The artifacts resembled tiny lizards, but Kat knew what they were. The carvings were crocodiles. And even worse, she knew what was missing from the fourth alcove.

The white stone carving inside the cat food sack in Harlin's apartment!

Please, Nathan! Find me before Doctor John finds the stone!.

Nathan was her only hope. She feared she knew what would happen when the witch doctor acquired the fourth and final stone.

But, why her? What had she done?

* * *

"I thought you were going to help me find Kat." Nathan glared at Jake, angry over the turn of events. "I don't have time for a bunch of religious mumbo jumbo."

"I'm just about fed up with you, whelp." Jake stopped and put a finger in Nathan's face. "You don't understand what we're up against. You can either go with me, or you can find Kat on your own."

Nathan, though irritated, knew they were running out of time. "Fine. Let's go find this preacher of yours."

Impatiently, he followed Jake through the cobbled French Quarter streets reeking of the previous night's overindulgence. Nightfall approached and the vomit filled sewer drains would soon begin accepting the current night's deposits. A good time always exacted its toll. But Nathan didn't notice the stench, he was worried about Kat.

It had taken them a full day to get to New Orleans and Nathan feared what might have happened to Kat during that 24-hour period. Time, always a precious commodity, did not stand still for anyone. The only thing that kept him from striking out on his own to look for Kat was that he had no idea where to begin looking. So he followed the silver mane in front of him and hoped Jake knew what he was doing.

Jake stopped and looked at the building address in front of them. "This is it."

A group of young teens, dyed and pierced in every conceivable location, wandered past and into the building.

"Come on." Jake glanced at Nathan. "I think the service is about to begin."

Nathan winced. He hadn't been in a church for more than ten years and would be fine if he made it another ten years. Nathan's parents sealed that chapter in his life ages ago. The few remaining vestiges of his childhood beliefs, the ones not destroyed by his father's infidelity, had been stripped away in graduate school. No more foolish beliefs. Science made far more sense. So why waste time in church? It was merely a place for those people still searching for truth.

The gullible masses needed something to believe in to keep them from one another's throats. Organized religions filled that void. Society's glue, he'd heard it called. In spite of his belief that religion was a necessary evil, he still found it distasteful to watch some charlatan perform and then pass the hat.

But, right now, what other choice did he have?

None. He would suffer anything to find Kat. Without a word, Nathan followed Jake into the show and found a seat. A number of people milled around, Nathan pegged the crowd at around 200. He'd grown adept at estimating head count as a child. It was a topic of primary concern around the kitchen table.

How many did we have tonight, dear? I don't know, Nathan did you get a count?

Nathan could hear their voices. The next question would be about the offering.

How much money did we get tonight?

Always the same concerns. Head counts and dollar signs. Never a mention about the needs and prayer requests expressed by the congregation during and after the service.

Comfortable in his cynicism, he surveyed the crowd. It was an odd bunch, to put it mildly. Within his immediate field of vision he could see five or six transvestites, a hoard of punk rockers, a few tattooed bikers, and a sprinkling of emaciated addicts and burned-out whores. The dregs of society. The occasional "normal" looking individual stood out from the crowd and probably had some sort of mental disorder.

Someone started strumming on a guitar up front. Piano or guitar, the universal sign to take your seats. The show was about to begin. And heeeeeeere's Johnny!

Nathan glanced at his watch. Another hour wasted while Kat endured who knew what. Jake, until now sitting immobile beside him, pointed at the stage.

"That's Kevin." The corners of his mouth turned up in a smile. "He's the one who can help us."

Nathan's gaze followed Jake's finger to the mountain of a man now on the small raised platform. Incredulous, he glanced back at Jake. "Him? He's the preacher?"

"That's our man. Kevin Croix."

This should be good. Nathan's preacher expectations involved someone sporting the finest polyester leisure suit, a diamond stud tie tack, and what he'd dubbed a "preacher-doo." The fluffed bouffant 'I'm-a-cross-between-Elvis-and-a-used-car-salesman' look, complete with at least one full can of hair spray to hold it all in place.

Croix sure didn't look the part, but judging from the size of the crowd, Nathan knew he must be able to walk the walk and talk the talk. He sat back and waited for the performance to begin, the face to pinch, the voice to quiver, the tears to flow. He'd seen it all before. Choreographed classics, every one.

Nathan's father's performances, repeated every Sunday, were Oscar caliber. He'd scream and cry and spit for an hour and then pass the offering plate. Sunday morning, Sunday night, and Wednesday night. During the remainder of the week he'd spend time having sex with some troubled member of the congregation. Counseling, he called it. All the while, Nathan's mother pretending she didn't know anything was going on.

She was no better than he was!

Nathan got his fill of the hypocrisy early on, but endured until college, constantly struggling with his own demons.

How was it a sin for a young hormonal teenage boy to want to have sex and yet apparently God looked the other way while the old man bedded anything he could counsel the skirt off of?

Nathan, lost in his childhood thoughts, barely noticed when the music stopped. However, when Kevin took the center platform, Nathan decided to leave. Ten years had not been long enough. Nathan's heart raced and his palms began to sweat. He slid a finger under his collar and pulled, trying to gain some breathing room, before realizing he was wearing a tee shirt.

Pale faced and out of breath, he leaned over to Jake. "I'll meet you outside when it's over. I've got to get some fresh air."

Jake, obviously curious, shrugged. "Fine. I'll see you on the steps."

CHAPTER 31

Billy Blanchert wasn't as stupid as everyone thought. Even his own recently departed brother Lou, who had often accused him of being as sharp as a sack of wet mice, underestimated his intelligence.

He'd been smart enough to kill Tara Hocum and get by with it. Cut her open from gut to gullet with that big skinning knife he used for cleaning deer. That dumb skank deserved it. She should have never told him he was no good in bed. Every man was sensitive about that and she'd just kept on and on. Digging at him. Needling him.

So Billy cut her and watched as she screamed in agony and tried to hold her intestines in. It only took Tara a few minutes to bleed to death, and he'd enjoyed every minute of it. Afterwards, he dumped her body out in the gulf. He'd wrapped her in a tarp, stolen a boat, and carried her out past the barrier islands. A couple of concrete blocks weighted her down nicely and he pitched her in the water with a spool of fishing line attached just to see how deep she went.

He knew the bloody mess inside the tarp would make the little blacktip sharks go crazy. In hours there wouldn't be enough left for anyone to identify, even if they found her.

Tara's body reeled out 200 yards of fishing line and came to a rest on the bottom. Billy sloshed a few buckets of water across the deck to wash off a spot or two of blood and cut the line, severing all ties with his ex once and for all. He eased the boat back to the dock and, as far as he knew, no one even missed it.

Now, seven years later, not a soul could pin it on him no matter how hard they tried. He'd never whispered a word to anyone, and didn't intend to. That's how people got caught. Blabbing about everything.

Yeah, it was true he'd killed Tara, but he hadn't killed Lou.

The more he tried to relive that night in his mind, the more he thought Lou must have hit his head on a stump and drowned. After that, some big gator had made quick work out of that free meal, however scrawny and tough it was.

Lou was too mouthy anyway. It was only a matter of time before somebody killed him, but Billy didn't intend to take the fall for no accident. He needed to get out of here and fast. And he had a plan.

Long Beach's finest planted the seed of the plan last night when they'd thrown that greasy stinking longhaired drunk in the same cell with Billy. The guy mouthed and cried all night long until Billy was sick of his whining. So it didn't bother him one bit when he strolled over to the sleeping drunk and brought the edge of his hand down sharply across the guy's throat, crushing his larynx like stepping on a grape.

What a wake up call!

The guy fell off the bunk and started flopping around on the floor like a freshwater eel in the bottom of a boat. His eyes bugged out and his hands went to his throat, the greasy hair fanned out on the floor under him. Seeing Billy, he reached for him, begging for help. The man tried to speak, but managed only a low croaking sound. Satisfied, Billy yelled for the jailer.

"Hey! Abram! Get in here! This dude is throwing some kind of fit."

Billy positioned himself at the cell door and plastered a frantic look on his face. "Hurry up! I think the guy's dying or something!"

Abram, the ancient jailer, sure wasn't going to win any races. Billy could hear him shuffling down the hall at the speed of a disabled terrapin. Made a man feel confident about the penal system. At least from this side of the bars.

By the time Abram arrived, Billy's cellmate struggled feebly against the unseen antagonist that suffocated him.

"Back away from the door, Billy." Abram, retired years ago, supplemented his meager income by moonlighting at the jail. Like a hard rain pounding on a freshly plowed field, time had eroded Abram's body. The major structure still stood, but stooped over now, with the muscle tissue beaten loose and washed down the stream of life. The old man posed no problem for the younger and stronger Billy.

The polished key ring jangled against the bars as Abram fumbled with the lock, nervous because Billy's cellmate no longer moved. His job would be in danger if a prisoner died on his watch and he knew his pitiful social security check would no longer support him.

Finally, the tumblers clicked and the lock submitted to the polished steel. Abram, moving a little faster now, bent over the prone form. He forgot about Billy standing beside him as he felt for a pulse.

The heel of Billy's size-13 boot landed squarely on Abram's right temple, driven with all the force 240 pounds of beer-enhanced physique could muster. It was enough. Abram's head, too close to the frame of the cell's beds, smashed into the metal upright and the old man dropped to the floor like a hundred pounds of chicken feed landing in the bed of a pickup.

Billy wasted no time giving Abram a pat down, confiscating the old man's wallet and keys. A few loose coins and a pocketknife later, Billy shut the cell door behind him. He didn't bother to check Abram's pulse.

What difference did it make whether they stuck him with one, two, or three murders?

The death penalty didn't discriminate and the state of Mississippi could only kill him one time anyway.

CHAPTER 32

Ed Hebert's head throbbed unmercifully. The little man inside wanted out and he pounded with a vengeance. The four aspirin taken earlier served only to scale back the internal intruder's activity. The little man still wanted out and Ed contemplated another handful of pills, but decided against it. He suspected a concussion, but refused to get it checked. He deserved it. Letting that college boy get the best of him.

The vile sanitized smell of the hospital waiting room helped very little. Earlier, a custodian rolling a bucket of dingy chemical-filled mop water, spent a few minutes swishing the waiting room grime to a different area of the floor. As far as Ed could tell, other than an exercise in shifting dirt and looking busy, the purpose had been to fill the air with the sinus-clearing odor of ammonia. Might as well shoot for the aroma of cleanliness if not the appearance.

Ed, worried about Abram, paced the floor and waited.

That old man better not die!

They found Abram an hour ago locked inside the cell with the dead prisoner. Billy Blanchert, driving Abram's beat up old pickup, had at least a three-hour head start. Ed wasn't worried though. The Mississippi, Louisiana, and Alabama state police had all been notified. A description of the truck and its plate number hit the wire minutes after they found Abram.

For now, he'd play the waiting game. He could do little else at the time. Ed sank into one of the uncomfortable vinyl chairs in the emergency waiting room, laid his head back, and closed his eyes.

"Ed? Are you alright?" Dr. Nesbit's hand tapped his shoulder. He must have dozed off.

Ed tried his best to wake up. Dr. Nesbit, a little blurry at first, came into focus. "Yeah. I'm fine." Ed rubbed his eyes with his hands. "I just need a little rest."

"You really should let me look at you, Ed. You know you've probably got a concussion."

"And what would you do about it if I did, Doc?"

"You would need to get some rest and take it easy."

"Well, there's no point in checking me out then, because I don't have time to rest." Ed stood up, suddenly remembering why he was there. "How's Abram?"

"He'll be fine." Dr. Nesbit removed his cloth shoe covers revealing a pair of red sneakers. "We put a few stitches in his head, and he'll need to lay around a few days, but he should recover completely. That's one tough old man."

"Thanks, Doc." The relief showed on Ed's face. He thrust out a hand. "I appreciate everything. Now I've got to get to work. I've got two fugitives to catch."

"Ed? Before you go I've got something you need to see."

"What is it?"

"Follow me." Nesbit turned and headed back into the emergency room surgical area. Ed obediently trudged along behind him. His feet felt like they were encased in cement.

Nesbit stopped beside a sheet-draped gurney and pulled the covering back, revealing the contents. A man's body, fortyish, sporting a neatly trimmed black mustache and goatee in sharp contrast to the blood drained face. The corpse looked vaguely familiar.

"Is that Tommy Robideaux?"

"Yes, but that's not what I wanted you to see."

Nesbit pulled the sheet off the man's legs, or what was left of them. Both legs were gone, torn off by some incredible force below the knees. Jagged shards of bone protruded from the mangled limbs. The sight had become all too familiar to Ed in recent days.

"The ambulance brought him in about two hours ago. He was DOA. Lost too much blood."

"Why'd they bring him here?"

"Believe it or not, when they found him he was alive. Looks like the wounds are a couple of days old but somehow he managed to get tourniquets on his legs and drag himself up onto Highway 39. The first vehicle that happened along was one of our ambulances. The boys brought him here stat, but it was too late."

"Why didn't you call me?"

Nesbit looked at him wryly. "We did, Ed. You were out of pocket. In fact, I think our phone call caused the dispatcher to find Abram."

Ed nodded. It had indeed been a hectic night. He rubbed his temples. "Who could do this type of thing, Doc?"

"I don't know, but I've got someone you need to talk to." Nesbit walked back to the nurse's station. "Will you page Grayson for me, please?"

Grayson soon appeared. The old janitor Ed noticed earlier.

"Grayson, this is Chief Hebert. Tell him what you told me."

Grayson, cutting his eyes back and forth, began. "Years ago, when they bought all that land to test them rockets, they bought my farm."

He paused for a moment, remembering. "It wasn't much of a place. Mostly swamp, but a few good acres to run some cows on, and it had been in my family for years."

He looked at Ed. "You know the government made us sell it to them. Told us we didn't have no choice. I guess they was right."

Grayson stopped and took a deep breath, sweat beaded his upper lip even in the cool of the emergency room. Ed allowed the old man's tale to unravel at his pace. "It all started then. There was a bunch of killings. Mostly cattle and such. But then people started getting killed too."

Grayson nodded his head in the direction of the gurney. "They was just like that one. Legs and arms all ripped off, if they found anything. Several people just disappeared."

He looked at Ed. "Them cops back then tried to pin it on

that college professor, but he never done it."

"Who do you think was responsible?"

"For a while, a bunch of us thought it was the government trying to make us sell. Scaring us, you know." Grayson's eyes took on a faraway look before focusing back on Ed. "But that ain't what it was. And there ain't no who to it. It's a what."

The old man's eyes looked haunted. Grayson leaned against the counter, his wrinkled face saddened. "The government woke it up then, Mr. Hebert. And somebody done woke it up again."

CHAPTER 33

Nathan glanced around Kevin's Spartan apartment looking for some clue as to why Jake insisted this man could help them.

What can he do to help?

Kevin looked more like a biker than the stereotypical preacher. The long hair, the teardrop tattoos and the muscled physique didn't fit the mold.

Nathan's inspection of Kevin's apartment didn't assuage his fears either. A sword, nearly six feet long and burnished to a mirror sheen, leaned in a corner by the doorway as casually as similar locations in most homes sported a collection of umbrellas.

Nathan barely noticed the tattered, broken down couch and a duct-taped recliner, both ready for curb side pick up, that lined the walls. However, along with the monstrous sword, the solid oak casket in the middle of the living room certainly posed some interesting questions. Jake appeared nonplused by the unusual home furnishing, but the *Dark Shadows* motif unnerved Nathan.

Don't most people have coffee tables? Not coffin tables?

Nathan's face must have exposed his concern because Kevin, glancing his direction, volunteered. "I sleep in it."

Nathan recoiled from the statement as Kevin offered more explanation. "This life is temporal. I don't ever want to forget that." The big man lifted the lid on the coffin. "Spending every night inside this box is a constant reminder of mortality."

Nathan would have looked for the hidden camera if his situation hadn't been so serious. Kat, kidnapped and in danger, could expect no help from them. Two lunatics, and a fugitive from justice, who were fast running out of options.

What could they hope to do?

Nathan plopped down on the decrepit couch. He'd failed Kat.

Kevin seated himself in the recliner and turned to Jake.

"It's good to see you, Jake. But I know there's a reason for you coming here."

"I needed an expert on voodoo, Kevin, and you're the only one I know that is not a practitioner."

Jake pulled the scrap of paper with Nathan's replication of the crude drawings in Kat's apartment from his wallet and handed it to Kevin. Nathan, skeptical yet hopeful that Kevin might be able to provide some clue, watched the big man. The massive beard and long hair masked most of Kevin's facial expressions, but Nathan thought he saw the man's brow furrow, with concern or curiosity he didn't know.

"Where was this?"

"It was on my wife's living room wall. Above the door."

Realizing Kevin didn't know the full story, Nathan gave him a quick rundown of what had happened that night. From Nathan's viewpoint, Kevin had gone from lunatic to their best hope of finding Kat.

Why hadn't Jake told him the man was a voodoo expert?

Kevin studied the paper. A small stick figure appeared to be on top of a mountain, or maybe an erupting volcano. Lines emanated away from the mountain, toward the stick man. A primitive knife, or possibly a cross, hung above both images. Kevin held up the sheet of paper. "What color was the paint?"

Nathan realized he'd left out that crucial detail. He swallowed the lump in his throat. "It was blood. Not paint."

Kevin didn't appear surprised when he looked up at both men. "Then it's bad. I've never seen these symbols before but blood always means sacrifice. They intend to kill her."

Nathan's stomach churned. He felt sick. "That kind of stuff still happens?"

"You hear whispers about it." Kevin stood and paced the floor of the tiny living room. "As far as I can tell, it's a pretty rare occurrence, and always rumored to be some illegal from one of the freighters. That way no one knows they ever existed."

"But why Kat?"

"That's what we have to ask ourselves." Kevin stopped his

pacing, his eyes boring into Nathan. "What's special about your wife? Why did they want her?"

Jake, an odd haunted look on his face, spoke. "I'm afraid I can answer that. I mentioned part of this to Nathan and Kat the other day."

He continued haltingly, struggling to verbalize his fears. "Kat's a Native American. Her grandmother once told me she was a descendent of the lost Biloxi tribe. Legend maintains the Biloxi worshipped a river god who controlled the Chinchuba. No one agrees on what the Chinchuba was or is. Some say a disease. Some say a creature of some sort."

"Get to the point." Nathan knew that Kat's time was running out.

Jake shot a hard glance his direction. "I believe the Chinchuba is a luecistic crocodile."

"What does this have to do with Kat?"

"In time, whelp. Now, shut up." Jake clinched his jaws to control his temper. "There's a part of the legend I haven't shared with the 'Professor' here. A sacrifice, from the Biloxi tribe, is said to appease the Chinchuba."

"Do you really believe that crap, Jake?"

"It doesn't matter whether I do or not." Jake pinned Nathan to the couch with his eyes. "All that matters is that whoever kidnapped Kat believes it."

Nathan realized that Jake was right. He'd been an idiot. It didn't matter whether he believed the legend or not as long as some psycho out there believed in it.

Kevin, silent until now, spoke. "There's a parallel legend in the Acadian culture. The 'ghost gator' is rumored to be controllable by voodoo. The ritual is said to involve the sacrifice of a 'goat without horns.'"

"What does that mean?"

Kevin looked at both men. "A newborn baby."

Nathan jumped from his seat and grabbed the sheet of paper from Kevin, peering intently at the drawings. A low moan escaped his lips. He handed the paper back to Kevin.

"Kat's pregnant."

It was a simple statement, but the knowledge gave the drawing new meaning. The mountain was not a mountain. Nor was it a volcano. It was the mound of a pregnant woman's stomach. The stick figure, a child, had been surgically removed from the womb. The simple pencil rendering bore an uncanny resemblance to a primitive and ghastly c-section.

* * *

Humsinger's hands shook so badly he could barely hold a cup. No matter, the whiskey ceased to have the dulling effect he sought and the cup was empty. His bloodshot eyes bore mute testimony to the lack of sleep and his wounds had begun to fester for lack of attention. The bloody bandage on his arm had yet to be changed and he didn't care. Days of not bathing or changing clothes left him indistinguishable from a number of other French Quarter homesteaders.

A well-dressed woman, still attractive in her early forties, pulled a ten-dollar bill from her purse and stuffed it in the cup when she walked by. Humsinger took the bill with his free hand and pocketed it, not saying a word. He watched her nose wrinkle when she passed, offended by the stench of his body odor.

His right hand slipped into his pocket and clutched the small white carving stolen from Harlin's apartment. Reassuring himself that it was still there. For two days he'd searched every possible location for the stone. Starting with Kat's apartment, then Nathan's, and then finally Harlin's. That stupid yowling cat finally led him to the stone stuffed in the cat food sack. Humsinger sat on the tiny kitchen floor and wept when he found the artifact.

He no longer cared about anything except deliverance. The stone in his pocket was the last piece of the puzzle, and relinquishing it to Doctor John would hopefully buy his pardon from the witch doctor. At the very least, maybe the shaman would kill him, ending the mental torment and granting him sweet release. He preferred death to the status quo. Or prison, his other likely alternative.

The sun blasted the narrow streets, squeezing gallons of moisture from every living creature in the Quarter. Humsinger included. He plodded on in the heat and humidity, followed the directions to the letter, found himself in front of Doctor John's compound. Dreading to go in, and yet hopeful that his services would no longer be needed.

Taking a deep breath, he steeled himself against the known, opened the gate and entered the narrow plant-lined corridor leading to Doctor John's inner sanctum. The oppressive heat followed him like an obedient puppy unnoticed by its master. Humsinger's head felt light and he could barely place one foot in front of the other.

Humsinger reached the small courtyard, strangely bright after the darkness of the tunnel. He clawed at his collar trying to unbutton his already-loose shirt.

He needed oxygen!

Earlier he had prayed for death, but now he realized he really didn't want to die. He stumbled and fell, still careful to protect the stone carving. The precious stone carving, so much like the one he'd killed Crawley over.

Humsinger, his face pressed against the brick cobbles, gasped for breath. A small parakeet with bright green plumage hopped in front of him. The last time he'd seen one of those was in Australia on a collecting trip.

Why couldn't he have been satisfied with that life?

Was this it? Was he dying?

Neil Crawley, Specky Vore, and Harlin Radkin all flashed through his mind in various stages of decomposition.

Who knew how many others had already been killed? And how many more would die as a result of something he put in motion?

The oxygen-starved Brian Humsinger lapsed into

unconsciousness under the watchful eye of the big voodoo priest.

"Retrieve the stone." Doctor John commanded. Quin pulled the small white carving from Humsinger's pocket and handed it to the big man. Doctor John's eyes glinted with pleasure.

The final piece!

Now he could go. His destiny awaited him. The power that would soon be at his command intoxicated him. Only a few minor preparations and the sacrifice could take place.

Doctor John nodded at Humsinger. "Load him in the van with the others."

Quin nodded and grasped the filthy Humsinger by his feet. Unceremoniously, he dragged the older man across to the waiting van, his head bouncing across the cobbled courtyard. Quin opened the doors and hefted him in, depositing him squarely on the lifeless form of Madame Jean whom he'd loaded yesterday. Surprisingly she hadn't started to stink yet.

He started to close the door and then remembered something. The dragon's blood stick in his pocket. Quin removed the *gris gris* and threw it on Madame Jean's body.

A hundred dollars wasted!

The toothless old hag hadn't helped him at all. Her magic was worthless compared to Doctor John. He might be a slave, but at least he was still alive. That was more than he could say for her.

And Humsinger wasn't too far behind!

He shut the van door and waited. Doctor John would bring the girl soon and they would leave. Quin knew that the day after tomorrow, when the sun rose over the banks of the Singing River, Dr. Kat Abnaki would provide Doctor John with a child sacrifice.

Quin stifled an involuntary shudder and glanced around to see if Doctor John witnessed his weakness. The witch doctor had already gone back inside his compound. But Quin's actions hadn't gone unnoticed. A pair of eyes, invisible through the courtyard's foliage, retreated from the parapet three stories above.

CHAPTER 34

Billy Blanchert propelled the small craft with a long pole, expertly planting one end on the muddy river bottom and thrusting, all while maintaining a precarious balance standing at one end of the pirogue. He ditched Abram's old pickup after the fuel pump went out, foiling his planned escape.

He'd steal a better truck next time.

The lightly traveled dirt road he'd been on led across the Louisiana line straight into the middle of nowhere. He knew all these back roads far better than any stupid cop and would have been home free if the truck hadn't conked out.

Billy found the pirogue behind a ramshackle old fishing cabin and thought of his appropriation as liberating it from the oppression of its current owners. He chuckled at the thought.

Sounded like something Jesse or Al would say on CNN.

The 14-foot wooden boat slowed his timetable down considerably, but in the land of the blind the one-eyed man was king. And he had no other options. So he poled the pirogue closer to his new destination, the Mississippi coastal waterway.

The small tributary would soon run into the Singing River, and he could pick up the pace a little by staying in the current. With luck, he'd make the coast by tomorrow afternoon and he could hop a boat out of here. This time he'd lose himself in South America. Hole up with some young and tender senorita and let her wait on him hand and foot.

He'd hidden the truck well enough that it shouldn't be found for a few days. By hitting the starter with the truck in gear, he'd managed to inch the decrepit vehicle around behind the old fishing cabin. Fortunately no one lived there, except maybe on the weekend.

Billy hit the river about midday and the water's depth forced him to switch to the nearly useless broken handled paddle he found in the front of the boat. He could use it for a rudder and little else. But with the swift current, due to the recent rains up north, he needed little else.

Another time and another place and Billy would have a hook in the water, enjoying a lazy float down river, trying to roust out a few fish. But the pirogue came unequipped with fishing gear, a fact he regretted when he passed the occasional other boat carrying anglers one direction or the other.

The afternoon waned when he finally spotted Harmon's Landing, a little one-horse store carrying an assortment of bait, tackle and beer. All the necessities. Billy started to drift on past, but his stomach rumbled disapproval with that decision so at the last minute he banked the boat and clambered ashore.

Billy hadn't seen Dan Harmon in ten years and doubted the old man still owned the place anyway. After a cursory look around the outside to make sure no one else was there, Billy mounted the rickety wooden steps and went inside. Old man Harmon sat behind the counter watching a 25-year-old black and white television.

"Howdy, Billy." Just like he'd been in here yesterday. "Been a while since I seen you."

Harmon smiled, revealing what was undoubtedly the worst set of dentures Billy had ever seen.

The old man looks like a horse!

The teeth appeared longer than normal, and slightly protruding, and were a far cry whiter than Dan Harmon's blackened teeth of ten years ago.

"Hey, Harmon. How you been?"

"Pretty good, Billy." He bared his teeth again. "Got me some new dentures and I'm trying to break em in."

"I bet that's a pain."

"Worse than a man thinks." Harmon popped the dentures out of his mouth and took a pocketknife to them, whittling away at some unseen irritant. He looked up and smiled, now revealing raw red gums. "What can I do you for, Billy?"

"Why don't you make me a couple of them bologna sandwiches and gimme a six pack of beer."

Finished with his project, the old man replaced his new teeth, and grabbed an open loaf of bread. He reached into the plastic bag, snagged four slices of the bread, and spread them on the crusty countertop in front of him. "Mustard or mayonnaise?"

Billy, eating a candy bar and trying to decide whether Harmon had taken the time to wipe his hands on his dirty jeans, mouthed. "Both."

Harmon pasted liberal amounts of both condiments on every surface and reached for the bologna. Momentarily sidetracked by a wayward fly, he killed the pest and then rummaged around in the cooler a few seconds before yelling toward the back of the store. "Vera! We got any bologna?"

"Yeah. Just a minute."

He turned and winked at Billy, "I got me a new wife." Conspiratorially, he continued. "Traded in the old one for a younger model."

Vera appeared with a fresh stick of bologna. Billy took one look at Harmon's younger model and he almost lost his appetite. She sported a long, coarse ponytail that looked like it would fit better on the north end of a south bound horse. Too much time in the sun had turned her skin copper colored with the consistency of poorly-tanned leather. Apparently, Vera had decided she didn't need hormones either. The younger model sprouted hair in places women didn't need hair, including a few wiry strands visible above the low cut tank top.

Vera smiled at Billy revealing a row of rotted teeth that stuck out like one of those hairless mole rats on the animal shows. She slammed the stick of bologna on the counter and gave an exaggerated wink. "Here's the pig snouts and lips you wanted."

If he'd been Harmon, he would have spent the orthodontia budget on the old lady. Billy suppressed a shudder as the hideous creature ran her tongue over her hair-covered upper lip and leered at him. Obviously an invitation, Vera turned and sashayed toward the back room, her knee length go-go boots clicking on the wood floor. Hypnotically, Billy's gaze followed the woman's cottage cheese thighs out of sight.

Harmon caught him looking and grinned, proud of his new choppers, and his new wife. "Now you know why I couldn't resist."

Billy suppressed another shudder and held his tongue. The old coot needed glasses worse than he did teeth. A woman that ugly might not could help it, but she could stay home. His recently departed male cellmate looked better than Vera.

Harmon slapped two thick slices of bologna and two pieces of cheese on each sandwich. Finished, he stuffed each sandwich into a zip lock bag and sealed it shut.

A pocket calculator appeared and he tallied up the damage. "Let's see. Two sandwiches, a six pack of beer, and one candy bar. That'll be ten dollars and 75 cents." The old man winked at Billy. "I won't charge you no sales tax. You don't tell the governor and I won't either."

Billy threw a twenty that he'd pilfered from Abram's wallet on the counter. "Gimme another candy bar and, in case anybody comes asking, you ain't seen me."

Old man Harmon snatched the twenty and grinned again, revealing the pearly white horse teeth. "Seen who?"

"That's what I'm talkin' about." Billy grabbed his sandwiches and turned to leave. "See you, Harmon."

Billy didn't see Dan Harmon pick up the phone after he walked out, but he did see the Chevy van pull past the Harmon's Landing. Right down the rutted dirt road leading to nowhere. Fishing, drinking beer, or smoking dope; it didn't really matter to Billy what they were up to. He was ready to make a little better time than the river offered and that van would do nicely.

He popped a beer and downed it in three quick gulps, retrieved a sandwich and devoured it in a similar fashion, and then started off down the road following the van. The road ended in a couple of miles at a bend in the river, but Billy didn't want to risk missing the van if it turned around and came back out.

Billy popped the top on another beer and began to whistle a tune as he walked.

It was a beautiful afternoon.

* * *

"We don't have much time then." Nathan, frantic over Kat, pleaded. "We've got to do something fast. Jake? Kevin? One of you please come up with something soon or . . . ."

Nathan's voice trailed off. He couldn't bring himself to finish the sentence.

Kevin paced the floor of his tiny apartment. Who could have kidnapped Kat?

He knew most of the practitioners of voodoo in New Orleans, but knew very few elsewhere.

Who could he contact to provide him with information about a voodoo priest or priestess in southern Mississippi? One capable of human sacrifice?

The silence, broken only by the muffled voice of New Orleans night life, contributed to the ominous tone. Kat was in real danger and they could do nothing about it. All three men, lost in their own thoughts, searched desperately for an idea. Nathan glanced toward Kevin, his head bowed and his eyes closed. He appeared to be praying. Nathan sighed. They didn't have time for this.

The knock, timid at first and then louder, fixed all eyes on the door. Kevin opened it slowly.

"Well, come in." Kevin's voice revealed an unexpected tenderness for such a big imposing man. The girl, no more than ten or twelve years old, entered the apartment. Seeing the coffin, she stopped a few steps into the living room and appeared ready to run. Kevin noted her chagrin. "Don't worry about that thing. It's just furniture."

Fear cloaked the small child like an oversized garment. She stood in the middle of the living room quivering, very near to an emotional breakdown.

"They said you could help me." She managed to squeak out. "They said you have good magic."

Kevin, his concern for the child evident, spoke. "I don't have magic, honey. But I will help you. Just tell me what you need."

The girl, still frightened, glanced back over her shoulder at the closed front door.

"Doctor John took Madame Jean three days ago." Tears erupted and streamed down the small child's cheeks. "I don't know what to do."

Kevin knew Doctor John. Who didn't in the Quarter? If he'd taken Madame Jean three days ago, Kevin could do nothing for her now.

"Do you know if she's in his hotel?"

"They were until today, but they left. I watched his place ever since he took her, trying to find some way to help her." The girl's sobs interrupted her account. Kevin patted the child on the back to comfort her.

"Do you know where they went?"

"No. Doctor John and that man Quin Laroche loaded her into a van. Her and another man and woman. And then they left."

Nathan came off the couch. "Did you say Quin?"

The girl jumped, startled by Nathan's sudden reaction. "Yes sir."

The name on the fishing pole. It wasn't Qun, it was Quin. How many Quins could there be?

"What did she look like? The woman?"

"She was small." The girl stammered. "Pretty and very dark with black hair. Probably a coonie."

Nathan looked at the other men. "That's Kat."

Kevin resumed the questioning. "Now think hard. Do you have any idea where they might be going?"

"No sir." Her tide of tears began to slow. "Do you have something to eat?"

Kevin rounded up some cheese and crackers while Nathan and

Jake discussed the new development. He gave Darius, his friend and cab driver, a quick call and asked him to take the child over to Karyn's place. Kevin knew Karyn would watch the girl and that she was off work tonight. He'd seen her at church earlier.

Darius picked the child up, but not before she exacted a promise from Kevin that he would do everything he could to find Madame Jean. Kevin rejoined the men in his living room.

"Any luck?" Jake and Nathan had yet to come up with a plan on how to find Kat, and Madame Jean.

"It's like looking for a needle in a haystack." Jake blurted.

Nathan looked up sharply. "What did you say?"

Jake, a perplexed look on his face, repeated. "It's like looking for a needle in a haystack?"

Nathan's face expressed his hope. "That's it! We've got to get to Stennis."

* * *

Ed's radio crackled on. "Ed? You there?"

He picked up the receiver before the dispatcher could yell again. "Yeah, I'm here. What's up?"

He'd gone home and slept a couple of hours, but his headache refused to abate, so he went back out on patrol hoping something would break in at least one case. He was in luck.

"Dan Harmon called in. He just saw Billy Blanchert. Says he's headed down towards the Brown Hole on the Singing River."

Ed turned on the lights and siren. Billy wouldn't get away this time. Not after he'd killed a man in Ed's jail.

CHAPTER 35

Billy peered through the underbrush at the van parked under a huge live oak. The river's normally sluggish path lay just beyond a small knoll and on the far side of a small thicket of cane. For the last several minutes he'd watched the van and seen no one.

The van's occupants must have gone down to the river. He waited a few more minutes, listening for voices, and finished his last beer. Hearing nothing, he decided to make his move and get the van.

Hopefully it would be better than the crappy pickup he'd stolen off Abram.

Billy stepped out of the woods and strolled to the van. If anyone caught him now they couldn't accuse him of anything. Until he reached the van. He scanned the small meadow while he walked and, satisfied no one was near, opened the driver's side door. He should have taken the time to look inside the van before he slid behind the wheel. And he didn't have time afterwards. Billy's time was up. Doctor John, watching the man approach from the small tinted window in the back, was waiting for him. Billy, normally the predator, had become the prey.

Billy didn't see the long sinuous arm or the flash of the razor sharp blade. He merely felt a gentle tug at his throat and a warm sensation spreading down the front of his chest.

What is that red spurting on the windshield? On the inside?

His mind, already slowing from the alcohol and now the blood loss, finally registered. Recognition hit a second before the severed jugular pumped the last bit of vital fluid into Billy's lap. He managed to turn slightly, trying to get a look at his attacker, before his eyes glassed over. Kat witnessed the entire incident with one of Quin's strong hands clamped over her mouth. She bit down hard on her tongue attempting to scream. Quin relinquished his grip and she found her voice. She screamed.

Doctor John ignored her ear piercing vocalizations and continued his task. With a few quick strokes of the blade he removed Billy's head and cradled it in his lap. The darkened van did not hide the big man's glee as he admired his new trophy. Kat felt herself fading out as the witch doctor began to remove the skin from his grisly prize.

"Tie her up and go build a fire." Doctor John commanded Quin. "I will need some hot sand to finish my task."

The finished product, Billy's shrunken head, would make a fine addition to his collection. Doctor John didn't have one that was partially bald.

* * *

Jake and Kevin crowded around the map table in the remote sensing room at Stennis listening to Nathan explain the operation.

"Okay, guys, here's what we're doing. ADEOS II is our dedicated bird. ADEOS stands for 'Advanced Earth Observation Satellite.' The II is because she's a second generation.

ADEOS II carries an optical sensor that observes reflected solar radiation. She orbits frequently enough that we can get a decent picture of environmental changes on a minute scale."

He paused to see if they were following him.

Jake, quick to become impatient, asked. "Yeah. We get it. But how is that going to help us?"

"What we're interested in is the reflected infrared radiation. We can use ADEOS to identify something as minute as plant stress. A stressed plant gives off a different heat signature than a healthy one."

"So?"

Nathan continued to talk while opening several of the map drawers. "Harlin identified illegal dig sites using ADEOS. The other day when I was trying to remember where he might have gone I looked at several photos."

He spread two large photos on the map table. "Check out these two." Nathan pointed to spot on the map still marked with a sticky note. "This one is from about a month ago."

Next, he pointed to another one. "This one is from a week ago."

Jake and Kevin studied the photos while Nathan continued. "See the difference? The most recent photo shows where someone did some digging since the shot from a month ago. See how it shows up as a different color on the spectrum."

Jake shrugged. "Okay, so someone dug a hole. Big deal. How does this help us find Kat?"

"This didn't click with me the other day, but the newer one has a much larger heat signature than it should have." Nathan pointed at the photo. "And see how it's separated by a band of cooler earth?"

He looked at both men. "I've been out to that site and there's only one hole in the ground. Do you know what that means?"

Jake knew. He peered at the second heat signature on the newer photo. The familiar shape, suddenly recognizable, leapt off the table. "Nathan? Did you notice the shape?"

Nathan looked at the photo again. It was true. The aerial remote sensing shot revealed a shape not unlike a huge alligator.

"Hand me those calipers." Nathan carefully measured the object and placed the caliper against the scale printed at the bottom of the photo. His mouth dropped open.

The creature was at least 50 feet long!

Shocked into action, Nathan scrambled for the computer, explaining as he moved. "ADEOS II completed another pass overhead almost an hour ago. I've got to download those photos and then we've got to find that same heat signature."

"You two pull the aerial photos from those drawers while I download the most recent data. We'll have to compare the two in order to find it."

The task was daunting and time was running out for Kat. Nathan attacked the keyboard with fervor.

Kat's life depended almost solely on him, and everything Humsinger had taught him in the last two years.

Kevin, quiet until now, spoke. "Can you only download the ones near water? That's where we'll find it."

Nathan rejoiced inside. Kevin's one comment could save them hours.

CHAPTER 36

Kat tested the rope used to bind her to the large oak tree. Daylight succumbed to darkness and she knew her time was growing short. The mosquitoes exacted their gallon of blood, but she paid them little mind. The three bodies stacked like firewood to her right, one of them headless, foretold her future. She would die soon if she did not escape. And her child with her.

I have to think of something! Think!

During the afternoon, Doctor John left her alone, busy with the task of removing that poor man's skin from his skull. The witch doctor finished his gruesome chore nearly an hour ago and placed the leering skull atop a nearby fire ant mound. Kat could see it all too clearly about 20 feet to her left. His next step had been to scrape the flesh away from the skin, just like she'd seen her grandmother do with a raccoon or mink hide.

Sickened, Kat watched Doctor John meticulously suture all the skin's orifices closed. The mouth, eyes, nostrils, and ears were all sewn shut with tiny stitches. His skill level rivaled that of many plastic surgeons. Now he was in the process of filling the skin sack with hot sand. He looked up from his task and smiled at her, revealing the golden fangs.

Fear kept her eyes open. Even the grotesque sight in front of her was better than her imagination of what might happen. Her mind raced as she fought the rising panic.

She had to remain calm! That was her only hope.

She tested the rope again. It was no use. The man called Quin made sure the bonds were secure when he tied her up, even while mouthing the words 'I'm sorry.'

A rustling sound to Kat's right caused her to steal a glance that direction. One of the bodies sat upright. She thought they were all dead. He was an older man with both hands now pressed against his temples, yet he looked strangely familiar. He turned to face her direction and Kat gasped.

Dr. Humsinger!

Doctor John looked up from his grisly creation and then stood and walked away toward the river leaving them alone. He appeared unconcerned about the new development. Humsinger watched the witch doctor's retreating back and then stared at Kat, trying to focus.

"Dr. Humsinger! Untie me. Quickly."

Brian Humsinger, mentor and boss, recognized Kat and started crying. "I can't Kat."

"Please! Dr. Humsinger, you have to help me! He intends to kill me!"

"I'm sorry, Kat. I can't." Humsinger choked back the sobs. "It's all my fault. I got greedy."

"Just untie me!" Kat's whisper became a coarse command.

"I physically can't." Humsinger nodded in the direction of Doctor John. "He controls me."

Kat, near hysteria, could not comprehend. "What are you talking about?"

Humsinger, able to stop the flow of tears, began. "I was robbing graves and this sadist found out. I don't know how. But somehow he can control my actions through voodoo. I don't understand it." "How could that happen?"

"The artifacts were priceless. Sapphires, rubies, emeralds. All huge stones carved for ceremonial purposes. I'd locate the sites with the aerial photos and send in a team of diggers to loot it."

Humsinger wiped his face on his shirtsleeve. "I lined up a buyer so I could subsidize my retirement. Doctor John found out and had me retrieve all the stones I'd sold."

"Did you kill Harlin?" Not that it really mattered, but Kat wanted to know for some reason.

His haunted eyes turned to Kat. "No. I didn't kill Harlin. I'm not sure what happened to him. But I killed a man in cold blood, Kat. I watched my body do it while my mind screamed at him to run. He was my buyer in Chicago. I can't live with what I've done, Kat. But I've tried to kill myself and can't. Doctor John won't let me." Humsinger's robotic statement chilled Kat. She knew the man had fallen over an emotional precipice.

Humsinger paused again and looked away. Kat could see his throat move as he swallowed. "And worst of all. I helped him kidnap you."

Brian Humsinger, a man Kat had looked up to, put his head in his hands and wept. Kat felt pity in spite of her predicament. She might die, but she would die proud, knowing she had not betrayed anyone.

* * *

Madame Jean's eyes fluttered open. Total blackness surrounded her. She blinked several times to focus her vision. The darkness remained.

Had she crossed over to the other side?

She moved her hand and felt the rough texture of carpet and smelled the strong scent of cinnamon.

Was she still in Doctor John's bathroom?

Careful to make no sound, Madame Jean tried to move. Her arms were constrained in some manner. Suddenly she realized she had been rolled up in the rug from Doctor John's bathroom. Beyond that she knew nothing. Madame Jean strained to hear something, anything that might provide her a clue as to her location.

Silence. Total silence.

Madame Jean attempted to move again and discovered she could inch her way toward the head of the carpet tube by slightly bending her knees and pushing herself along. If she cocked her head to one side, she could see the opening, a subtle difference in the shade of blackness. Slowly she wormed her way toward the opening.

The noise of cicadas welcomed her and she realized she must be outdoors. Where, she did not know. But Madame Jean knew one thing. Somehow she had managed to cheat death, and she was glad to be alive. Weak from lack of food, gums sore from the recent teeth extractions, and head throbbing from her near overdose, Madame Jean was glad to be alive.

The puffer fish toxin, used to create zombies, accomplished one of two things. It either killed the user, or it slowed their metabolism to the point where they appeared dead. She herself had never used it before, but had stumbled on the correct dosage for her body size.

Inch by inch Madame Jean worked her way toward freedom. Her head, now out of the carpet tube, rested on the headless corpse of Billy Blanchert. Surprised by nothing, she made a quick survey of her surroundings before continuing her task. A bank of coals from a campfire glowed orange in the dark night. An occasional flame escaped the glowing embers and made a run for freedom, only to be snuffed out by some unseen force.

Doctor John was nowhere in sight but to her left a man lay leaning against a huge oak tree. An older white man, sleeping fitfully. Madame Jean watched while the man battled the nightmarish demons that chased him in his dreams. Next to the man, a young lady lay bound to a tree. Her hands appeared to be tied behind her back while a hemp rope encircled her entire body, strapping her to the tree.

Satisfied no one watched, Madame Jean continued her quest for freedom, inching her way out of the carpet tube. In seconds, her hands and shoulders were free, allowing her to proceed with greater speed. Still cautious, still watching for Doctor John. A few more minutes and she would be free. The carpet tube was stiff enough that it did not collapse when she exited. Hopefully no one would miss her for a quite some time.

Madame Jean crawled to the safety of the nearest tree and stood up. Immediately dizzy, she stopped for a moment to recover her balance, and noticed the woman watching her. A silent pleading with mournful eyes for the same freedom she now possessed. Madame Jean held a finger to her lips for silence and made her cautious way to a position behind the woman's tree.

Doctor John's maniacal laugh pierced the night. The cicadas halted their music. Bullfrogs ceased their courting rituals and opted for silence. And Madame Jean froze behind the tree.

Now she could hear chanting. From a considerable distance though. Nervous about lingering any longer, she slid around the huge oak and untied the woman's bonds.

"Good luck." She whispered to the woman. "Give me a few minutes head start."

Madame Jean eased back behind the tree before standing. Doctor John laughed again, closer this time, and it provided her with renewed strength as her fear threatened to overtake her will. A few feet away she began to run, stumbling at first, but then gaining her balance rapidly. Distance was what she wanted.

Behind her, Kat mouthed a silent "thank you" as she listened to the receding footfalls. The chanting grew louder. Nearer. Kat could wait no longer. Humsinger's eyes searched her face, and he was rewarded with a cold stare. It would be impossible to forgive him for what he'd done to her and her unborn child.

With a final cold glance to Humsinger, she whispered. "Keep your mouth shut." And she jumped and ran. Kat ran like she'd never run before. Limbs slapped her face in the darkness and briars tore at her flesh. The thin nightshirt, ripped open by Doctor John, offered little protection. Her bare feet were quickly stone bruised and lacerated by the rocky path.

Kat didn't care. She was free. Somehow she found the road and picked up her pace, running even faster. Her lungs cried out for oxygen and Kat slowed her feverish pace. Lights from a car flickered on, catching her in the beams. Kat stumbled to a stop.

Please God! Don't let it be Doctor John.

Caught in the middle of the road, Kat darted to the side just as the flashing blue lights came on. She sank to her knees in relief and burst into tears. A uniformed officer approached.

"Ma'am? What's going on?" The small man, concern in his voice, could tell she hadn't been on a late night walk. Her nightshirt, now hanging in shreds, did little to cover her. Blood oozed from countless cuts and scratches and tears of relief streamed down her cheeks.

It was over. Kat stood, still silent, and watched in mute horror as Doctor John appeared behind the much smaller man. He'd made no sound, materializing out of the woods like a ghost. The witch doctor blew a fine powder in the officer's eyes when the cop turned to face Kat's nightmare. Doctor John flicked a metallic fingernail blade toward Ed's throat and Kat saw a thin line of blood appear. Stupefied, Kat could only watch and cry as the officer wilted in front of her, holding his throat as blood seeped out between his fingers.

The blue lights, still flashing on the police cruiser, reflected off Doctor John's golden fangs. He smiled, holding out his hand to her.

"Come. Soon it will be daybreak and time to meet your destiny.

CHAPTER 37

Nathan studied the handheld global positioning unit. Another mile and they would be there. He'd programmed the site coordinates before they left Stennis in a vehicle appropriated from the chain link fence surrounding the motor pool with a pair of bolt cutters.

He hoped and prayed they'd picked the right target. Even with eliminating all landlocked sites it had taken them hours to sort through the remaining satellite images. After all, most of south Mississippi and south Louisiana was near water. The search yielded two possible locations and Nathan feared they would not have time to check them both. Kat's time was running out.

Nathan rounded a bend in the road just as the sun peeked over the horizon. A portion of the orange orb was barely visible through the trees. His anxiety mounting, he pressed the accelerator even harder. The four-wheel drive vehicle bounced down the rutted road picking up speed. They sideswiped a tree and ripped the passenger side mirror loose. Nobody said a word. Who cared?

A straight stretch of the road offered even greater opportunity for speed and Nathan watched the speedometer reach 70 miles per hour, on a road designed for 20 mile per hour speeds, before he had to hit the brakes to round the next bend.

There was no time to stop. Nathan had the truck going well over 50 miles an hour when the Bay St. Louis police cruiser appeared in front of them completely blocking the narrow dirt road. Reflexively Nathan swerved the truck, barely missing a man's body lying in plain sight behind the car.

The truck plowed over about a dozen small trees, each no more than three or four inches in diameter. The trees, while totaling the truck, absorbed much of the impact. Nathan, his hands tight on the wheel, cushioned the collision shock with his arms and shoulders. Kevin Croix, his hands on the dash, managed a similar feat on the passenger side.

Jake did not fare as well. He managed to raise his arms only slightly before his head slammed into the dash and knocked him cold. A small stream of blood trickled down his face. Nathan felt for a pulse.

"He's alive."

"Come on. We'll take care of him later. Our time is about to run out. I can feel it."

Kevin wasted no time in getting out and grabbed the large sword from the back of the truck and ran up the road. They would check on the body later.

* * *

Kat lay spread eagle in the center of several animal skins, her arms and legs tethered with rawhide strips to four pegs driven into the riverbank. Quin removed the last remnant of her tattered nightshirt when he tied her down. Trance-like, the man had scrubbed the mud and grime from her body, preparing her for the sacrifice.

The four stone carvings surrounded another small skin not too far away. Each stone lay on a small platform with a lit candle. One green, one red, one blue, one white. Each candle, the color of the corresponding stone. The sun climbed ever higher until its light was visible over the eastern tree line.

Kat's tears were all gone. She could cry no more. Instead she prayed. Prayed for forgiveness and salvation, either in this life or the next. She believed in the afterlife, but didn't know what it would be like.

Doctor John approached, wearing a shirt for the first time. In another time and another place, Kat would have commented on the beauty of the soft leather garment. Fine beadwork decorated the front and back adorned with remarkable images of the luecistic crocodile like the one in Jake's pen.

What happened to Nathan and Jake? Have they been killed?

Kat, unwilling to give up, tested her bonds one more time as Doctor John strode over chanting all the while. A bejeweled knife glistened in the morning sun. Kat shuddered involuntarily. A gag in her mouth prevented her from screaming but threatened to choke her.

Doctor John stood over her. He knelt, the dagger lifted high, and then stopped. A strange look crossed his face when he noticed Kat's tiny tattoo. He studied the multicolored butterfly, no more than one inch across, tattooed just above her bikini line. Gotten in a moment of stupidity as a rebellious teenager, Kat rarely thought about it any more.

Kat didn't understand the significance. A similar small butterfly, symbolic of the soul winging its way to eternity, had recently been painted in blood on Doctor John's face. The woman in the cemetery, whose heart he had eaten to gain her strength, had cursed him.

Would the mother of the goat without horns be allowed to live? How could it be possible? The Old Ones could not lie!

He must kill her quickly. Doctor John raised the dagger high and began to thrust it down towards Kat's heart. Kat's body tensed, and she closed her eyes, waiting for the pain.

Preoccupied with the tattoo, Doctor John didn't notice Kevin and Nathan's breathless arrival. Nathan, lighter and faster than Kevin, never slowed his pace. While still at a full run, he reached for the gun in his waistband that he'd taken from the cop in Kat's apartment.

The gun was gone!

Nathan had no time to waste looking for a weapon. He launched himself into the air, executing a perfect tackle and hitting Doctor John in the chest just as the dagger started down.

The adrenaline rush kept him from feeling the blade as it entered the fleshy part of his shoulder.

The blow knocked Doctor John's grip on the knife loose and both men rolled on the ground, the knife still protruding from Nathan's back. Doctor John came up fast as Kevin hurtled in, the six-foot sword held high, a mighty blow swinging to intersect the witch doctor. Had it connected, the blow would have easily cleaved Doctor John neatly in two.

Doctor John, agile for such a big man, ducked the blow and came up underneath Kevin, allowing Kevin's momentum to propel him towards the river. The huge bouncer tucked his head and rolled, losing his grip on the sword as he tumbled down the embankment. Kevin rapidly recovered and charged up the slight hill toward Doctor John.

Doctor John smiled in anticipation as he waited for Kevin to reach him. He recognized the man from New Orleans. A worthy adversary whose head would make a fine addition to his collection. The long locks and the massive full beard would make the shrunken head look like a hairy ball.

As soon as Kevin came within reach of Doctor John's long legs, he launched a roundhouse kick aimed at Kevin's head. Kevin ducked and swept the witch doctor's leg on past with his left forearm before quickly stepping in closer and landing two powerful jabs to Doctor John's kidneys.

Doctor John winced but continued to smile as he brought his right elbow back around and slammed it into Kevin's head. Kevin staggered and threatened to go down but regained his footing as the witch doctor sprang at him. He feigned another stumble just as Doctor John leaped his direction and came up under him with his head in the shaman's ribs. Kevin felt the bones give but still felt no difference in the witch doctor's fury as he pummeled Kevin's back and kidneys with ham-sized fists of hardened steel.

Kevin, knowing the punishing blows would rapidly siphon his strength, threw Doctor John forcibly off of him. Doctor John landed on his back, but was on his feet so fast that Kevin began to wonder if the man was hopped up on drugs. He seemed to feel no pain.

The two gladiators circled one another warily, each respecting the other's strengths. Kevin faked a left jab and followed with two fast rights, all neatly blocked by Doctor John. Purposefully, he left himself slightly open after the last punch and Doctor John complied with his plan and threw a massive right hand at Kevin's face. He allowed the punch to connect but pulled himself away to reduce the force of the blow. Kevin faked a knockout fall from the punch and landed on the ground with one hand supporting him as he swept Doctor John's legs out from under him with a powerful sweeping kick.

The witch doctor, not anticipating the ploy, landed flat on his back, the wind knocked out of his lungs. Kevin wasted no time. He rolled to pin the big man's arms with his own massive legs and grasped Doctor John's throat in his hands. Kevin's thumbs pressed into the big man's trachea for the kill. Doctor John, panic in his eyes, bucked with his lower body. The man's power was incredible.

He threw Kevin over his head and back down the embankment. This time Kevin landed in the center of the four stones. The animal skins did little to cushion his fall as the force of the fall knocked the wind from his lungs. He recovered rapidly though and scrambled to his feet, gasping for breath, just as the river water parted and the giant luecistic crocodile surged forth.

Kevin, his back to the river, did not see it coming. His sword, lost earlier and now laying only a few feet away, drew his attention. Kevin felt the water hit his back seconds before the ghostly reptile clamped down on his leg and retreated toward the river, towing the big man to his watery grave. Kevin clawed frantically at the ground, managing to grab a small bush, only to see the roots pull free from the ground. He began reciting Psalm 23 as the creature dragged him closer to death.

Strapped to the stakes and gagged, Kat watched the entire battle from a few feet away.

Unable to scream.

Unable to help.

Doctor John, at the sight of the 50-foot-long creature, stood motionless and watched the creature drag the hairy preacher toward the water. He did not watch long however before reaching down and wrenching his dagger from Nathan's back. Doctor John returned his attention to Kat, approaching her with the now-bloody dagger hanging at his side. He knelt and raised the dagger over his head, mumbling something unintelligible.

The dagger started down and Kat tried again to scream. Sunlight flickered off a blade arcing towards Doctor John's head. Nathan, regaining consciousness had retrieved Kevin's sword and he now swung it with all his strength at Doctor John's neck.

The razor sharp blade sliced through the witch doctor's neck and severed his head from his shoulders as neatly as a guillotine. The witch doctor's arm, holding the ceremonial dagger, fell neatly cleaved to the ground beside Kat. His shaved head, complete with visible gold fangs, bounced down the embankment and landed in the mud at the water's edge.

Jake, bleeding from his head wound appeared from nowhere and vaulted past Kat, Nathan, and Doctor John's headless corpse to grab Kevin's outstretched arms. He dug in his heels to no avail as the creature pulled Kevin under the water. Jake, still holding Kevin's arm, grabbed for a rock on the bank with his free hand. All he managed to do was dislodge Doctor John's severed head as he himself followed Kevin under the water. He refused to let go.

Nathan fell to his knees beside Kat and fumbled with the gag in her mouth. She burst into tears again when Kevin Croix popped out of the water like a fishing cork. He splashed to the bank, and using his upper body strength, pulled his massive frame out of the water. Nathan ran down and grabbed his arms to help him. Together they scrambled up the bank, Kevin's mangled leg leaving a clear blood trail.

Both men collapsed near Kat, still tied to the ground. Jake had not surfaced.

"Nathan?" Kat cried out now that the gag was gone. Nathan and the stranger laid unconscious beside her. She could see blood pumping from both men's wounds.

"Somebody! Help!"

Quin appeared and looked down at Kat, a vacant expression in his eyes. Where he had been during the battle, Kat did not know. He reached down and pried the dagger from Doctor John's severed hand and turned to Kat, bending toward her with the knife.

Kat screamed. And then Quin cut the rawhide tethers holding her to the ground just as Jake, bleeding from his head wound, bobbed to the surface. Quin looked around at the bedraggled bunch.

"Come on lady. You got to help me get these people loaded in the van. They all need a doctor."

CHAPTER 38

Gathered around Miss Ella's bed, they were a ragtag bunch of stitches, bruises and bandages.

Jake sported two black eyes from the dashboard-broken nose and a stitched up cut connecting his eyebrows. His pride was intact though, since his heroics saved Kevin's life. He refused to admit that Doctor John's head entering the water had anything to do with the croc releasing Kevin. Kevin disagreed but allowed Jake his moment.

Kat was a mass of purple and blue accentuated by scabbed-over scratches, all received in her frantic escape through the dark woods. She couldn't wear shoes yet with the thirty or so stitches in her right foot she'd gotten from stepping on broken glass. In the excitement and fear she hadn't even felt the cut.

Kevin, in an oversized wheelchair, propped his mangled foot high in the air. The doctor said to stay off of it for a month, so Kevin would be down at least a week. He had a lot to do back in New Orleans, but it would be a while before he could go back to working as a bouncer with the metal pin in his ankle and the 400 stitches. He could preach on Thursday night sitting down though so the meeting would go on.

Ed Hebert carried another knot on his head from hitting the ground and a thin red necklace of stitches where Doctor John cut his throat. The fine white powder that Doctor John had blown into his face had saved him. The powder made him fall away from the big witch doctor, which kept the blade from penetrating his jugular. Another fraction of a millimeter and he'd be dead. The scar would be a constant reminder of his brush with death.

Nathan, one arm in a sling and the other around Kat, had been lucky. The knife missed all the vital organs, but hit a vein and nearly caused him to bleed to death. Four units of blood filled him up and he was beginning to regain some strength.

Quin, with the help of Kat, had somehow managed to pile them all in Doctor John's van and make a run for the hospital. Only five days ago, their ordeal seemed like a distant memory. Ed had gathered them all together to give them an update.

"It looks like your buddy Humsinger is going to spend the rest of his days playing with crayons in a rubber room." Ed looked around the room, noting that his callousness about Humsinger bothered no one.

"The state is currently doing an evaluation to see if he's mentally competent to stand trial. I've seen him through the observation window. He'll never set foot in a courtroom."

"What about Quin?" Kevin asked. "He helped drag us all back to get patched up."

"He violated his parole so he's going back to jail." Ed lifted his hands palm up, questioningly. "As soon as the prosecuting attorney figures out what to charge him with, he'll be sucking up some more state resources."

Kat had been wondering. "What about Madame Jean? Has anyone seen or heard from her?"

Kevin fielded that one. "I talked to Karyn on the phone this morning. She said Madame Jean showed up and got the girl. Her house is locked and the word on the street says she moved to California. I guess she had her fill of New Orleans."

"What about Harlin?" Nathan still wondered about his friend. No one had heard from him.

"I've got the divers dredging the bottom of that slough near the dig site where Hawk disappeared. Quin told me he saw the croc get Harlin and his friend Specky. I don't know if we'll find any remains or not."

"Did you ever find out why he had those artifacts in his apartment?"

"We searched his place and it looks like he was gathering evidence against the grave robbers. I can only speculate that he'd pilfered those artifacts to try to set up a sale and see who was behind it all. I guess he never made it that far."

"What about the croc? Has anyone been able to hunt it down?" Nathan would never forget the giant beast rising up out of the river and seizing Kevin's leg. He shuddered at the thought.

"Not a trace. We've been cooperating with Stennis, and they've loaned us some expertise from your department, but so far we haven't found anything." Ed shook his head. "I certainly would have liked to have seen the croc myself, but the one Jake donated to the zoo looks ferocious enough and proves they exist."

Ed continued. "What I'm not certain about is the spiritual connection you folks claim existed. I'm not sure how or why Doctor John could control that croc."

"He couldn't." This was Kevin's area of expertise. "Not yet, anyway. Had he been successful with the sacrifice, he very well could have controlled that croc."

"I'm not calling you a liar, Kevin. But I am a skeptic."

Nathan, curious, asked. "Why did you bring the sword?"

Kevin shrugged, knowing they would never believe him. "Three nights before you and Jake came to the meeting, the Lord spoke to me. Not audibly, mind you, but clear enough. The scripture Isaiah 27:1 came to mind while praying one night and I felt as impressed as I've ever been to do something. I knew I was supposed to be obedient and buy the sword."

"So what is Isaiah 27:1?"

Kevin recited the scripture from memory:

> "In that day the Lord with his sore and great and strong sword shall punish leviathan the piercing serpent, even leviathan that crooked serpent; and he shall slay the dragon that is in the sea."

"I thought I might use the sword in an illustrated sermon, but then when we went to Stennis I felt impressed to bring it. But I'd say Nathan using the sword to kill Doctor John was a good illustration of good conquering evil." Kevin paused and shook his head in amazement. "I didn't realize the leviathan meant anything until afterwards."

"Kat? Are you there?" Shocked, everyone turned toward the voice. Miss Ella's voice.

Kat rushed to her bedside. "I'm here, Grams."

"Did you find Jake Lloyd?"

"I'm here too, Miss Ella."

"Kat? Meet your father."

Kat, incredulous, turned to Jake. Jake, equally incredulous, turned to Miss Ella. "What?" He managed to stammer.

In a weak voice, Miss Ella continued. "When your mother learned she was pregnant with you, she had broken up with Jake. They were fighting like two lovers fight and your mother, my sweet daughter, was too stubborn to tell Jake about the pregnancy."

The old woman took a deep breath and continued. "In the latter stages of the pregnancy, she stayed inside, ashamed for anyone to know about it." Grams smiled lovingly at Kat. "You were born at the house. No one knew but me, your mother and your aunt."

Kat sat dumbstruck as Grams related the story. "Your mother was killed shortly after you were born, before we had a chance to record your birth. You were such a tiny baby and your mother was walking down by the bayou, near where she and Jake used to eat lunch, when she was killed."

The old woman tired fast, but continued. "Your Aunt Anna and I feared that if Jake found out about you, he would take you away from us, so we forged your birth certificate and listed Anna as your mother. We had a friend at the courthouse that helped us file it. To this day, I've never told anyone."

The old woman looked at Jake with mournful tear filled eyes. "I'm sorry, Jake. That's why I wanted Kat to find you. I had to let you know the truth."

Jake, tears welling up in his eyes, patted the old woman's arm and hugged his new daughter. "Thank you, Miss Ella."

Nathan thought about his own father whom he hadn't seen in over ten years. Maybe the time had come to look him up.

"Kevin? Do you mind renewing our wedding vows?" Nathan looked at Kat. "That is, if Kat's willing."

A mischievous smile graced Kat's mouth. "Only if Daddy can give me away."

Jake chimed in. "You haven't asked for my daughter's hand, whelp."

Nathan held up his hands in defeat. "Okay, okay. I give in. Dr. Lloyd, sir. May I have your daughter's hand in marriage?"

"Only if I get to keep my grandchild on weekends."

EPILOGUE

The big male was 75 years old. At 14 feet long and 1600 pounds there was nothing to challenge the bull alligator anymore. Smaller males usually knew instinctively to evade him. Those that did not typically got no larger in size. Occasionally one would escape with his life, a few scars, and a lesson learned the hard way. Although long since forgotten, he had learned just such lessons himself.

The bull gator needed to eat. There had been no meal now for almost three months. He had gone six months before, but never by choice. But he would eat today. At least a little. The bull could smell a nest, and a nest meant some small morsels of food. The fact that those small morsels were his own kind never entered his tiny brain. The small newly hatched alligators were simply nourishment to him. The female could be nasty tempered about it, but driven off none the less.

He drew closer, the smell stronger in his nostrils. His considerable bulk glided effortlessly through the stagnant water. The smell seemed a little different somehow, but it was still a nest. No doubting that odor of decaying vegetation and newly hatched shells. Hopefully there were some yet to hatch that he could dig up and devour. He was almost there.

The huge male pulled himself out of the water, plodding ever closer to the nest. It was taller than any nest he had raided in the past, but still fresh. A small gator, about two feet long, appeared to have beaten him to the nest site. Normally the females drove off those little gators. A big female could make short work of a smaller nest raider. He had nothing to fear.

The smaller gator chirped at him when he approached. The female must not be around. He bellowed at the underling to get out of his way or suffer the consequences. Suddenly something was moving and moving rapidly. Trees and brush cracked and popped as the large animal approached. The bull's attention was diverted to the larger meal coming his way. Much better than raiding nests. Possibly a deer, or a stray cow.

The brush parted and the big male would have registered surprise, were he capable of it. Past experiences failed to surface. He had been dominant for too long. Lunging, he attacked the approaching foe, only to be engulfed in the giant maw. Huge jaws, much larger than his own, easily grasped the big bull gator and whipped his considerable bulk from side to side, shaking him like a rag doll. The hindquarters of the bull flew into the adjacent brush, while the head and front half were gulped down to be digested whole. The mother sniffed the still-chirping youngster and appeared satisfied. Her young were no longer threatened.

LOOK FOR THESE BOOKS BY EMPORIUM PRESS AUTHOR TIMOTHY D. WISE:

SEASON OUT OF TIME
By Timothy D. Wise
In June of 1977, Jaime Mitchell died in a traffic accident following an alleged UFO crash in the mountains of Miracle Springs, Arkansas. Twenty years later, Dr. James Koslow is still haunted by the death of his childhood friend. His search for answers ultimately hurls him through time to confront the tragedy again. Can he prevent it or will he be forced to relive it?
ISBN: 0-9725549-4-7
$7.95
110 pages

THE SIGN OF THE SWORD
By Timothy D. Wise
On an icy November night, four high school students and their teacher take a carriage ride through a foggy forest and find themselves in another world. Chased through the forest by silver-eyed cyborgs, attacked by a werewolf, and rescued by a ragged stranger who claims to be the heir to King Arthur's throne, the travelers find that their only chance to return home lies in restoring the kingdom of Camelot on an alien world.
ISBN: 0-9725549-6-3
$12.95
216 pages

THE
INTREPID FORCE
SERIES

INTREPID FORCE
By Timothy D. Wise

Each of them joined the team for their own reaso▉
Eisman joined because of Wendy Blake. Wendy▉
avenge the crime that led to her cybernetic recon▉
Jared Thomas joined because of his drea▉
mysterious woman from another time. Rever▉
Sheppard saw leading the team as a kind of ▉
Now an interplanetary criminal has seized cont▉
Venus dome and the lives of over 25,000 peopl▉
the balance. To defeat their foe, the men and ▉
Intrepid force must face and defeat their own inn▉
as well.

ISBN 0-9725549-0-4

$12.95

INTREPID FORCE: INVASION

It began with a signal from an ancient wreck o▉
Saturn's large moon. A survey ship went to in▉
and vanished. Two years later, Earth is invade▉
armada of ships led by a being who calls himsel▉
and claims to be the Antichrist foretold by C▉
prophecy. Aided by Neema, a young woman wh▉
to have come from a dark and terrible future, the▉
Force races to discover Gogue's true nature and▉
Neema's future from becoming their own reality.

ISBN 0-9725549-1-2

$14.95

396 pages

www.ingramcontent.com/pod-product-compliance
Lightning Source LLC
Chambersburg PA
CBHW021511240626
47154CB00002B/588